Inn the Spirit of Murder

by

Rhonda Blackhurst

The Spirit Lake Mysteries

Inn the Spirit of Murder

Cover Art by *The Wild Rose Press, Inc.*

The Wild Rose Press, Inc.
PO Box 708
Adams Basin, NY 14410-0708
Visit us at www.thewildrosepress.com

Publishing History
First Edition, 2024
Trade Paperback ISBN 978-1-5092-5641-9
Digital ISBN 978-1-5092-5642-6

The Spirit Lake Mysteries
Published in the United States of America

Dedication

To Clint—my one and only; Ben & Alex, who taught me how to love unconditionally; and my grandbabies, who give me a second chance to get it right.

Chapter 1

Dying is often worse than death itself. Particularly in romantic relationships. Not that I would call the relationship with my boyfriend, Brad, romantic. Not anymore. The romance part had all but died.

As I stood barefoot on the edge of the porch that overlooked the lake, waiting for his expected arrival and the likely breakup, movement behind the darkened window of the boathouse ripped my attention from my conflicted thoughts.

At my near-silent gasp, Aspen, my red retriever emotional support dog, sprang to a sitting position and touched my hand with his cool nose. I buried my fingers in his fur as I squinted and peered closely at the boathouse, focused on the possibility. *Could it be*? I'd been searching for signs of the infamous apparition since I'd moved here. Had the ghost finally shown me favor and allowed me to see it? I tugged the strings of my hoodie, shivering. Aspen kept his gaze glued between me and the boathouse.

The ghost activity at the inn in Spirit Lake, Minnesota, drew people like hummingbirds to sugar water, resulting in profits for the entire town. Or storm chasers to a tornado funnel. When I was little and stayed with my grandparents, Grandpop stood by the screen door, his hands on his hips, during a tornado warning. I'd sneak up behind him, careful that he wouldn't know I was there, and send me back downstairs. I would clasp my hands in front of me, adrenaline pumping as we waited for the tornado to materialize, yet desperately hoping it didn't. The anticipation got my blood pumping just as much as the fear of *what if it did.*

When I saw nothing more in the boathouse window, my heart resumed its normal pace. I sat on the edge of the porch beside Aspen, crossing my legs in front of me, my attention torn between the boathouse and Brad. It had been a long time since we fed our relationship significant attention, much less romance. We'd taken plenty of withdrawals from the account over the past year, but few deposits. It'd be fair to say we deposited nearly zero since my parents gifted me the Spirit Lake Inn six months ago, which they inherited from my grandparents. The last time Brad and I spoke three weeks ago, he'd said something had to change, that we were phasing out to nothing. Yet, neither of us so much as made a phone call to the other until today. Our relationship was breathing its last dying painful breath. I figured Brad's visit this evening was to take off the tourniquet, stop the slow bleeding, and put the darn thing out of its misery.

Still, I wasn't sure I was ready to let it go. What if this was only a phase, and we got the train back on the track? It had been Brad that carried me through my initial sobriety six years ago. And it had been Brad who was the stable, practical one, talking reason when I'd lost it. It had been Brad that I used to go to with everything. At one point, he had been my best friend. And now I wondered if we could even call what we had friendship.

Owning the inn had fulfilled me in ways Brad never had. I hadn't even known my life was void of anything until I'd moved here. The industrial ovens for baking when I couldn't sleep, the gardening shed, the employees, the guests—all of it. Even my name proved this was my destiny—Andie Rose Kaczmarek, Polish for Innkeeper.

There. The curtains fluttered in the boathouse window. I drew a deep breath and held it, afraid to even blink. I remained motionless, waiting...

The flutter stopped as suddenly as it started, now eerily still. I let out the breath I'd been holding and shook my head. Despite Grandpop and Honey—a name everyone called my grandmother, including me—being solid believers in the spirit world, (more in the form of angels), I'd never been convinced of a spirit presence, so why—*Wait*! There it was again. This time it wasn't a mere flutter, but more a draft fanning the curtains back and forth. "Of course, you dummy," I muttered. "That's exactly what it was, a draft." If the window was open, even a crack, that explained it.

I exhaled slowly and leaned into Aspen, who hadn't yet relaxed enough to lie back down. I wrapped my arm around him and buried my cheek in his fur. I'd begun having panic attacks six years ago after a devastating health diagnosis of the "C" word that rendered me three months to live. It eventually turned out to be a misdiagnosis. But while the limited lifespan was off the table, the anxiety remained all too real. I could entertain *what if* scenarios better than Stephen King could write them. Three years ago, at the suggestion of a therapist, I'd found Aspen to be my certifiable support animal, near-constant companion, and best friend.

Now, we both gazed at the monstrous weeping willow tree along the lake's shoreline and near the boathouse. A slight breeze in the evening air stirred the graceful droop of the willow's silvery leaves. Though after the adrenaline rush moments ago, the willow's leaves now resembled bony fingers, scratching and reaching, looking rather sinister in the setting sun. Aspen finally got comfortable and lay on his side, snoozing. Finally, I leaned over and laid my forehead against his, looking into deep brown eyes that comforted me more than a security blanket ever could. I slowly stood, stretched, and looked at the boathouse one more time. Nothing.

I glanced behind us toward two couples on the lawn as they finished a game of croquet in the last embers of daylight, and a young man and woman, clearly in love, as they huddled together in front of the fire, her head on his shoulder. The movement from the boat shed didn't appear to catch anyone else's attention. After one more look, I turned to go back inside, Aspen beside me.

Seeing as there had been only speculation and unprovable claims without solid proof of ghosts at the inn, the verdict was still out on whether I believed. Yet, I'm not sure how one could *prove* a claim. It's not like you could chain up a ghost, then run and get everyone to come and see it. Although, if I decided I didn't believe, I would never admit it. They'd run me right out of the town. The townsfolk took this paranormal stuff seriously. Halloween and the accompanying harvest festival had been the hot topic of conversation since I'd gotten here in April: who was handling what, improvements they could make from last year's festival, friendly competition—and some not so friendly—on the business decoration contest, and plans for ghost hunting. As a child, when I visited my grandparents on school breaks, I'd learned that the inn was booked solid through the entire holiday season, from September through December. Also, many locals made frequent trips to the inn, hoping to catch sight of the ghost as early as August. They claimed to drive out to our on-site restaurant or our coffee bar, but I knew the ghost was the chief attraction. Now that we were at the beginning of October, the town's energy had ramped up to astonishing—and often frightening—proportions. The founders of Spirit Lake had proclaimed it to be the Paranormal Capital of the country since Anoka had earned the title of the Halloween Capital of the World.

Aspen and I checked in with Jade, the twenty-something gal working the front desk, before heading to my room to get ready to go meet Brad at Brewski's Pub. The pub was next door to the protestant church and halfway down Spirit Lane, the main street that ran through town. It was disconcerting that he'd chosen a pub to meet since I was a recovering alcoholic. I have six years of sobriety under my belt and can frequent alcohol establishments without a problem, but I don't go to one unless I have a good reason. I knew that if we were indeed ripping off the Band-Aid, which was probable and about time, I wouldn't be tempted to drown my sorrows or celebrate with a glass of champagne. That alone told me the relationship wasn't a healthy one, and it was time to let it go gracefully.

As Aspen and I walked past the library to my room, the copy of *The Woman in Black* by Susan Hill that I'd just re-shelved the day before lay under a lamp on the table between two reading chairs. I re-shelved it and finished the trip to my room at the far end of the inn. Last room on the left.

A mere fifteen minutes later, I emerged in a pair of

black jeans and a clean hoodie, my long curly red locks tied back in a ponytail. No need to waste time and energy on getting ready for a breakup. While I had dressed, Aspen laid on my bed with his nose on his front crossed paws, one eye open watching me. He'd come to know that when I dressed down, it meant he would go with me; when I dressed in my glad rags, there was a chance he would have to stay home—which wasn't often. His behavior said it all. Today I needed him with me.

When I walked into the foyer, Ivan, the inn's chef, stood beside Jade at the front desk. His elbows rested on the counter, and he leaned on them, towel clenched in his hands. When he saw me, he stood.

"I was just leaving for the day," he said, his tone chillier than the evening autumn air.

Jade's eyes widened ever so slightly. She and Ivan were friends, and she was more than aware of his resentment of me and my intrusion into his professional life. Before I acquired the inn, everything involving the kitchen was his turf, and no one dared to go near that line, much less cross it. As far as I was concerned, the inn was mine, and if I wanted to use the bloody kitchen while he was gone, I would use it. I cleaned up after myself, so he had nothing to fuss about. If I used the last of something, I ordered new. He would have to get used to it—or not.

"Don't rush on my account," I said. "Aspen and I are just heading to Brewski's Pub." It was no secret that I abstained from alcohol because of addiction issues in my past, so it wasn't a surprise when Ivan snorted in response.

"The pub?" Jade inquired.

"Yup. Meeting someone. Jade, I'll see you shortly."

I turned toward Ivan and smiled, my usual attempt to soften the hardness there. "See you tomorrow."

"The pub serves food," he stated.

"You're right. I'm aware of that." I frowned, unsure where he was going with this.

"So most people don't like dog hair in their food."

I cocked my head to the side. Though I didn't bring Aspen into the inn's kitchen, Ivan had made it clear since I'd been here that he didn't like Aspen in the guest area of the inn at all.

"He's a service dog, Ivan. You know that." I tipped my head. "See you tomorrow."

I left before hearing any cynical comment he might have uttered. I wasn't in the mood for his moodiness.

I opened the driver's door of my forest green Kia Soul, and Aspen hopped in and over to the passenger seat, sitting tall and proud like he owned the place. He graced me with a brief glance of his chocolate brown eyes, the ones I could never resist. I slid in behind the steering wheel. It had been tempting to walk the mile and a half, knowing that Brad could give me a ride back home, but walking on the back road that led into town at dusk held no appeal. Animals didn't scare me, but people did. What people can do to other people is astonishing. And there were many tourists here, meaning they were people none of the townsfolk knew. Not to mention that far too many people admit to not seeing well driving at dusk or after dark. Add to that, most drivers don't exactly look for pedestrians on a back road.

I found a parking space in the narrow strip around the side of the pub. I took a deep breath and looked at Aspen, who watched me closely, seemingly in tune with my every emotion. "Come on, dude, let's get this over with, shall we?" He tipped his head to the side as if asking, *Do we have to*? I jerked my head toward the pub. "The sooner we get this over with, the sooner we can move forward." I slid out of the car, my devoted canine right behind me.

Chapter 2

Brad's car wasn't there yet, so Aspen and I continued into Brewski's and snaked around tables in the dim lighting. The lighting varied depending on the barkeep running the place for the day. The servers don't have a say in the matter. I knew this because on one occasion—the *only* one before this evening—when I came in from the bright late afternoon sunshine, my eyes hadn't had time to adjust to the dim lighting, and I nearly tumbled over a table. All that got hurt was my pride and my wallet; my pride because I'd had to explain that I hadn't been drinking before I came in; my wallet because I'd replaced the table of drinks I'd spilled. I'd asked the server about it, and she'd said they don't have a say in the lighting issue, that it's up to the bartender—the bartendress in this case—since the person behind the long bar was a woman. I'd been here with Brad that time as well because there was a Minnesota Twins baseball game on TV he'd wanted to see.

After ordering a Diet Pepsi, I sat at a table in a corner and near the door so I could spot Brad when he came in. Aspen hunkered down beside my chair, half under the table, and laid his nose on his crossed front paws. My phone chimed with an incoming text.

Brad: —*Running late. Be there as fast as I can.*—

No surprise. I couldn't remember a time he was ever early and few that he was on time. It had become the

9

norm. As an attorney, he often got derailed by a client or by needing to complete and file a document by a deadline. So he said, anyway. I had no reason to doubt him. He stayed connected to his phone for business, but he didn't carry that over into the rest of his life, which is why it surprised me when he texted this evening.

The breakup wouldn't disrupt my life very much. Nor his. His job kept him so busy that he was rarely at his own apartment, much less able to visit me. And I was too busy getting established at the inn and didn't want to take time away from it yet. I'd already suffered the loss of him as my best friend, so there wasn't even that anymore. This was simply a formal letting go, so we could both move on.

I focused on a football game on the big screen TV, not paying much attention. I was a die-hard Minnesota Vikings fan. The game held little interest if they weren't the team playing.

Finally, I glanced around the pub and then at my watch; Brad was forty-five minutes late, later than usual. I wanted to get this done and over with. The waiting just gave me anxiety. And for an alcoholic, anxiety while alone in a bar could lead to disaster and embarrassment from unintended consequences, no matter how much time was under one's belt. Which reminded me it was high time I began looking for a new sponsor since moving here. Asking someone to be your sponsor was akin to asking someone out on a date. Terrifying yet rewarding if you get the "yes." I rolled my eyes and finished my Diet Pepsi, preparing to leave. If Brad got hung up, it could be another hour. I'd rather wait at the inn, and he could meet me there.

I pushed my chair back, and Aspen roused to a

sitting position. When the door opened, I expected to see Brad. Ivan surprised me instead.

"Ugh," I muttered. I looked down and took a deep breath. To address him or pretend I didn't see him—quite the dilemma. It was a choice I didn't have to make after all since he marched toward my table, a snide grin on his face.

"Alone?" he asked. "Or stood up by someone?"

"What do you want, Ivan?" I said, meeting his eyes. "Because I'm not in the mood for your—"

"I'm meeting Roman," he said and looked around the bar, then back at me. "Appears he's not here yet." He craned his neck, looked around the corner of the bar, and then nodded with a wave of recognition. "I guess he is."

Roman had been to the coffee shop at the inn a time or two with his dad. He was a barista at Hallowed Grounds Coffee Shop on the edge of town. A self-proclaimed coffee junkie, I'd been there too many times to count, and Roman had been my barista numerous times. He seemed like a good kid, though quiet. But with a dad as a church deacon, I would expect nothing less.

"He's twenty-one," Ivan said, as if reading my mind. "Looks young for his age." He made to leave.

"Do you have time to chat for a minute first?" I stood so I was at his level, a trick I'd learned in my life coach training and leadership courses. At five-foot-eight, I was nearly the same height as him. "I'd like to figure out how we can move forward and get along. We work at the same place—of which I'm the owner."

He nodded and stuffed his fists inside the pockets of his jacket. "You've reminded me of that too many times for me to forget."

"So what's the problem? It can't be something so

little as the dog biscuit issue." The Spirit Lake Inn had been baking specialty dog biscuits for the past several years and sold them to the public. When I'd taken ownership, Ivan saw it as a chance to do away with them, claiming my grandparents hadn't hired him to bake for dogs and that he was a professional chef.

He stood a little taller and squared his shoulders. "This thing you call a *little issue* is demeaning to my profession." He took a hand from his pocket and pointed to Aspen. "Dogs don't belong in food establishments. And I didn't go to school to learn how to bake for *them*." He spat the word and made a face as if he had burped something up.

I took a step back, Aspen stood, and I laid my hand against his neck. "Which is why I told you I'm happy to do it, Ivan. I love baking."

"I know that because you use my kitchen. *My* kitchen. I've been the chef there for seventeen years. I've asked you not to use it, but you disrespect me and use it anyway."

His tone grew louder, and the patrons next to us turned their attention to our way. I smiled an apology, and the man nodded his understanding before he continued to open a bottle of wine. No cheap wine there. Apparently, they were celebrating and not breaking up. Ivan held up a finger to Roman, indicating he'd be there in a minute.

I took a second to gather my wits. "Ivan, I'm not disrespecting you. When I use the kitchen, if I use the last of something, I replace it. And I clean up after myself, so you'd never even know had you not seen me that once."

"A chef always knows when someone else has been

in his kitchen. That is *my* territory, and you have no business being in *my* territory."

Apparently, we were dogs now and marking our territory. Aspen sat on my feet as if telling me to stay calm.

"Well, I'm sorry we can't agree to disagree with this. I own the inn, and I *will* use the kitchen. If you can't accept that, maybe it's time to look for work someplace else." I looked at the table next to us as the man finished opening the wine bottle and discreetly slid his knife toward the opposite side of the table, as if one of us would use it as a weapon.

"Are you firing me?" His tone was low yet threatening, and he cracked his knuckles on one hand, then the other. "I don't think you want to do that. I was there long before you owned the place. And the inn will never survive without me."

"My grandparents made it as successful as it is, Ivan. Not you. You are one of a team of people who makes the inn run as well as it does. *One* of a *team*."

He turned his head to the side and then looked at me with eyes that turned my blood cold. "I will sabotage your business if you get rid of me. I'll go somewhere else in Spirit Lake, and the inn will have no business at all."

"Somehow, I doubt that," I mumbled. And after this altercation, I knew Ivan staying at the inn wasn't an option. He had to go. The sous-chef, Tony Valentino, had skills near that of Ivan and was much easier for everyone to get along with. I took a breath. "Ivan, it's clear you're not happy with me at the inn. Go someplace that makes you happy, Spirit Lake or not. Life is too short. But please leave me the recipe for the dog biscuits." At the mention of the word biscuits, Aspen's ears perked up, and he gave me a hopeful glance.

"I will not leave the inn or the dog biscuit recipe. The only way that'll happen is over my dead body," he said, jamming his fists in his pockets again. Aspen made a low, guttural sound. He didn't appreciate Ivan's refusal to cooperate any more than I did. I took another step back and nearly tripped over Brad's foot. I'd been so focused on Ivan that I hadn't even noticed he had arrived.

Chapter 3

"Whoa," Brad said and kissed my cheek. "You sure ticked him off. I'd ask what that was about, but I think everyone in the vicinity heard the exchange."

Aspen turned away from Brad in an apparent state of disapproval. I swear he was more human than animal. "How long have you been standing there?" I asked him as I watched Ivan stalk over toward Roman. The two men exchanged a few words; Ivan nodded, showed Roman his phone, then left with a look toward me that sent shivers down my spine. Had he recorded our conversation? My mind sputtered to remember everything I'd said, confident I had said nothing he could use against me. I hoped, anyway.

When I turned back to Brad, he'd settled comfortably in a chair, waving the server toward him as he watched the game. "The Seahawks are going to have a fantastic team this year," he said. "Just wait and see."

"I can hardly wait," I grumbled.

"What's wrong?" he asked with a frown. He held out a hand to me. "If you're mad because I'm late, you know these things happen."

"Pretty much every time."

"Andie Rose, that's not fair." He sighed, stole a glance at the television screen, then turned his attention back to me. Kind of. "You know I don't control the timing of filings and contracts."

I exhaled and looked over to see Roman finishing a can of Coke before I looked back at Brad. "Ivan just threatened me, and you're acting like it was nothing."

He offered a small smile. "Andie Rose, those things happen in the workplace. Because the inn is a small business, that doesn't make you immune. It'll blow over."

I wasn't sure which disagreed with me more, the "small business" statement like this was some silly hobby or the one about it "blowing over." Like it was a squabble over a scheduling conflict. I stewed for a minute before deciding that, given the circumstances, I was probably being overly sensitive. Brad had a sense of business, which is why he was so successful at his firm.

"I sure hope you're right," I said, seeing him steal another glance at the television. "If you want to watch the game, let's go back to the inn. That way, I can work while you watch." I had some preparation to do for Ivan's impending departure. Like, look for the dog biscuit recipe before he came back in the morning—*if* he came back. I had no doubt he would shred it before giving it to me.

Brad's gaze lingered on the television until the play ended before turning back toward me, waving his hand as if dismissing the TV. "Sorry. It's been a stressful day. Zoning out to a game is what I do. You already know that. But no more game." He stroked the back of my hand with his thumb. "I'm here with you, so let's do us."

The server brought over a bottle of Miller Lite and set it, along with a napkin, in front of him. After I declined the offer of another soda, she breezed away.

Yes, let's. Getting straight to it, I said, "Not that I'm unhappy you're here, but what was so urgent that you had to see me this evening?" In anticipation, I held my breath and caught my lower lip between my teeth. My evening could potentially go from bad to worse. Or not.

He stared into my eyes, a small smile in place. "You have the most gorgeous, unusual blue eyes. Maybe it's because of the contrast to your red hair. Which looks nice tonight, by the way."

I narrowed an eye. "Brad, it's in a ponytail. And I'm sure you didn't come to talk about my eye and hair color." His apparent nervousness was disconcerting and made me even more sure he'd come to break up. When he looked down for a lengthy moment, I finally said, "Brad?"

He reached into his suit jacket pocket, his hand still for a moment, before pulling something out, hiding it in his hand. He slid out of his chair and onto his knee. My breath caught, my cheeks burned, and I thought I might faint. Surely, he wasn't —

"Andie Rose Kaczmarek," he said as he lifted his hand, a gold band pinched between his forefinger and thumb. "Will you marry me?"

My hands flew to my burning cheeks. As much as I wanted to say something to Brad, unlike Aspen, who let out a whine and tucked his nose beneath his folded paws, sound refused to come out of my mouth. Not even a gasp. My night had just gone from bad to completely unexpected. And I wasn't sure which surprised me more, the proposal or the size of the diamond.

"Andie Rose?" he asked, shifting his weight on his knee. The confident look in his eye a moment ago turned to one of discomfort. "Andie?" he asked again when I still couldn't utter a peep.

"Uh—well—um—" Thank goodness the people

from the table next to us left so as not to witness this awkward exchange. The server had yet to clear the table, so I snatched the corkscrew lying next to the empty bottle of wine and nervously clutched it in my hand, seeking comfort like a toddler with a stuffed animal. A proposal was the opposite of what I'd expected.

Saying nothing, I laid it back down, took the ring between my fingers, and held my hand out to help Brad get back up.

"That wasn't the least bit embarrassing," Brad mumbled once on his feet. He looked around, straightened his tie that he had yet to remove, and sat back down.

I finally found my voice, though shaky by the unexpected turn of events. "I thought you were coming to break up with me, so imagine my surprise when that wasn't the case. Quite the opposite."

He jerked his head back. "Break up? Why would I break up with you?"

"It's not like we spend much time together, Brad. You have your job, I have mine, both in different cities…"

He frowned. "I don't understand. I thought we were good. You wouldn't have to work anymore. My sister loves it that her husband brings in the dough so she can stay home with the kids. You could do whatever makes you happy and focus on starting a family."

Just when I thought I couldn't be more surprised, his words stunned me, feeling like a refrigerator landed on my chest. "Brad, the inn is what I love. It's been in my family for decades. And kids? We've never mentioned kids before. I'm not even sure I want children. Also, you know I'm planning to get my life coaching business set up here from my office. And what do you mean you thought things were good? You're the one who said things needed to change."

"But Andie," he said, getting excited, "getting married does change things. And you can do your life coaching gig from anywhere. You wouldn't even have to do it anymore at all. Think of the possibilities."

I exhaled and sighed. "But, Brad, those things are what I like. They *are* my possibilities. I love running the inn. I've found a great AA meeting in town where we laugh and have fun. I love helping others be the best they can be by coaching them." I tossed my hands up in the air. "This life I have in this town is what I want. And I'm assuming you won't move here."

"You know I can't. My job is in the city."

"And my job is here. Mine's not any less important than yours."

"Honey," he said, as if soothing a child. "Be reasonable here. I make more than enough money to support us. Substantially. And are you really cut out to deal with the employee conflicts you had just a half hour ago without drinking over it?"

My jaw dropped. "Excuse me? I'm not newly sober, Brad. I have a solid foundation."

"But you hated that conflict. Admit it. You wouldn't have to worry about that anymore."

No, the altercation with Ivan hadn't been enjoyable. But I loved my life here and the friends I made. I couldn't imagine a single thing missing. And I still hadn't seen the infamous ghost.

"Tell you what," he said, setting the ring firmly in the palm of my hand and folding my fingers around it. The diamond cut into my palm. "Take some time to think about it. You don't have to decide tonight. When I got here, things were pretty tense with that guy. Go home, unwind, think about it, and get back to me."

"You're not coming to the inn?"

He shook his head. "I have to get back home. I have an early morning meeting."

He stood, held out his arms, and I stepped into them, my fist still clutching the ring with the monstrous diamond. "You're right. I need some time to think about it," I whispered into his hair.

"Of course you do, honey. And that's okay. But I didn't want to wait another day before asking. No regrets, you know?"

I pulled back and looked into his eyes. "Why?"

He frowned. "Why, what?"

"Why was it so important to ask me tonight and then rush back to the city?"

He cocked his head to the side. "I told you why. I didn't want to wait another day."

"But why, Brad?" Something made me uncomfortable. And I was never uncomfortable with Brad. That's one thing my cousin Babs always accused me of—sticking with him because it was comfortable. "Why do you want to get married?"

He smoothed his hand over my hair and let my ponytail run through his fingers. "It makes sense, babe. It's the next logical step. We belong together. I want to take part when the guys at work talk about their families. Be part of it. You know?"

"So you proposed to fit in with the guys." The insult slammed me right between the eyes. "Brad—"

"I'm tired of never seeing you, Andie Rose. If you lived with me, we could have dinner every night and—"

It hadn't escaped me that he said if you lived with *me*, not if we lived together, and it felt like I was suffocating. "You're rarely home by dinner."

"Because I have nothing to get home for. If you were there—well, Andie Rose, promise me you'll at least think about it. And remember the argument with the guy tonight? You'd never have to deal with that kind of thing again." He pulled me into his arms again.

"I promise I'll think about it." But I already knew I would never leave Spirit Lake unless it was in a body bag. I love it here. And I wouldn't give up on my dreams so that Brad *fit in* with the guys.

****

I watched Brad's car disappear and then stood in the chilly night air. I slouched against the brick exterior of the pub, and Aspen leaned against my leg. Sister Alice from St. Michael's strolled past Sweet Temptations Bakery across the street. She looked up, and I waved at her.

"Good evening, Andie Rose." she called over to me. "Lovely evening, eh?"

"Sure is," I called back as, thankfully, she continued her stroll without crossing the street to me. Sister Alice was one of my favorite people, but I had a lot to process right now—alone. I thought of her greeting—I wouldn't call the evening's *events* lovely, but everything else was. And that's what I chose to focus on. As I'd coached my clients, it was all about perspective.

As I closed my eyes and deeply inhaled the scent of fallen leaves, pine, and pumpkin—every business and home in Spirit Lake bakes pumpkin-something-or-other, so the scent wafted throughout the entire town—it solidified my decision. I was staying put, all right. I lingered a bit longer, watching the townsfolk strolling in the near-perfect evening air. Some of them I'd met before, and we exchanged greetings, but many I didn't know—including the couple who had just witnessed my exchange with Ivan inside the pub; they passed by without noticing me, sharing the one thing I feared Brad and I lacked—love. Just a tiny important piece of the equation. I sighed.

We walked farther down Spirit Lane, which was lined with fully decked-out businesses with pumpkins, bundled corn stalks, gourds of every shape, size, and color imaginable, orange and yellow lights, fall garlands, scarecrows, you name it. It surpassed even my expectations. Ghosts of all kinds hung from doorways, streetlamp posts, tree branches, and everywhere else one could hang something. Businesses pulled out all stops and spent extravagantly hoping to win the decorating contest at the end of the week-long Harvest Festival.

I walked with Aspen down the block past the darkened windows of Spirit Vineyard Protestant Church and the decorated windows of Lakeview Pharmacy and Hallowed Grounds Coffee before turning back toward the car. As I passed an alley and glanced into the seemingly endless darkness, gooseflesh covered my arms as I spotted what looked like a moving shadow. I shook my head and continued forward. *You've got yourself all wigged out, girl.*

By the time we returned to the inn, the work stress was long gone. I could deal with Ivan in the morning. Tonight, I was going to settle in my room with my journal, Aspen by my side. Jade had left for the night, and the front desk was beautifully quiet. Yet it looked alive with the orange lights circling the desk, the pumpkins placed throughout the inn, and, my favorite, enough sunflowers and daisies to stock the shelves of the floral shop in town.

I looked through the bank of dining-room windows that lined the wall facing the lake. The stars speckled the sky, and the moon hung, suspended. Even a bat or two zipped beneath the trees, snatching the remaining mosquitoes. The view was stunning. A few people were still enjoying the bonfire, green and black plaid blankets supplied by the inn covering their laps as they held roasting sticks with marshmallows over the flame. I smiled.

"Come on, my good boy," I said to Aspen. "Let's grab you a biscuit to take upstairs for a bedtime treat. I have a feeling it's going to be an early, stressful morning."

Aspen followed me into the kitchen, dark save for the light over the giant ovens, which emitted just enough light to see without having to turn on the overhead lights. As I walked over to the large jar that held the dog biscuits, Aspen let out a low growl in the doorway. I startled.

"Aspen? What's wrong, boy?" I wasn't sure he'd *ever* growled. Ivan be damned, I motioned Aspen toward me and kneeled beside him, looking into his eyes. "What's wrong, boy? We have to hurry. I don't want to chance Ivan popping in and finding us in the kitchen." Aspen stared at something past me, panting and unsettled. I followed his gaze behind me and gasped. Ivan wouldn't be catching me here in his kitchen ever again. He was dead.

Chapter 4

I gasped and circled my arms around Aspen's neck before I duck-walked toward Ivan, his body sprawled on the floor, to feel if he had a pulse. Given the shiny red pool accumulating by his head and no trace of life, I'd guessed correctly. He was as dead as they come. I scooted closer to investigate what caused the bleeding, expecting to find a gash on his shaved head from a fall. I caught my breath. Lying on the floor beside his neck was a bloody corkscrew. This was no accidental fall at all. Ivan was murdered.

I bolted back to where Aspen sat, rooted in place, still uneasy. My fingers fumbled with my phone. It slipped from my shaking hand and clattered on the floor, skittering under the stainless-steel workstation that ran dead center down the length of the kitchen. My already frayed nerves twinged even more from the noise. Aspen panted and whimpered quietly, enough to let me know he was not a fan of dead bodies.

I used to do the hair and makeup of the deceased at a funeral home in Birch Haven, Minnesota, to prepare for viewing. Most of them didn't upset me, which was unsettling in itself, I supposed. But having just argued with Ivan mere hours ago and that he was an employee of mine, this was different.

And then reality punched me, the weight of it bowling me over onto my hind end. I sat there, wondering what to do. There wasn't any way I wouldn't be a suspect in this. If Brad was right, everyone in Brewski's heard Ivan and me arguing. Not that the pub was packed with people, but all it took was one. And there was far more than one.

My breathing quickened, and I grasped onto Aspen for comfort. Given his dislike of the situation, I was pretty sure I'd become his emotional support human. What a pair we were. Unsure if shortness of breath would precipitate a panic attack, I steadied myself by focusing on Aspen until I could function. Finally, clutching my phone, I punched in 911 and stayed on the floor with Aspen, remaining still in the dim lighting of the kitchen, until sirens shattered the quietness of the night.

****

The guests, awakened by the screaming sirens as they approached the inn, huddled in a group to get a glimpse of the commotion, but soon found themselves in police interviews instead. By the time the interviews ended, police and crime scene investigators finished, and the coroner had removed the body, it was midnight. The mention of murder made most of the guests uneasy. But some of them were a little too excited—making *me* uneasy—and one was convinced it was a Halloween prank.

After I'd gotten everyone from the inn calmed down, it was almost two in the morning. It wasn't until the last guests retired to their rooms for a few remaining hours of sleep that it hit me. None of the staff knew about Ivan's death. The only two who were close with him were Tony, the sous-chef, and Jade, with whom people suspected the connection to be more involved than friendship. But it was a rumor I chose not to entertain.

Unless I knew something for a fact, I had no time for rumors and cut off all the talk about it whenever it came up. *But what if it wasn't only a rumor?* I wondered. *Could she have had a motive?*

My thoughts zipped back to Tony, and an additional concern arose. We had to think of a breakfast alternative for the guests and hope they wouldn't be disappointed since the kitchen was still a crime scene and we had to keep it closed for business until the evening meal. Breakfast was the most extensive and elaborate meal the inn served, dinner a close second. In fact, we often had diners who weren't guests at the inn. With a murder at the inn, breakfast was probably the last thing on anyone's mind though, so the worry may be for naught. Even so, we'd need to have something available. I'd have to call Tony and brainstorm workable solutions. I wondered how he'd take the news about his friend. I'd wait to tell Jade until she came in. Small town and all, I hoped they wouldn't find out before then.

I took a deep breath, and once again turned to Aspen for comfort. Who needed Brad? Aspen was there whenever I needed him, and he never let me down. Even if I was in a foul mood, he trotted me right out of it. I rolled my eyes—what a sad perspective on how I felt about Brad. We had been all but over for months now, and I knew I needed to tell him soon and not string him along.

Deciding that waiting even a minute longer to call Tony didn't put off the unpleasantness, I picked up my phone from the table beside my reading chair and punched in his number. He picked up on the fourth ring. "Yelllo." His voice was thick with sleep and a bit slurred.

"Tony?"

He cleared his throat. "Yeah?"

"It's Andie Rose."

He coughed, then said, "Hold on. Wait a second for me to get my bearings."

After a minute of silence, I feared he'd fallen back to sleep. "Tony? Are you there?"

"Yeah. I was out kinda late last night. What's up at—almost two in the morning?"

"Bad news, I'm afraid. Are you alone?"

He snickered. "That's kind of a personal question coming from my boss. But, yeah, I'm alone."

I laid the back of my hand against the warmth of my cheek. "That's not exactly what I was—Ivan died last night." There was a loud crash on his end. "Tony? Are you okay?"

"Uh—yeah—as okay as I can be after that bombshell. Definitely awake."

"Sorry. I don't know of an easy way to give news like that. I know he was a friend of yours."

"Friend? Not exactly."

I reared back at the intensity of his retort. "I thought you guys were tight."

"We worked together; that's it."

Tony snickered bitterly, and I had to wonder if he was in shock. When I didn't say anything, he continued.

"That's water under the bridge. Especially now," he said. "So what happened? Who did he tick off?"

His question shook me. He guessed it was murder? "Tony, what makes you think he ticked someone off?"

He groaned. "Listen, thanks for letting me know, but can we talk about this tomorrow when I come in? I'm sleeping off a hangover. Last evening was a nightmare."

For me too. I thought I'd gotten to know Tony well over the past few months and liked the guy, so his lack of sympathy stunned me. I bit my lip at his probable response to the request I was about to make. "Well," I began, "I was hoping we could brainstorm on how we can improvise. Obviously, the kitchen is closed until tomorrow's dinner. Crime scene."

He groaned. "Oh, man. I hadn't even thought of that. I'm the lead chef now."

Oh, boy. *Had* he thought about it? He insinuated he knew Ivan was murdered and had a complete lack of sympathy. Now he assumed the position he'd always wanted was his. Tony hadn't made it a secret that he should have Ivan's job. Had he killed Ivan to get it? And what about the friendship I thought was there but apparently wasn't? In fact, the opposite. I made a mental note to ask him about it in the morning. Or later *this* morning, to be precise.

"Neither the restaurant on the edge of town nor the café on Spirit Lane open early enough to place an order the size we'd need to feed everyone. Any suggestions?"

"If the guests know there's a murderer running loose, they've probably been awake all night to be sure they're not the next victim. You really think they're gonna be hungry after that?"

"All the same, we need to execute a plan. I'll get cracking in the morning to look for Ivan's replacement."

"Wait, what?" His tone changed to one of confusion. "What do you mean? Why would you look for a replacement for Ivan? I'm right here."

"You can't take two shifts. It's not sustainable. And I can't cover yours for an extended timeframe."

"But I—"

"Can we talk about this later, Tony? Right now, I'm solely focused on ideas for what we can do for breakfast."

He huffed, then exhaled. "All right."

"What if we did something of a continental breakfast like we did at the hotel I used to manage?"

"Like every other hotel?" he said. "That's hardly special."

I gave a long, frustrated sigh. "We made it special at the hotel I worked at. Besides, got any other ideas, hotshot?"

"The headache I had before you called was bad enough. Now it's a tsunami." After a moment of silence, he said, "Lakeside Grocery is open 24/7. I'll stop and pick some things up and we can set them out in the dining room. I'm going to give you the receipt for reimbursement, though, because I can't afford it on a sous-chef salary."

Relief calmed me. His somber joke told me he forgave me for waking him up and for not giving him Ivan's job on the spot. I had no doubt we'd be having that conversation before the day's end, but right now I just couldn't. The crime didn't only rob Ivan of his life, it sucked every ounce of strength and every brain cell from me.

"I'll even add on a bonus," I said. "Like a buck or something."

"Funny," he said dryly before hanging up.

I held the phone in my hand. Aspen snoozed contentedly beside me. I had to know more about this intense relationship between Tony and Ivan to be comfortable that it wasn't Tony who killed Ivan before letting him take Ivan's place. "Oh, Grandpop, this never happened when you had this place. How would you handle this?" I whispered as I petted Aspen and listened to his even breathing as he slept.

I lay down. Somehow, I had to grab a few winks. A couple of hours were better than none. Before I'd had a second to think anymore, my alarm went off at four thirty, and I was in the exact position I'd lain in two hours earlier. I groaned at the disruption, slapped the snooze button, and tossed my arm over my eyes, but another wink was not to come. Who'd played the prank by setting my alarm clock so early? *Ugh.*

Before coming to the inn, I managed a hotel in Minneapolis. Back then, I woke up at four forty-five every morning to work out before going to work. It hadn't taken long to adjust to my new schedule here at the inn, where I woke at six, either went for a run around Big Spirit Lake with Aspen, or did some yoga, again, with Aspen at my side. A wide running trail separated Big Spirit Lake and Little Spirit Lake. Depending on how much time I had, sometimes we ran around both. Aspen loved the run. The yoga, not so much as he'd lay and watch me with an accusatory stare that seemed to convey, *You get your workout, I should get mine.*

Lost in my memories and grateful for being here at the inn, the reminder of why my alarm sounded so early kicked me in the gut. Gratitude vanished as I bolted upright. My stomach churned with anxiety. Last evening's murder killed any appetite I usually had in the morning.

I got up and saw Aspen was not his usual chipper self. He'd never made it a secret that Ivan wasn't his friend by his standoffish demeanor whenever Ivan was around. Often, he'd even sit on the floor and face the other way.

After I took him outside to pee, we returned to the back stairwell that led directly to my room. I put some food in his bowl and filled his second bowl with fresh water. Then I threw a banana, some strawberries, oat milk, chia seeds, and protein powder into the blender to make a smoothie for some nourishment, washed my face, slipped into a fresh pair of jeans and a long-sleeved T, pulled my hair back in a ponytail again, and sat down with my smoothie while I read today's devotional from my *One Day at a Time* book. But I could not comprehend a single word I read. I'd say the words went "in one ear and out the other," but they hadn't even gone *in* one ear. All I could think about was how long until the police interrogated me about my argument with Ivan at the pub. I didn't cough up the information last night. It seemed like a good idea at the time. Now I realized it wasn't one of my most brilliant decisions. It only made it look like I had something to hide. Which I kind of was, to be fair.

After one final failed attempt at reading, I closed the book and waited for Aspen to finish his breakfast. He was the slowest eater I'd ever known a dog to be. On more than one occasion, if I was hungry enough, I'd been tempted to finish it for him.

His bowl finally empty, I snatched his harness from the chair, and we headed downstairs to begin the day that I hoped brought answers. And a day of being there for the team as they processed Ivan's death, whether or not they liked him.

I half expected the guests to be lined up at the front desk to check out, but no one was there. Heck, they were probably afraid to leave their rooms. I also half expected a rumor that the ghost killed Ivan.

Clattering and scraping sounds came from the dining area. Tony. At least, I hoped it was Tony. I trembled, clenched Aspen's harness, and headed that way. It was time to find out about the hostility between the two chefs.

Chapter 5

As I passed the kitchen, the crime scene tape still crisscrossed the doorway. I shuddered and looked the other way. Tony was deeply focused on rearranging a few tables in the dining room on which to arrange the newly purchased continental breakfast items. When he started lifting item after item out of the large brown bags, I stepped beside him.

"Hey, Tony," I said.

He jumped and dropped a bagel on the floor. "You scared me to death." he said, scowling.

"Don't worry. It's not the killer. Just me and my sidekick here." I nodded toward Aspen.

"I thought you were the ghost who probably killed Ivan," he said.

And there it was with the ghost joke I had expected. "That was lame," I said with an eye roll. It was as if he'd heard my thoughts from a moment ago. "No ghost. Just me."

I bent over to pick up the bagel. Aspen had barely sniffed it, then turned away from it.

"He's not normal," Tony said. "You know that, right? And do not even think about putting that on the plate," he warned.

I narrowed my eyes and set it on a napkin, handing it to him. "Here. Just for you." He took the napkin by the corners and tossed it into the trash can. I cocked my head to the side. "Tony, are you okay?"

He tucked in his chin and leveled his gaze on mine. "Sure, why?" I didn't say anything, encouraging him to talk. He briefly glanced at me, then back to the table. "Because of Ivan?"

"Well, yeah. It's not like he called in sick. He's dead." He appeared to not hear a word I said. "Tony?"

He stopped and looked at me. "Andie Rose, I'm sorry the guy's dead. I wouldn't wish that on anyone. But Ivan had a lot of enemies. He was a class one jerk."

"Who didn't like him?"

"Me, for one. But it doesn't mean I killed the dude."

"Who else?"

"I'm sure Jade's husband wasn't too fond of him, given the circumstances."

My eyes opened wide. "Tom knew about Jade and Ivan?"

He looked at me as if I'd lost the last shred of sense I had. "No offense, but what rabbit hole have you been hiding in? Of course he knew. How could he not? It's a small town. People talk."

"Who else didn't like Ivan?"

"Luka Molotov, for starters." He went back to retrieving items from the bags.

My jaw dropped. "*Deacon* Luka Molotov? Roman's dad? I hardly think he'd be capable of murder."

Tony continued without giving much of a reaction to my surprise. "Why, because he's a deacon? Are they not human like the rest of us?"

"Well, yeah, but—well, I can't see it. Luka Molotov seems like such a calm guy."

"With a flash-bang temper." He glanced at me before pulling a tub of butter from the bag. "I don't know why I couldn't go in the kitchen just to get the things we already have instead of buying all new."

"Detective Griffin said forensics hasn't been completed yet. It's not like I could argue with that. Or that I'd want to."

He shook his head. "Well, I guess it won't go to waste."

"What can you tell me about Luka Molotov's temper?"

"Roman can tell you some stories. Things that have made him afraid of Luka."

"How can he stay on as a deacon then? Why haven't they asked him to step down?"

"It's religion, Andie Rose. Who knows why they do anything they do? There are too many rules to count."

"Not a fan of the Catholic church, eh?"

"Not just the Catholic church; people who call themselves Christians in general."

There were two churches in town, St. Michael's Catholic Church and Spirit Vineyard Protestant Church. St. Michael's held most of the town's population in its membership, but most of both memberships believed in the ghost of Spirit Lake. My grandparents were die-hard Catholics, but even though my AA meetings were in the basement of St. Michael's, I hadn't declared the church my home.

Knowing the history of Christianity, I had nothing solid to hand Tony to change his mind. Nor was it my place to do so. I liked Tony just as he was. Again, I hoped the police would rule him out as a suspect in Ivan's murder. With my help, maybe it would happen faster. When I said nothing further, he went on.

"If you asked the entire town, you'd probably come

up with half of them who didn't like Ivan. And now that includes Jade, too. I overheard them talking in the kitchen yesterday, and she was pretty torqued. She told him she might be pregnant, but it couldn't be her husband's because he's sterile, and Ivan wanted nothing to do with a baby. He even went so far as to ask her if it was his, insinuating—well, you know the insinuation. I don't have to spell it out for you."

I held my hand out. "Wait. If Jade's husband is sterile, how can they have a child?"

He frowned. "Please tell me you don't live such a sheltered life. She was pregnant when she met her husband. The father of the baby left her."

"I assume the guests know." Tony said. "About the murder, not Jade's drama."

"Yes. After the police questioned them, and I assured them they were safe."

His eyes widened. "How do you know that?"

"How do I know what?"

"That they're safe. Someone killed Ivan last night in the kitchen. How do we know that *someone* isn't still here? Maybe we should check the rooms—the one with the *un*barricaded door is probably the killer." I stared at him. "Because it means they're not afraid," he explained.

I nodded. "Oh. I can't imagine any of the guests killed him. And the staff wasn't here. That means the killer is probably someone else, and they're not just gonna hang around, waiting for someone to discover them."

"Unless it was the ghost," he said, wiggling his thick black Italian eyebrows.

"Seriously?" I squinched my face.

"All I'm saying is that no one knows if it's a friendly

ghost."

"Or if there *is* a ghost." I shook my head. "And this is hardly the time to joke."

Tony stopped what he was doing, and his eyes grew wide again in mock horror. "Don't let anyone in Spirit Lake know you question the ghost. They'd hang you."

I stared at him, at a loss for words. Finally I said, "Inappropriate much?" Yet, the Tony I knew was a good man, and I hoped it wasn't him who killed Ivan. I enjoyed having him as part of the team. "So tell me about this spat between you and Ivan you mentioned on the phone. And how is your hangover, by the way?"

"Ibuprofen does wonders."

"And the spat?"

He ripped off a sheet of plastic wrap and began wrapping the bagels and sweet breads. "The scum stole a recipe of mine. Entered it in a contest and won some serious money. Not only did he steal from me, but he didn't even share the money the recipe won."

"That must have made you so mad." I held my breath, waiting for his reply.

He gave me the side-eye and said, "Yeah, but I wouldn't kill over it if that's what you're getting at." He forced a smile and winked. "We Italians are lovers, not fighters." He looked around him. "Where did it happen, anyway?"

"In the far east corner of the kitchen." I shuddered as I remembered Ivan's lifeless body. Aspen looked up at me, then sniffed the air with all its breakfast smells— I nabbed a dog biscuit from my pocket and handed it to him, snickering when he only sniffed it. "Don't be a snob, Aspen. You're a dog. This is what dogs eat." I turned my attention back to Tony. "What do you know about Jade's husband?"

"Seems like an okay guy. But don't they all? Some people only let you see what they want you to see. Chameleons."

"That, Tony, is not you." I smiled. "You tell it like it is."

"That's me. King of honesty." He studied me as he folded a now-empty paper sack. "So, about the lead chef position. What's up with that? You can't seriously give it to someone else. I've earned that position fair and square. You know I'm good."

I poked my tongue inside my cheek and squinted as I studied him.

"No," he confirmed, "I didn't want it so bad that I'd kill for it."

"I didn't say you did."

"I know what you were thinking."

"Apparently not." I smiled at him, but I still wasn't a hundred percent convinced. "Tell you what, if you can take over and somehow carry both positions without killing yourself until I can get someone else in here to help you—"

"Help me," he repeated. "Does that mean I'm not the lead, or I *am* the lead?"

"If everything goes well, then yes, you will be. Let's move in that direction. I'll get started today on filling the sous-chef position." *That would give me a bit of time until either the police or I catch the murderer. And hopefully to prove Tony's innocence.*

He smiled, satisfied. "But you're able to cover me this afternoon, right? Ibuprofen only works so long. I'm pretty sure my head will split wide open by then."

I grimaced and shook my head. I didn't miss that

part of my drinking days. Not even a little. "Yes, I'll cover this afternoon and can help as much as possible after that. I know my way around a kitchen. We don't need you dying, too," I mumbled.

"Yeah, I know. And Ivan hated that. That you knew your way around *his* kitchen."

"I'm aware. But so we're straight, I *will* use the kitchen to make the dog biscuits and anything else I want to bake. I will not get in your way, will clean up after myself, and replace used items. You won't even know I was there."

He grinned. "I don't care if you *are* in the kitchen." He nodded toward Aspen, who sat beside me. "Just make sure there's no dog hair anywhere. Meaning, keep him out."

"Give me some credit. You know I don't bring him into the kitchen with me." I looked at Aspen, then cocked my head in defeat. "Well, except last night when we found Ivan. But hand to God," I lifted a hand in the air, "I don't bring him into the kitchen."

Emotional support animals had become controversial since I've had Aspen. They aren't allowed the same privileges as guide dogs and other support animals. While I don't discount the importance of guide dogs, mental health is an illness, too, and it sticks in my craw that they aren't considered as such.

Tony chuckled. "I know. I'm just teasing you."

"Good, because just so you know, if I wanted to, I would."

Tony snickered. "No rebellion in you, no sir."

I offered a bemused smile. "Call it what you will."

I was still a little shocked by Ivan's hostility toward Aspen in the pub last evening. I knew he didn't like dogs, but didn't know how strongly he felt about them.

Aspen and I went to the front desk so I could look at the reservation book. Unless people heard about the murder and canceled because of it, we were booked solid well into January. I'd have to act fast. Getting my life coach business up and running here would have to be put on the back burner for now as I helped Tony in the kitchen whenever I could and conducted a search for a sous-chef.

I made a list of people I could call for suggestions on temp replacements but would have to wait to make the calls until a decent hour. I checked in with Tony again, who assured me he had everything under control. Although, I was sure he'd be hitting a proverbial wall within a few hours. The shadows under his eyes looked as gray as the ash in the fire pit.

With nothing left to do downstairs at the moment, I told Tony I'd be up in my room for an hour, but back down before Jade arrived. Aspen would not get his run this morning, and once he figured that out, he'd likely give me an attitude for a bit. While sleep was my fix, chasing bunnies and squirrels, and marking everything raised by an inch or more from the ground, was his. But his disappointment would pass. Animals were so much more forgiving than humans. That thought circled me back to Brad, and I wondered how forgiving he'd be when I told him no. Would he want to go on as usual, or will my "no" to his proposal be the end of us? Not that there was really an *us* anymore, anyway. I realized it was up to me to pull the plug. I thought about calling him and getting it over with, but decided to wait since he'd likely still be sleeping.

When I went past the library, the copy of *The*

Woman in Black lay on the chair again. And, again, I re-shelved it but then pulled it back out. A guest might be reading it, leaving it here between reading sessions.

Once inside my room, I lay face down on my bed. Except for kicking off my sneakers, I remained fully clothed. Aspen jumped up and curled in beside me. But he wasn't as still as I'd hoped, probably dreaming of the squirrel that got away. Finally, I got up. If I didn't have the energy to take him for a run around the lake, at the very least, I could take him for a walk in the woods. No shortage of rabbits and squirrels there.

As we tromped through the fallen leaves on a trail that cut through the woods, daylight peeked through outstretched, partially bare limbs. Soon they would be naked, waiting for springtime clothing again. But now, in the dawn, they'd gone from looking beautiful to sinister, thanks to the state of my mind since Ivan's murder and knowing the killer was out there somewhere. I desperately hoped the killer wasn't out here in the woods, watching. I shivered and looked in every direction.

Satisfied we were alone, I thought about the potential suspects so far—Tony, Jade, Jade's husband, and Luka Molotov. Good gracious, a deacon. Was there no safe place? I hoped more came to light during the investigation because I didn't want any of them to be the killer.

Twigs snapped in the distance ahead of us, and Aspen stood deathly still. If I didn't know better, I'd have thought he was a pointer. My breath caught in my throat, and I kneeled beside him, my arm around his neck, and whispered, "How about we go back to the inn, my friend? I think you've seen enough wildlife for now." As if he understood me, he turned quickly without argument, and we began our journey back. Thankfully the daylight was brighter by now.

By the time we got back to the inn, there was only about half an hour before Jade arrived; Lily, the other front desk employee, would arrive three hours later. Lily usually worked the earlier shift, and Jade closed, but they switched schedules today so Jade could go to an appointment. I wondered if the appointment was about the baby. Selfishly, I wished they hadn't switched shifts, because once Jade learned about Ivan, I wasn't sure if she would have to go home without finishing hers. Not that I'd blame her, especially after the news.

I glanced at my watch. I had fifteen minutes to plan for Jade's potential meltdown.

Chapter 6

At ten minutes past the hour, I considered whether to call Lily or handle things myself when the front door opened. One look at Jade, and I wondered if she'd already heard about Ivan. If not, the news would for sure send her over the edge.

"Jade? Are you okay?" Aspen strolled over to give her a little lovin'. At first, Jade didn't appear to notice.

"I'm fine." But her tone said she was anything *but* fine. She reached down and absently scratched Aspen's head.

"Umm—you heard the news?" I asked.

She studied me through glassy, bloodshot eyes. *Tears or booze?* My hard guess was she'd been crying. She could have been drinking with Tony, but I dismissed that notion out of hand.

Finally, she said, "What news, that Ivan is scum?"

Her brutal honesty rattled me, and I swallowed a gasp. "Excuse me?"

She took a deep breath and sighed before settling into the chair behind the desk. "You're going to find out anyway, so I might as well tell you."

"Tell her you're pregnant?" Tony asked across the room from the doorway to the dining room.

"Eavesdrop much?" Jade said, eyes narrowed.

But the anger gave me hope she was going to be okay. It beat not feeling anything at all.

"What are you doing here, anyway?" she asked him. "Where's Ivan?"

"Not here," I blurted before Tony could say anything. I didn't think he would, but since he was now standing beside me, I didn't want Jade to haul off and crack him one.

Jade turned toward me. "What, he's sick? Well, I am too, and because of that dirtbag, I have a good reason to be."

"Takes two to tango," Tony said.

Jade's eyes radiated hostility.

"There's no easy way to tell you this, Jade, but Ivan won't be coming back." I studied her eyes carefully, but there were no telltale signs of anything. "He's dead," I said. Her expression didn't change in the slightest.

Finally, she sniffled, shook her head to clear the apparent puzzlement, then squinted and said, "What?"

"Ivan's dead."

She shook her head harder. "He can't be. I just saw him last night. What happened?"

Tony wiped his hands on a white hand towel before tucking a corner into the belt of his apron.

"Tony, where did you get the apron and towel?" I hadn't even noticed them earlier. "Tell me you didn't go into the kitchen," I warned, crossing my arms.

"Okay," he said with a shrug.

"You did, didn't you?"

"You told me not to tell you."

"Tony." I gave an exasperated sigh and shook my head. "Unbelievable. You know the kitchen is off limits right now."

"I needed the apron and towel. I swear I didn't touch anything except the drawer handle where the aprons and towels are," he rationalized.

At a loss for words, I took a deep breath.

"Where did you see Ivan last night, Jade?" Tony asked.

Jade looked from him to me. "Here."

My jaw dropped. "Here?" I croaked. "Why here?"

Her eyes clouded with confusion. "Why not here? When I called him, he said he'd just left Brewski's and was on his way to the inn to get a recipe. Made sense since I live so close. It was convenient." She looked from me to Tony, then back to me. "I don't understand why that's important. How did Ivan die? What happened?"

"Maybe you can tell us that," Tony said, voice low.

Jade glared at him. "What is it you're asking me, Tony?"

"I didn't think it was a confusing question," he answered.

He didn't sound accusatory to my ears, but I could see where Jade might think so.

"Listen," I said, stepping between the two, a hand on Tony's chest and one on Jade's shoulder, creating more distance between them. "Why don't we all take a breath?"

"I didn't mean anything by it; it was just a question," Tony said.

"And I didn't appreciate the insinuation," Jade snapped.

"If you have nothing to hide, then you wouldn't assume I was insinuating anything."

He had a point, but in this context, it wasn't helpful.

"Tony," I said, "please go back to the dining area and finish up. Guests will start arriving any minute."

"Everything is done. I displayed the breads and

bagels, and the rest is ready to go. It's not like there was a lot to do without a kitchen."

Jade looked at Tony. "Why are you without a kitchen? Blow something up? Fire?"

"Hilarious," he scoffed.

"Please go anyway," I said before he could say anything more.

Jade began crying quietly by this time, and I rubbed small circles on her upper back. "Let's go to the library and talk."

"What about the desk?" She sniffled and yanked a Kleenex from the box.

"I'll radio Marcie. I saw her fixing something in the gardening shed."

Jade frowned. "Where's Frank? He's the gardener."

"I assume it's something mechanical, since Marcie's working on it." I picked up the handheld radio and called Marcie. In less than three minutes—three silent minutes between Jade and me that felt more like thirty—Marcie stood beside the desk, her coveralls stained with dirt, and God only knew what else. "Something broken in Frank's palace?" I asked.

"Just an electrical issue that a squirrel could have fixed. But not Frank." She chuckled and shook her head. "So, what's up?"

"Ivan's dead," Jade blurted.

"What?" Marcie said. Her eyes grew wide for a split second before she added matter-of-factly, "I guess what goes around, comes around."

Now it was my turn. "What?" When no one spoke, I said, "How is it everyone seems to know things around here except me?"

"Because you don't let us tell you about those

things," Jade said as she tucked a strand of loose hair behind her ear.

Jade hadn't made it a secret that she thought I was old and boring when I didn't engage with her gossip. Never mind the fact that I was mere months older than her. If she only knew me back in the day; if there wasn't drama, I cooked some up. And how life was so much harder back then. As far as I knew, Jade may have started the rumor about her so-called secret relationship with Ivan.

"Not if it's gossip, no," I said. "We've gone over that. Gossip is toxic in the workplace. Anywhere, for that matter."

"Well, not everything is gossip, Andie Rose," Marcie said. "Some things we all *know*."

I sighed and rubbed my temples. "I wish I could ask my grandparents why they kept Ivan on as long as they did if he was such a menace and cross to bear."

"I can tell you that one," Marcie said. "Your grandparents didn't see the bad in anyone."

"That's the truth," I agreed. "Can't say as I take after them in that regard."

"You can ask Sister Alice for anything beyond that. She'd know."

I tilted my head. "Why?"

"Sister Alice and your grandparents were tight," Marcie added.

"Why didn't I know—" I shook my head and waved a hand, dismissing the question I had been about to ask. "Forget it. Marcie, can you watch the desk for a few minutes while Jade and I step out? It shouldn't be long." Given what I knew about Jade and Ivan, I wanted to tell Jade alone, giving her some space to process and emote without an audience.

"No problem," Marcie said.

"If anyone dares to unlock their doors after last night and check out," I said facetiously, "let them know I'll be right back to address any concerns."

"What concerns?" She tilted her head and leaned forward. "It's not like they'd know Ivan. He thought it above himself to be friendly toward anyone except his reflection in a mirror." She glanced at Jade. "Well, with you, too, apparently."

I flinched and waited for the verbal arrows to fly from Jade toward Marcy, pleasantly surprised when nothing came. If it had been Tony who said that, there would have been a second murder on the premises.

Marcie's tone about Ivan wasn't lost on me, however, and I wondered if something had gone down between the two of them. But it also gave me pause about leaving Marcie alone at the desk without full disclosure of the events. The last thing I wanted was for Marcie to hear from a traumatized guest on scene last night.

"Okay, you know what? I'm just going to tell both of you something right here, and then, Jade, you and I will talk privately, okay?" When neither said anything but waited for me to continue, I did. "Ivan's death was not an accident."

Jade's shoulders stiffened. "What are you saying?"

"Someone murdered him."

Jade gasped, and her hand flew to her mouth. "Murdered?" she repeated in disbelief. "But why?" The glint in her eyes revealed something had mentally clicked into place. "That's what Tony meant this morning." Sparks of anger surfaced. "He thought *I* killed Ivan?"

"I don't think that's what he meant at all, Jade." I rested my hand on her tensed shoulder, and she shrugged it off.

"Yeah, right."

"We're just trying to find answers to this senseless tragedy."

"Senseless tragedy, my butt," Marcie grumbled.

My jaw dropped as I looked at her. "Maybe I should look into employee sensitivity training."

Marcie adjusted her cap. "I'm just saying, you can't be like Ivan and expect it not to nip ya in the arse."

"Did you and Ivan have a falling out?" I asked her, wondering if yet another employee could be a suspect.

"Nope. So long as we each stayed in our own lane, we got on fine."

A man and a woman strolled toward us, rolling their suitcases behind them. Our conversation ceased, and Jade excused herself to use the restroom. Just as well. I couldn't trust she wouldn't have a meltdown in front of the guests.

"We're here to check out," said the man.

"Are you sure? You're paid through the next two days," I said.

"Keep it," said the woman. "After last night, we decided our lives are worth more than two nights at the inn, no matter how nice it is here. I don't want to go through another night of propping furniture up against the door and still getting no sleep."

I thought about how all the rooms must look, and I cringed. The cleaners would have their work cut out for them today.

"I understand," I said. "I can refund you for the two nights and put it on the same card you paid with. That's the least I can do. Or a voucher for two free nights to use whenever you want. Just call and schedule anytime." I knew I was rambling, but I didn't want to lose customers.

"Either is fine with us," said the man. "And thank you. I'd hope it's not the fault of anyone here, but all the same, we're out."

But *was* it the fault of someone here? I couldn't say for sure, because there were a lot of things about Ivan and the rest of the crew that came to light in the past six hours. To say it was unsettling was an understatement.

"Can we at least send you off with some breakfast in travel containers?" I asked.

They glanced at each other; the woman gave a subtle nod to the man. "Sure. We'd appreciate that as long as it's not from the kitchen." They craned their necks to look through the dining room doorway. "Thank you."

After settling up with them and watching as they walked out the door, another couple came down the stairs lugging a suitcase.

I forced a smile. "Checking out?" I asked, despite the obvious answer.

"We got little sleep last night for clear reasons," the man said. "We're going to head on to the cities."

"No crime in the city," Marcie muttered.

I jabbed her with my elbow and stepped in front of her, forcing another smile for the couple.

I repeated the check-out and partial refund process with them and another couple after that, providing both with the same breakfast offer. Both couples declined, not that I could blame them. Not only had there been a murder at the inn last night, but it happened in the kitchen. If I were a guest, I'm not sure I'd want to accept food from here either—at least not without some definitive answers.

Right after they left, Jade returned to the desk, face splotchy, mascara smudged.

"Feeling better?" I asked. Not one of my brightest questions.

"Given the circumstances, I suppose. But I wanna know who killed him. And why?"

After another ten minutes, faint breakfast smells of bread and cinnamon wafted our way, along with muted talking and occasional nervous chuckles. Tony picked up cartons of coffee from one of the coffee shops in town, but I longed for the scent of coffee brewing on site. I wondered if anyone from outside the inn would come by for breakfast as usual or if the word had gotten out, keeping people away.

Finally, I decided it was safe to leave Marcie at the desk while Jade and I went somewhere quiet to talk, ultimately deciding on one of the picnic tables outside a back door that the staff used for breaks.

Jade sat on the table, feet on the bench, elbows on her knees. I dropped beside her. Aspen trotted off, exploring for critters.

"How long had you and Ivan been seeing each other?" I finally asked.

"A while. We've only been—intimate—for a few months, though. Wouldn't you know, *this* happens." She put her hand on her stomach.

"Does your husband know?"

"I told him last night after I got home from talking with Ivan."

"Where did you and Ivan talk?"

She looked at me and frowned. "I told you. We

talked here."

"Where here, though? Which room?"

"The kitchen. That's where Ivan was going to get the recipe. Why do you keep asking me that?"

I sighed and released a long exhale. "Jade, I found Ivan's body in the kitchen."

Her hand flew to her mouth. "Ivan was alive when I left, Andie Rose. I swear it." As if it suddenly occurred to her, she said, "That's why Tony couldn't use the kitchen."

"Yes. It's still a crime scene until the forensics team tells us otherwise. What time did you leave?"

"I don't even know. I wasn't paying attention to the time. I was just so upset at him I was seeing red."

"Jade, did—"

"No," she said, her voice loud. "I didn't kill him."

"I believe you," I said. *But did I?* "You know the detective will find out, right?"

"I have nothing to hide, Andie Rose. Nothing," she insisted. "I didn't do anything."

I thought about my disagreement with Ivan at Brewski's last evening, and a twinge of hypocrisy at the fact that I had mentioned nothing about that, either, surfaced. But I knew *I* didn't kill Ivan. A weak rationalization, I supposed.

"Then you have nothing to worry about," I said, then groaned inwardly. I was a pro at giving advice but not following it. "A Detective Griffin will contact everyone who works here today to ask questions as part of the investigation process. He'll follow up with any of the guests. If you want me to, I can see about staying with you during your interview."

"Yes. You know I didn't do it, right?" She looked at

me with wide eyes and adjusted her position.

"Jade, they will find who did this, and then you won't have to worry about it, okay?" She nodded. "I have to ask—what was your husband's reaction when you told him about Ivan?"

She shuddered. "I've never seen him so mad. But can you blame him? He thought he could trust me and found out he couldn't." She stomped a foot on the bench. "I'm. Such. An. Idiot."

I stood and faced her. "Why?" She looked at me in astonishment. "I mean, why did you do it? Have an affair."

She breathed deep, looked down, and scuffed the bench with her shoe. "That's a loaded question."

I held up both hands, palms facing her. "Absolutely no judgment going on here. My boyfriend proposed to me last night, but I don't want to be married. Not to him, anyway."

She looked at me, then off into the distance. "Tom and I have been having problems for a while. He's just so emotionally absent. All. The. Time. I guess I just needed to feel connected to someone and didn't think beyond that." She looked at me and smiled wanly. "If you're not a hundred percent sure you want to marry a guy, Andie Rose, don't do it. Like the old drug slogan, *Just say no.*"

"I plan to. I just haven't yet."

"What are you waiting for?"

"The right time."

"Is there such a thing?" she asked.

I looked off into the woods. "Nope."

Jade's admission about Ivan hung in the air. I didn't see him as the emotionally engaging type. Fact was, if she thought he was, Tom must be super bad. "Do you think Tom is capable of murder?"

Jade's gaze wandered again, this time toward the tree line of the woods. "Hmm. I don't know," she whispered, a tear falling down her cheek. She wiped it with the cuff of her jacket.

I took a deep breath. "All right, then. We should probably go back inside so Marcie can get back to work."

Jade sniffed, nodded, and followed me inside.

Chapter 7

After telling the remaining permanent staff—Lily, the sixty-something-year-old woman who worked with Jade, and Frank Flowers, the gardener—about Ivan's murder, I decided taking an hour away for an AA meeting was in my best interest. I needed a dose of the ribbing, bad jokes, and laughter we all shared there. Jokes others deemed highly inappropriate, offensive, and in poor taste, but had us ex-boozers nearly crying with laughter. We were an odd lot who, under normal circumstances, wouldn't mix. But we got each other like no one on the outside ever could.

I pulled open the heavy oak door of St. Michael's church and attached Aspen's leash to his harness. Except for service dogs, which included Aspen for the meetings, animals weren't allowed. I guess it's because they sucked up the attendees' attention, leaving the speaker talking to air. Couldn't blame them, really. Dogs had that effect on humans. Except for Ivan. And Brad. It's not that Brad didn't like Aspen, he just didn't particularly notice him, even if they were in the same room. He never had a dog growing up, so I couldn't fault him.

Maybe that's a partial explanation of why his marriage proposal shocked me. Why would a man ever assume a woman would give up everything for him? What an insult. We'd been together for several years, but during that time, we'd grown into completely different people.

The lingering smell of incense from the church and terrible coffee from the basement greeted me as I descended the spiral staircase. Today the brick walls caused me a bit of claustrophobia as they appeared to close in, but the smell of coffee propelled me forward. I was a self-proclaimed coffee snob since I'd quit imbibing, but over time, I'd become accustomed to AA coffee. I could honestly say I even enjoyed it.

Everyone greeted Aspen first with baby talk that we humans seemed to reserve for animals. I snickered, and it echoed in the hush that had fallen over the room as they all looked at me. Then all of them started speaking at once.

"What the heck happened at your place last night?"

"Was it murder?"

"Knowing Ivan, just about anything could have happened."

"Do the police know who did it?"

"People," Sister Alice interrupted. "Give the girl a chance to get some coffee and catch her breath." She poured a cup and handed it to me, giving me a side hug after she did. "Now, what do you know?"

"What about the part about letting me catch my breath?" I asked her.

"You're a runner. You've caught it by now."

I laughed a hollow sound that echoed in the darkness beyond and sat in one of the few empty chairs in the circle. Aspen settled in and made himself comfortable at my feet.

"AA traditions, people," I said. "No outside topics."

"The meeting hasn't started yet," one of them complained. "Dish."

I exhaled and shook my head slowly. "I found Ivan dead this morning. But apparently, you already know that." I took a sip of coffee and grimaced. "Sister Alice, did you make the coffee today?"

"Yep."

"I can tell."

"Because it's that good, right?"

"Because it's that strong. More than usual even. The potent stuff must have been your booze of choice back in the day."

She grinned. "Everclear vodka. If you're going to drink, why bother with the stuff pansies drink?"

Everyone laughed.

"So give us details," a man named Scooter said.

"First, am I the only one in Spirit Lake who didn't know all the enemies Ivan had in town?"

"Probably," said Wes Wilson.

I'd met Wes last spring when I visited Spirit Lake with a friend. He was quite the colorful character. He strived to be helpful to others, often to his detriment. He'd too freely loan money, pushing his way into someone's space to help them even when they'd asked him not to. He possessed loud energy that annoyed folks, and language—well, suffice it to say he had *colorful* language. And yet, if anyone needed anything, it was Wes to whom they turned because they knew it was a given.

"Sister Alice, why did my grandparents keep Ivan on for so many years if he was such a nuisance? Marcie said you'd know."

"He wasn't a nuisance to them. He admired and respected them."

"I didn't know he was capable of that. And let me

tell you that admiration and respect didn't carry over to me."

"You know how they were—they gave everyone the benefit of the doubt and wanted to give everyone a chance. Besides, he's a heck of a cook."

"What are you going to do for a chef?" Wes asked.

"Tony will take over. But I'll need to fill Tony's spot ASAP."

"Maybe it was Tony that offed him so he could have the position," Evelyn said.

"Tony's as good as they come," Luna said. "He'd never do that."

"I saw Ivan at the bar the other day," said Bill. "He was in a heated conversation with Mike Swanson. Maybe it was him. Mike."

Sister Alice swiveled her head to look at him over the bright red frames of her glasses. "While that's a concern, Bill, you in the bar concerns me more."

"It's all good, Sister," Bill said. "I've got this."

"Those words are the kiss of death for an alcoholic, Bill," she said, and sighed. "You've been in this program enough times to know that."

"This time's different."

"That's what you said the last two times." Sister Alice shook her head. "Let's get started, shall we? And Andie Rose, can we speak after the meeting, please?"

"Ooh," Wes said, laughing like an obnoxious teenager. "Someone's in trouble."

Sister Alice and I shook our heads and sniggered. *Boys*.

After the initial matters and the routine way we started our meetings, Sister Alice said, "Andie Rose, want to start us out?"

I shrugged a shoulder. "Sure. My name is Andie Rose, and I'm an alcoholic. And by the time the day's over, I'm gonna need a drink." Nervous chuckles gave way to laughter when I said, "Oh, My-lanta, people. I'm kidding."

The strange looks I received at one of my favorite sayings—and one I used often—set the tone for the rest of the meeting.

****

After the meeting wrapped up and the last person trickled out, I stayed with Sister Alice and helped clean the table from the coffee and cookies she'd laid out earlier. Or rather the cookie crumbs, since the cookies inevitably were gone before the meeting was halfway over. I slipped the plate with the crumbs on the floor for Aspen, trying to be discreet, but my effort to escape Sister Alice's attention failed.

Sister Alice cleared her throat. "Dogs don't eat from dishes, Andie Rose."

I met her gaze and smiled sheepishly. "The dishwasher sterilizes it." She stared, not budging in her apparent disapproval. "Aspen is only part dog," I tried again, attempting to win her over. "The human part requires human treats. On human plates." She shook her head slowly. "So what's up?" I asked her. "Why'd you wanna talk?"

"I've come to accept that you're not going to ask, so I'm offering to be your sponsor. You've been free-falling long enough. Your grandpop and Honey would never forgive me if I let you crash and burn."

"Speaking of my grandparents, I don't remember seeing you when I visited as a child. Why have you never told me how close you were to them?"

"You never asked."

If I could sum up Sister Alice in one word, it would be spunky. Or feisty. Or rambunctious. Quirky? Maybe mischievous. Okay, there wasn't just one word that fit her. She had short spiky white hair and favored brightly colored frames for her eyeglasses that sometimes included matching lipstick. She wore a crucifix around her neck and drove a moped almost everywhere she went. She didn't wear the customary habit, which didn't surprise me, but she was sure to wear her headpiece to church on Sundays and while working her shifts at Lakeview Hospital.

From the meetings I'd been to since moving here, I'd learned that Sister Alice grew up in an orphanage and turned to alcohol when she was seventeen until she reached the age of thirty when she got sober and became a sister. "Traded one habit for another," she'd joked. I'd discovered she'd worked at Lakeview Hospital for almost thirty years and lived in a modest house behind St. Michael's church with two other nuns, Sister Ida and Sister Eunice.

"How did you become so close to my grandparents? Other than they were long-time members of St. Michael's."

"They took me in when I first moved here."

She snatched a towel from the countertop, removed her glasses, blew heavily on the lenses, and wiped them off. Thank the good Lord, because the lenses were so smudged, she couldn't have spotted a walrus five feet in front of her.

"They let me stay at the inn free until I got my feet under me." She put her glasses back on.

I smiled as I thought of my grandparents. "That

doesn't surprise me at all. I just wish Grandpop could have been as forgiving with my uncle." She cocked her head to the side and waited, encouraging me to continue. "My uncle and Grandpop had a falling out years ago, and it never got resolved."

"Two people were involved, not one. You can't pin it all on your grandpop."

"But he could have ended it."

"Don't be so quick to judge something you know nothing about," she said, laying her hand on my shoulder. "They were the best people I've ever known."

"Until you met me, right?" I teased. "Do you know what the falling out between Grandpop and my uncle was about?"

She shook her head and sat down in one of the remaining chairs. "Nope, and I never figured it was my place to ask. But I know it was excruciating for him."

"Hmm," I said.

"So?"

Aspen nudged my leg, snapping me out of my thoughts of Grandpop and my uncle. "So, what?"

"Are you going to let me sponsor you?"

"Well, yeah. I was just afraid to ask."

She jerked back a bit. "Good heavens, child. Why?"

"Asking someone to be a sponsor is kinda like asking them out on a date."

"Well, honey, neither of us swings that way, and I'm already married to God. I'da had to say no to that. But I'd say yes to being your sponsor."

I laughed. "Well, in that case, I'm happy to be in a relationship with you."

"Besides," she said, grinning, "you're going to need my help to find out who killed Ivan."

"Why would you think I'd work on that?"

"Because I've been keeping my eye on you for the past several months and know you're the curious type."

"Are you calling me nosey?" I smirked.

"If the shoe fits. And from seeing Ivan leave the pub the other night and then you and your pup not long after. You looked like you had the weight of the world on your shoulders. Something went down between the two of you in that pub, and I assume you'll need to eliminate yourself as a suspect."

I squinted. "Sister Alice, were you spying on me?"

"Good heavens, no. I just happen to catch a show once in a while when I walk through town."

I nodded. "Hmm. I'm sure you do. Free entertainment."

"I don't make enough on a sister's salary to pay for it," she said. "Now, what have you got so far on Ivan's murder?"

"From what I've heard, it could be just about anyone in this entire town. Including some of my staff." I shook my head and exhaled. "I want to clear them and find out who the actual killer is. Tony went so far as to joke that it was the ghost."

Sister Alice smiled. "That sounds like Tony. He's a good one, that boy."

"And one with a motive to kill Ivan," I said, sighing as I slumped back in my chair. When she made a rolling motion with her hand, encouraging me to keep talking, I said, "He's been wanting the lead chef position. Also, he told me Ivan stole a recipe from him, entered it in a contest, and won pretty big bucks. And at thirty-one," I added, "he's hardly a boy, as you call him."

She shook her head. "Honey, all men are boys. But

I know Tony. He wouldn't kill over that. He wouldn't kill at all."

"Well, the police don't know that. That's why we need to clear him."

"And clear *you*. That's why I want to help you with this."

I gave her a sidelong glance. "This so-called partnership doesn't mean I have to ride in the sidecar on that moped of yours, does it? I want to drive."

"Of course you do. One of the biggest lessons we learn in AA is to stop trying to be a control freak." She winked, then grinned. "I'm large and in charge here."

I laughed. This was going to be one fun *relationship*. I only regretted not asking her sooner.

"What else have you got?" Her eyes danced behind the red frames.

"Are those even prescription glasses, or do you just enjoy being bold and colorful?"

"Both. I have prescription ones for when I drive. The rest are my unique style. Now come on, tell me what else you've got."

"Well, as you heard in the meeting, there's the guy he fought with at Brewski's a couple of days ago—Mike Swanson, was it?" Sister Alice nodded. "And Jade, who works at the front desk—do you know Jade?"

"Of course. It's a small town."

"With a ton of tourists," I added.

"Well, I hardly think a tourist works at your front desk."

I narrowed my eyes at her. "Am I going to regret having you as my sponsor?"

"Probably," she said. "What about Jade?"

"Gosh—that's a pregnant one there. Literally. But

I'm not sure I should spread my employees' secrets."
Sister Alice stared at me, her short, white spiked hair
sticking up more than ever as she ran her hand through
it. I sat up straight again. "Jade and Ivan were having an
affair. Jade turned up pregnant, confronted Ivan. Ivan
wanted nothing to do with it, and I assume an argument
ensued. In the kitchen, where I found Ivan's body."

Sister Alice whistled through lips, red to match her
frames. The red made the small mole on her upper right
lip stand out.

"Jade also fessed up to her husband last night.
Which means—"

"Tom could have confronted Ivan," she finished.

"How well do you know Tom?"

"Enough to know that his silent nature disturbs me
just a tad." She pinched her thumb and forefinger
together. "It's like something is lurking behind that
wall."

"A killer?"

She pressed her lips together. "Well, I certainly hope
not, but I couldn't tell you to be sure."

"And then there's—are you ready for this one?"

"Spit it out."

"Luka Molotov."

"Hmm. I've known about the falling out between
Ivan and Luka for years."

"Is Luka capable of murder?"

"I certainly hope not. He's the deacon at St.
Michael's." She pursed her lips and blinked rapidly.

"So I've heard."

"If you came to church, you'd *know* instead of only
hear about it." She winked at me. She did that a lot. Like
we were in a secret club, sharing a top secret. And I guess

we kind of were. Alcoholics Anonymous was kind of secret, hence the anonymous part, unless you were a member.

"The church will go up in flames if I walk through the doors. I haven't been since long before Honey and Grandpop died." My grandmother got the nickname because that's what Grandpop always called her. The kids in town thought it was her real name. I was into my teens before I learned it wasn't.

"If Luka's a killer, and it hasn't gone ablaze from his presence, I hardly think it would for you."

I cocked my head to the side. "Good point. I'll think about it; how's that?"

"It'll do." She smiled. "I want to hear about what happened in the pub last night. What was going on with you when I saw you a mere half hour after Ivan stormed out? And what were you doing in a bar?"

"It's where Brad—my boyfriend—wanted to meet."

"How considerate of him," she scoffed.

"It wasn't a big surprise. Brad's a sports nut and follows all the Minnesota teams. He knew the Vikings football game was going to be on the tube. But what *did* surprise me was I thought he was coming to break up with me. Instead, he proposed."

My heart flipped, then flopped. Not because of excitement, but because I didn't know what Brad would do once I gave him my answer.

Two parts of my brain I'd studied in life coach training played tug of war—the amygdala, incapable of rational thinking, asked me if he'd be out of my life entirely and was I ready for that? The prefrontal cortex, the part responsible for logic, reminded me it wouldn't be any different than it was right now if I didn't see him again. And then the amygdala began wedging itself back in control like a bad pair of underwear. Nope. It was no longer a comfortable fit for either of us.

"He proposed?" she asked, her eyes wide. "I hadn't realized it was that serious. You don't see much of one another, do you?"

I shook my head. "Not anymore. He wants me to move in with him and start a family. I don't want that. Not now. At least not with Brad," I added.

"Good. This town doesn't want to lose you."

"I'm not leaving this town, Sister Alice. Unless the ghost shows herself to me and demands it. Then I'd run like a scared little girl."

Sister Alice laughed loudly. "I'd pay a million bucks to see that show. What about—"

My cell phone rang, and I slipped it from the back pocket of my jeans, expecting it to be from the inn. I'd been gone longer than anticipated, and as short-staffed as we were, I needed to stop procrastinating and hightail it back.

Seeing it wasn't a familiar number from the inn, I answered, "This is Andie Rose."

"This is Detective Griffin. We need to talk."

This time, my stomach flipped, then flopped from dread. I knew what this was about, and it wouldn't be pleasant. I was gladder than ever that I had Sister Alice helping me. I was going to need all the help I could get.

Chapter 8

After phoning Lily to tell her I had to make a detour and couldn't be sure when I'd be back—I left out the part about the police station—I changed my mind about going there at all. My staff needed me right now. And I had to get back to relieve Tony so he could go home and get some sleep. The next few weeks were bound to bring about grueling hours for him.

Hoping not to upset him, I dialed Detective Griffin back and let him know I had to get back to the inn immediately and could he please meet me there. He hesitated, then agreed. Since he would be at the inn this afternoon, I hoped he interviewed everyone on staff today to get it over with. I didn't want it hanging over us like a malevolent cloud, causing nothing but anxiety.

Aspen and I had no sooner walked in the front door of the inn when Detective Griffin arrived. The guests who were outside enjoying the beautiful day strolled in shortly after him. I assumed out of curiosity. It's not every day there's a murder at the place one was staying—thank God. I couldn't fault them for wanting answers. It impressed me that more of them hadn't checked out, tires squealing as they made their escape.

"Good afternoon, Detective," I said.

He nodded his head in acknowledgment. "Do you have somewhere private we can talk?"

I felt all eyes on me. As a taller-than-average

redhead, I was used to people giving me a second look. I didn't exactly fit into what society considered the norm. Heck, not just my hair and height, but all of me was far from society's consideration of normal. I had legs *up to here*, which served me well in track and field during high school and college, so there was that, at least. But this was hardly the same. I shifted my weight from one foot to the other and felt my cheeks warm.

"Let me check in with Tony, and then we can go back to my office."

He waited by the front desk while I escaped the proverbial heat to let Tony know I'd be back to relieve him as soon as I finished the interview with Detective Griffin. Then he could beat it and get some rest.

"I can't imagine he won't want to talk to you before you split, though," I told him. "Has he called you yet?"

"Yeah, but he said he wanted to talk to you before the rest of us." He cast me a sidelong glance. "Probably to get the dirt on each of us."

"Well, you know I don't play that way. At least, I hope you know that by now."

"He's probably hoping it *is* one of us so he can wrap up the investigation and close the case fast."

Tony's words left echoes of discomfort. If his statement held an ounce of truth, Detective Griffin's focus would fall solely on us, and he might not investigate anyone outside the inn.

"There's nothing more to do here until we get the green light to reopen the kitchen."

"I'll ask him if he has any idea when that will be. I hope we can get the all-clear so we can prep dinner." I turned back toward the doorway and said over my shoulder, "We'll be in my office. Call if you need me for anything."

"Is your ringer back on?"

I turned back toward him. "Yeah. I turned it back on after the meeting."

My staff all knew about my AA meetings. Shortly after the start of my sobriety, Brad said I had nothing to be ashamed of and that if someone was going to criticize me for improving my life, that was on them. I smirked at the memory and the irony.

"Back soon." I waved and returned to the entrance area where Detective Griffin waited. Jade squirmed and looked uncomfortable under his watchful eye, like she wanted to be anywhere but there. Her pale complexion took on a greenish hue and I wondered if she might puke. And if so, from dis-ease or pregnancy? Lily, on the other hand, gave him no mind.

"Ready?" I asked him, eliciting a look of relief from Jade.

"Want me to keep Aspen?" she asked. "He'll like it better; I can guarantee it." Her offer earned a scowl from Detective Griffin.

If ever I needed an ESA, it was now. "No, I want to keep him with me. Thank you, though."

The detective stood and followed me to my office. I closed the door behind him. If he planned to confront me about my dispute with Ivan last evening, which I was sure he was, given his tone when he called, no one else needed to hear. I only wished Aspen could testify on my behalf.

I gestured to the chair in front of my desk, then went around and sat behind it. He sat back and tugged on the front of his button-up shirt as if loosening it from around his beefy neck. Jeans, no tie, no jacket; police appeared to keep things casual here in Spirit Lake. For that, I was grateful. Denim, whether on me or anyone else, always made me comfortable. And barefoot. Oh, how I loved to go barefoot whenever possible. I wriggled my toes, wishing I'd changed into my flip-flops.

"Are you interviewing my staff today as well?"

"Planning on it. But it depends on how our conversation goes. Perhaps not all today."

"Jade—the younger gal from the front desk—asked me to be with her when you do."

He looked at me over the rim of his glasses, a second chin protruding. "And why is that?"

"Ivan was a friend of hers. She's distraught."

"She looked like she was in her late twenties, early thirties. She's not a minor, nor are you her guardian. So, no, you won't be able to do that."

"If I'm sitting by her with my mouth shut, helping her to be more comfortable, what could it hurt?"

"She might not be as forthcoming with information if you're there. That and my interviews with everyone are private."

"Is that the law?"

"Mine," he said, his lips in a firm line. No budging room there, no, sir.

Despite my disappointment, I told him I understood. The last thing I wanted to do was argue with him and get on his wrong side, especially given my circumstances. I stayed silent, waiting for him to open his notebook and flip it to the desired page.

"Tell me about last night," he said.

"I wrote it all in my statement."

Again, he looked at me over the rim of his glasses. "*All* of it?"

"Yes, from the minute I got to the inn and found Ivan until you all arrived."

"Seems to be a pretty big piece from *before* you came back to the inn that you neglected to mention."

My stomach was getting to be a professional at flipping and flopping. I picked up a pen and began toying with it, focusing on it instead of Detective Griffin.

He cleared his throat. "Ms. Kaczmarek?"

I forced my gaze to meet his. "It's not how it might look. I was meeting my boyfriend at Brewski's Pub. While I waited for him, Ivan came into the pub, saw me, and walked on over."

"And?"

"He hasn't liked me since I took over the inn almost six months ago. When I arrived, he took that as an opportunity to stop baking dog biscuits."

He scrunched his face, a cross between a frown and amusement. "Come again?"

"You heard right. Dog biscuits. I told him we would continue making them because several businesses in town bought them from us. This town is very dog friendly," I explained.

"I know. I've been here for many years. And I've bought some biscuits for my own dog. But I don't understand how that created a ruckus between you two."

"So if you're from here, you know how popular they are," I said, grasping at the opportunity to connect with him on some level. "They're not a moneymaker, which Ivan thought made them a nuisance. He said professional chefs don't cook for dogs. I disagreed, told him I'll take over baking them so he didn't have to, and he blew a fuse."

Detective Griffin scribbled furiously in his

notebook. When he stopped, he looked up at me with a confused expression. "So the whole thing was over *dog biscuits*?"

I shrugged and broke eye contact.

"Ms. Kaczmarek?"

I fidgeted with the pen some more, cleared my throat, then said, "And my use of the kitchen to bake. I told Ivan that since he's so unhappy under my ownership, he might want to look for another job." I looked back up at him. "Life's too short, Detective. We spend far too many hours of our day at work to be miserable."

"Couldn't agree more," he said. "That's why I'm hanging it up within the next year. Maybe earlier."

"You don't like your job?" I asked, grasping at yet another opportunity to connect with him, hoping to help with my case.

"Time to move on and figure out what to do with the rest of my life."

"I'm a certified life coach who helps people find their purpose and passion. I'm also a relationship coach." One had to laugh at the irony of that, given my history with relationships, but I comforted myself on more than one occasion with the phrase my father used to say, *those who can, do; those who can't, teach.* "I don't have my office set up to accommodate it yet, but I will within the next few months. Just putting that out there for you." I slid a business card across the desk toward him.

He snatched it up, glanced at it briefly, tucked it in his shirt pocket, then said gruffly, "We're not here to talk about me. What else happened last night at the pub?"

"I asked him for the recipe for the dog biscuits, and he said I'd get it over his dead body."

Detective Griffin stopped writing abruptly and looked at me. "Well, that sure seemed to have happened, huh?"

"I didn't do this, Detective. I wouldn't kill over a recipe." *I sure hope Tony didn't, either.*

"What would you kill for, then?"

He watched me closely, but I didn't respond. I didn't appreciate his inference and wanted to withdraw my life coaching offer pronto. "From what I heard, he returned to the inn to retrieve a recipe after leaving the pub. My guess is it was that specific one. For the dog biscuits."

"Who told you he was coming back for the recipe?"

"One of my staff." I cringed when I realized what I'd done.

"Who?"

"I don't remember."

"Really."

"It was late. I got into a minor disagreement with my boyfriend—"

"First Ivan, then your boyfriend—sounds like it wasn't your night. But I bet if you tried real hard, you'd be able to remember who told you that."

I exhaled and sighed. "Jade," I mumbled.

"And how'd she come by that information?"

"Because they're friends—*were* friends—and they'd talked on the phone." *Innocent enough.* "I heard Ivan was in an altercation with someone by the name of Mike Swanson a couple of days ago; that one was also at the pub."

"Who told you that?"

"Can't tell you."

"Do I need to remind you—"

"No, I mean, I really can't tell you. I heard it in my

AA group. Anonymous?"

He shook his head and muttered, "How convenient. Any other incidents you know about?"

"I heard Luka Molotov and Ivan are longtime rivals."

His eyes widened. "The deacon at St. Michael's?"

I nodded. "The same."

He narrowed his eyes at me. "You seem to know more about the people in this town in the short time you've been here than I do in my long-term position. One of the small-town gossip mongers?"

"Far from it, sir."

He shook his head slowly and made a grunting noise. "Either way, you're going to be a problem and an obstacle during the remainder of my time at the police department, aren't you?"

"I don't intend to be. But I want to be sure my staff are cleared as fast as possible."

"How about you let me work on that," he warned. "Besides, you might want to be a little more concerned about clearing yourself. The murder weapon, the corkscrew, came from the pub. The name is stamped on it. Can you explain that?"

I shook my head and frowned. "How could I? I don't drink, so there's no reason I'd have had it."

"If you don't drink, what were you doing at a bar?"

I took a deep breath and counted to five in my head. "Just because I don't drink, Detective, doesn't mean I don't live a normal life. That's where my boyfriend wanted to meet, so we met."

"Can your boyfriend verify you were there and the timeline?"

"Yes."

"I'll need his contact information."

I grabbed a post-it note, wrote Brad's name and phone number, and then stuck it on the desk in front of Detective Griffin. "I have to go relieve my sous-chef so he can go home and get some sleep. I had to call him in early to cover Ivan's shift."

"Send him in before he goes home. Assuming I can use your office?"

"Of course you can. But Tony's exhausted." *Not to mention he has a nasty hangover.*

"We're both here, so it makes sense. Shouldn't take long." He opened a worn, brown leather cardholder, slipped out a business card, and held it out to me between his thumb and forefinger. "Call me if you come across more news. Which I have no doubt you will," he snarked.

I reached for the card, tapped it against my other hand, and asked, "I don't suppose I could ask you to do the same?"

He gave me an amused smile. "What do you think?"

I lifted a shoulder and let it fall back down, as I caught my lower lip between my teeth. "Doesn't hurt a girl to try." It looked like I'd be working this out independently. I hoped above hope that Tony didn't incriminate himself by an inability to think clearly in his exhausted, hungover state. "Do you know when we can use the kitchen again?"

"I'll check with the State police while I'm waiting for Tony to come in. They assist us with these cases since small towns don't have the fancy, pricy up-to-date technology."

I nodded. "Thank you, sir. I'll send Tony in."

"I'll be in touch," he said as he punched a number into his phone.

I entered the dining room through the side door so no one else saw me and badgered me with questions or concerns. Not yet anyway. I needed a minute to get my head together. I'd meant to ask Detective Griffin who told him about my presence in Brewski's but ultimately decided it didn't matter.

Tony was slouched on a chair in the corner, his legs stretched out on a chair in front of him. His head leaned against the wall.

"Tony?"

He opened an eye. "Yeah?"

"You're up. Detective Griffin is in my office."

His jaw dropped. "Are you kidding me? My eyelids won't stay open anymore, and my head is pounding."

"Sorry," I said, lifting my hands. "Better to just get it over with. I told him about Mike Swanson—I guess Ivan was in an altercation with him at the pub a couple of nights ago. And I told him about Luka Molotov. I'm hoping he'll stretch his investigation well outside the walls of this inn." I nabbed a bottle of Tylenol from a first aid cabinet that hung on the wall and tossed it to him. "Here, pop some of these first."

"He ask anything about me or Jade?"

I shook my head. "Nope."

"Jade's husband?"

I sighed. "As much as I wanted to say something about Tom, no. It serves no purpose except shedding more suspicion on Jade as having a motive, too." We looked at one another for a moment in silence. "Well? It's not getting any earlier. Give me a quick rundown of what you've planned for dinner and what I need to do."

"Kind of hard to do anything at all when I can't get into the kitchen. Once we know that, we can figure it out."

"Detective Griffin placed a call to the state forensic team to see when they plan to release the crime scene."

He groaned. "This day has been a nightmare."

"Tell me about it," I grumped back.

He stood, stretched, and shuffled out of the dining room toward my office. Oh, how I wished I had planted a recording device under my desk.

Chapter 9

I took up residence in the chair Tony recently vacated, my thoughts vacillating between planning dinner for that evening and murder suspects. I shifted my attention to a Suit who came through the door and strolled toward me. FBI? Attorney? Whoever, he was arrogant, if I had to say so. No bias, of course. I stood.

"Ms. Kaczmarek?" He extended his hand. "I'm with the BCA," he added as I shook his hand.

I squinted. "What's BCA?"

"The Bureau of Criminal Apprehension. I'm here to clear the crime scene. Give me a minute and I'll be out of your hair."

"Thank God." My hand flew up to cover my mouth, and he stared at me, none too impressed. "Sorry. It's just that I was at a loss as to how to serve dinner to our guests."

His eyebrows lifted as he looked around the empty room. "You still have some after last night?"

I nodded. "Surprisingly, yeah. The brave are in town or by the lake ghost hunting."

Now it was his turn to squint and ask what I was talking about.

"There's a ghost on the premises. Or so I'm told. I've yet to see it."

"Maybe the remaining guests are avid Clue fans, taking advantage of the situation to see if the ghost did it in the kitchen with the corkscrew."

I frowned.

"The board game?"

"I know what Clue is." I scowled my disapproval. Someone murdered my chef less than twenty-four hours ago and this guy was cracking jokes.

"My apologies."

After a moment of awkward silence, I said, "So I can go into the kitchen now?"

"Yes."

I turned and began my way there, feeling weights attached to my ankles. I was torn between relief that the kitchen was no longer a crime scene and returning to the gory image burned into my head. I stopped and pivoted at the footsteps marching behind me and the Suit almost bumped into me.

"Is there something else?"

"I should probably do a final run-through to be sure my people collected everything," he explained. "Will only be a minute."

I nodded my okay. Like he didn't have enough time to do that before he gave me the green light?

He ducked under the yellow and black crime scene tape and motioned for me to stay put. After he finished, he ripped the tape from the doorway, wadded it in his hands, and tossed it in the small trashcan by the door.

"You're good to go," he said. "Good luck to you."

What did he mean by that? Did he know something I didn't, like I was doomed to the inside of a jail cell? I took a deep breath to clear the accumulating anxiety. "Meaning?" I called after him.

He turned toward me. "No hidden meaning."

I kept my gaze glued to his back as he passed the

front desk and left, the front door closing behind him.

I took a deep breath to recenter myself and entered the kitchen. The corner where I'd found Ivan's lifeless body snared my attention and held it without mercy. Finally, I broke free from the memory.

****

With the Suit gone, I got down to work at the stainless-steel work island. I gave Aspen the freedom to roam the inn, but as usual, he stayed close to me, now snoozing on the braided run by the kitchen doorway. When he was particularly needy for attention, he hung out with Jade.

I no longer needed to fear getting caught by Ivan in the kitchen, and that thrilled me. Yet, relentless guilt shoved its way in, insistent on being my companion. As payback, the ominous corner where I'd found him seized my attention time after time.

Between getting desserts in the oven and chopping peppers and onions for fish tacos along with a topping bar—the quickest I could think of to make—I stole a valuable minute and searched for the dog biscuit recipe. Coming up empty, I wondered if Ivan had already tucked it in his pocket before his murder. I'd have to ask Detective Griffin. If the police had it, they would hold it as evidence, and he wouldn't release it to me.

Then an idea thwacked me: Ivan wasn't interested in keeping the recipe. He wanted it permanently gone. I crossed my fingers as I turned toward the garbage can. If it was less than half full when Tony left for the night, Ivan emptied it after he finished the breakfast preparation.

I stepped over to the large garbage can, picked up the lid, and peeked inside. *Sweet–my lucky day*. It hadn't been emptied on the day of the murder, and the police apparently found no reason to take it. If Ivan threw the recipe away, it'd be here.

I studied the gross, disgusting contents that only ripened overnight and decided then and there it was to be taken out every single night, even if it held a single paper towel. My nose wrinkled, and I gagged at the thought of digging through it. I thought of Aspen and how much he enjoyed the biscuits, not to mention the businesses that bought them from us to sell in their stores. Those were the ultimate deciding factors to get down and dirty with the trash.

I donned a pair of heavy-duty rubber yellow gloves from the sink, the ones that fit up to my elbows, and began. I'd gotten halfway through it when Tony said, "What are you doing? Can you say health code violation?"

I jumped and emitted a scream before turning to look at him, his eyes and mouth equally round. My cheeks warmed.

"The chef cannot be both cooking and digging in the garbage," he exclaimed.

"I was looking for the dog biscuit recipe. I looked everywhere else and came up empty, so I assumed Ivan may have thrown it away." I pulled off the yellow gloves and threw them in the trash.

He reached into the pocket of his apron and waved a card in front of me. "It's right here."

"How did you get that? And why didn't you tell me you had it?" I asked with an accusation born out of humiliation.

"Why would I? I was going to make a few batches before I left today, but obviously couldn't."

"Oh." Shame crept farther up my neck. "Where did you find it?"

He glanced away and mumbled, "I may have snooped around the kitchen a little when I came in to get the apron and the towel. To see if there was anything suspicious in there."

"Hypocrite," I grumbled.

"I wasn't digging through the garbage while I was cooking," he clarified. "Big difference."

"Whatever," I said, stuffing my hands in my apron pocket. "That stupid recipe was one of the things that caused the entire scene at Brewski's. I was positive he'd return to get it so I couldn't have it."

"What scene at Brewski's? And why wouldn't he have just waited until today?"

"Because I told him to start looking for another job."

Tony's eyes bulged. "Seriously?"

I filled Tony in on the argument between Ivan and me the prior evening. When I finished, I saw Tony's eyes glaze over.

"Look, why don't you head home and get some sleep? You look half dead—pardon the expression. I've got things covered here."

"No more garbage unless you're taking it out to the dumpster. Got it?"

"Yes, sir," I said, crossing my arms in front of my chest. "You sound like my dad."

He gave me a lopsided grin. "Don't go back to your office yet. Detective Griffin's got Jade in the hot seat now."

"Great," I muttered. "She wanted me to be in the interview with her, but he gave me a resounding no."

"He say why?"

"Claims witnesses are less likely to be forthcoming when someone else is in the room."

"He has a point."

"Yeah, but I don't have to like it." I tightened my ponytail by grasping it in two sections and pulling it tight.

"You, too, have a point." He slipped the apron from around his neck and tossed it in the laundry bin with the towels.

"Care to dish about your interview?"

"It'll have to wait. I'm in desperate need of sleep. Besides, neither of us needs the detective coming in here catching us comparing notes. Spotlight's on all of us right now. Especially you and me." He shook his head. "Peace out." With a wave of his hand, he was gone.

****

When Detective Griffin popped into the kitchen, I had just finished putting the food out for the guests with Lily's help. The desserts had five more minutes before taking them out of the oven. Aspen lay sprawled on his side on the floor outside the doorway, and the detective nearly tripped over him. I pressed my lips together to keep from giggling. Karma for making our lives at the inn so darn difficult.

"I'm heading out," he said. "I've spoken with your staff, and I'll tell you the same thing I told them—don't plan a road trip anytime soon."

If he talked with everyone, I'd need to keep my office door open tonight to let out all the negative emotions and vibes that might be stuck in there.

"No worries, Detective. I have a business; it's not like I can pick up and leave anytime I feel like it. Nor do I—or any of my staff, for that matter—have any reason to leave. We're innocent." But were *all* of us innocent? That's what I needed to find out—and fast before my business crumbled and everything Grandpop and Honey worked so hard for disappeared faster than I could run.

"So long, Ms. Kaczmarek. I'll be in touch. And, again, if you find out anything else, which I'm sure you will," he added dryly as he tapped the countertop, "let me know." And then he was gone.

While the guests ate, I puttered in the kitchen, periodically escaping to check on Aspen. He hung close to Jade at the front desk, making Lily and the guests happy as well.

When I breezed through the dining area, refreshing drinks, a couple of guests peppered me with questions about the murder. People at the tables nearby practically spilled from their chairs to hear.

I gave the same scripted answer to everyone; "We've been instructed not to talk about an open investigation, but no one here at the inn has anything to fear." Although the staff received the admonition to keep their mouths shut, it was unlikely it would keep them from talking about it among themselves. They'd just have to be discreet as possible. I agreed with Tony. We were already in the spotlight and didn't need to get caught talking about it openly. Plus, the last thing I wanted was to scare away the guests we had left.

Frank Flowers, the gardener, came into the kitchen a little after six. Frank was seventy-eight and the most benevolent southern gentleman I'd ever known. That said, he was the *only* southern gentleman I'd ever known. I tried not to play favorites with my staff, but Frank quickly became my most beloved employee. He'd made me a lucky gal by staying on when I took ownership of the inn.

"I'm headin' on out, Miss Andie. Anything you need me to do before I leave?"

I turned and smiled at the man standing in the kitchen doorway, dirt smeared on his overalls. His white hair contrasted with his weathered, light smoky quartz-colored skin. I quickly went toward him so he didn't enter the kitchen, inadvertently transferring the dirt.

The man could make grass grow in the desert, and our grounds were flawless because of Frank. Honey had discovered how many people found gardening therapeutic and relaxing, so she opened it to guests as well. Our greenhouse became an attraction to the Spirit Lake Inn all on its own. When Honey died, Grandpop kept it going. There were even clay pots in there that creatives could decorate. Frank thrived on the responsibility for it.

"No, you're good to go, Frank. I hope Detective Griffin didn't cause too much stress for you. He's interviewing everyone who worked with Ivan."

"No stress at all, Miss Andie." He smiled. "That Ivan wasn't a nice man and was a pain in my backside, but I'd never kill him. Heck, I free a trapped mouse if it's still kickin'. If I can't kill a mouse, no way I could kill a human bein'."

I smiled at him warmly. "I can't imagine anyone not being nice to you, Frank. Have a good evening."

"A'right then. See you bright and early." He smiled and waved as he turned and left.

No more than ten minutes later, Jade popped her head into the kitchen, a stark contrast to Frank.

"I'm out," she said.

"Interview with Detective Griffin go okay?"

"Yeah, I guess. I'm looking forward to spending time with my kid tonight. Get my mind off it all."

"Does he know? The detective."

Her gaze shifted to the floor. "Some of it."

"*Some* of it? Can I ask what part he knows and what he doesn't in case he says anything to me?" Again, keenly aware we weren't supposed to be discussing it, I didn't want to bury her if I admitted something to the detective that he didn't know yet.

"He knows about me and Ivan, but that's it. I didn't tell him about the baby, about my fight with Ivan, or about me telling Tom any of it."

I sighed through a long exhale as she turned to leave. "Jade?"

"Yeah?" She poked her head back through the kitchen doorway.

"I hope not telling the truth doesn't come back to bite you."

She frowned. "I told him the truth. Just not all of it."

"Lie by omission," I said gently. *You're one to talk, Andie Rose. Hypocrite much*? "I just don't want it to work against you if he finds out."

She narrowed an eye. "And how would he find out?"

"Not from me," I said, holding my hands out. "But keep in mind, I'm not the only one who knows about it."

"You and Tony. And he better keep his mouth shut."

"You're forgetting about Tom. What if he says something?"

"Why would they talk to him at all?"

"Jade," I said, talking to her as if reasoning with a child. "If they know about you and Ivan, they'd be stupid to ignore the scorned spouse."

Her shoulders fell. "Crap," she cried, blowing

through pursed lips. "I was so worried about the baby that I hadn't even thought of that."

"And not only that," I continued, "but you don't know if Tom has told anyone. For every person you think you can trust, that person has someone they can trust, and on and on."

"I will not get in trouble for something I didn't do," she said with emotion-driven anger. "It sounds like you want me to go down for it."

I crossed the kitchen to where she stood and laid my hands gently on her shoulders, looking her square in the eye. "That couldn't be further from the truth, and you know that. Give the police the truth, and trust that I am working on this behind the scenes, per se. To be sure the right person gets caught. I trust my staff, and I plan on working to clear every one of us." I was fully convinced this time. For the moment, anyway. My trust meter felt broken and unreliable. But while I believed in Tony and Jade, Tom was a very viable suspect.

"How do I tell the old fart now without making myself look even guiltier? I assured him I knew nothing more than what I'd told him."

I took a deep breath and thought about her dilemma. "Let me think about that one, okay?"

She nodded, sniffled, and left.

After dinner, I cleaned the dining area, straightened a few autumn centerpieces of calico corn and sunflowers in vases. I cleaned the kitchen and checked in with Lily, who was scheduled until closing at eight o'clock. She assured me she had everything under control, so I grabbed a jacket and strolled to the lake's edge with Aspen.

The big old willow tree beckoned us. Aspen's

attention darted toward the boathouse in the shadows. He stopped short and let out a barely audible growl. Glancing at what held his attention, I saw only my reflection, long and distorted in the darkened window. I kept my eyes glued there for anything of interest, but try as I might, I couldn't see anything. I shivered and looked behind us where seven adults sat around a blazing bonfire. No kids. But with a murder on the premises the night before, I'm not so sure I'd want my kids running around at dusk either. Usually, only a few people circled the bonfire at any given time. This evening, it was clear they believed there was safety in numbers.

Aspen still hadn't moved, but his stature loosened a bit. I looked at the window one more time and relaxed. Despite the anxiety demon, I considered myself fearless in most things, but clearly, the murder freaked me out.

We walked out on the dock, taking in the scenery from the edge of the lake. Not much moonlight tonight, just enough to draw sinister shadows.

I shivered again and folded my arms in front of me. I inhaled deeply and closed my eyes, savoring the freshness of the lake air. I wouldn't let anything, including murder, chase me away from this place. Especially since the murder victim had been my greatest threat.

My phone vibrated from my back jeans pocket, and I groaned, expecting it to be Brad again. I looked at the screen—an unknown number.

"Hello?"

"Ms. Kaczmarek."

I stiffened at the sound of Detective Griffin's voice. "This is she. How can I help you, Detective?"

"We need to talk."

Chapter 10

Pinpricks of worry zipped up my spine, my fingertips numb. I grasped for Aspen. "What is it?"

"When can you get here?"

It felt like my heart was about to leap out of my chest. "Am I under arrest?"

"I just have a few questions to ask. It shouldn't take long."

"You didn't answer my question, so I'll ask again. Am I under arrest?" Tunnel vision began closing in, implying an approaching panic attack. I wrapped my arm around Aspen and laid my cheek against his silky fur.

"Not at this time."

I began to do four-square breathing, a technique I taught clients—four seconds in; hold for four; four seconds out; hold for four. By the end of the second cycle, my heart rate slowed to a near-safe level, and the tunnel vision disappeared.

"Ms. Kaczmarek, are you there?"

"Yes. I'll be there tomorrow. I'm innocent and have nothing to hide."

This was the perfect time to call Sister Alice if there ever was one. As soon as I disconnected from Detective Griffin, I punched in her number and got her voice recording, so I left a brief message. "Hi, Sister Alice, this is Andie Rose. Call me when you get a minute? Um— thanks."

I kneeled beside Aspen, my arms around his neck, and laid my head against him. "I've gotta be dreaming and living someone else's life since last evening."

As if sensing my distress, he leaned into me and laid one paw on my leg. I sat down, crisscrossed my legs, and he lay down beside me, resting his nose on my knee. I ran my fingers through his silky coat as I mentally traveled through the events of last evening at the pub. And that's when it struck me like a hand grenade. I think I knew exactly what Detective Griffin wanted to talk to me about, and I thought I might be sick. The table next to Brad and me—they'd been drinking wine. I remembered what I assumed to be a pricy bottle of wine since it required a corkscrew opener, not the cheap Boone's Farm or Tj Swan I used to drink. I remembered picking up the corkscrew as a fidgeter during the uncomfortable conversation with Brad. But how was it that that particular corkscrew was the murder weapon? Had Ivan somehow gotten hold of it? But obviously, he didn't kill himself with it.

I tried to remember in more detail the people sitting at the table—I'd never seen them before, and they didn't seem to know Ivan. But that didn't necessarily mean anything. And I hadn't been paying much attention to them. I was too fixated on my situation.

I shook my head. No, that's ridiculous. There was no way it was the same corkscrew. This mess had my mind on an out-of-control rollercoaster. I pumped on the brakes before I hurtled off the rail.

The thrum of Sister Alice's moped, with the unmistakable rattle, neared. I hopped up, and Aspen followed suit. We trotted to the front of the inn, where Sister Alice unfastened her helmet, slipped it off, and spiked her flattened hair with her hand. She removed her goggles from over her eyeglasses.

"Darn bugs wreak havoc on my lenses," she said.

I pulled a tissue from my pocket and handed it to her. "Here. I thought maybe you were already in bed. Does Sister Ida or Father Vincent know you're out roaming the streets so late?"

"Ha," she scoffed. "Sisters aren't the boring, snoring folk people think we are."

"Oh, I knew that as soon as I met you."

She grinned, as if proud of the accusation.

"Sister Ida's the only one I need to sneak past, not Father Vincent. He holds no authority over us. But Sister Ida—*Uffda*. That woman is suspicious every time I leave the house."

Father Vincent was the beloved priest at St. Michael's, and undoubtedly, relieved he had no authority over Sister Alice. Sister Ida, the sister moderator, tried to keep Sister Alice in line—often unsuccessfully. Polar opposites, those two.

"Did you ever think she might have a reason for that?"

She cast me a look—the one that said *keep your opinions to yourself*—and draped the strap of her helmet on the handlebar. "What's up, buttercup?"

"It's been quite the afternoon, and then I got bombshell news right before I called you."

"I offer to be your sponsor, and you immediately hit me up with a problem."

"You didn't offer. You *told* me."

She grinned and hung her goggles beside her helmet. "That's neither here nor there. But I'm here. What can I do?"

Aspen lay at my feet as if sensing this could take a while.

"You could have just called me back, you know. You didn't have to drive out here."

"I didn't know if I'd be doing some kind of intervention."

I chuckled. "Not yet."

She grinned. "Inside or out here?"

"Out here while weather allows. I know all too well its end is near." As a Minnesota native, I knew winter weather could arrive unexpectedly at any time; the brutal cold, thigh-high snow lucky to melt before April or May, and roads layered in ice that meant ice melt that destroyed cars. I motioned toward the back. "Let's go on the dock. That's where Aspen and I were when you arrived."

"Better a ghost overhears than a guest, I guess."

I stopped and turned toward her. "Hey, I've been noticing the weirdest thing—"

She dropped her chin and locked her gaze on mine. "Weirder than finding a body in your kitchen?"

"Are you familiar with the novel *The Woman in Black*? Probably not," I answered before she could.

She frowned. "What, we sisters don't read?"

"Probably not those kinds of books."

"We read more than the Bible, you know. Hang out with me, and you'll know how exciting the life of a sister *really* is. Well, all except Sister Ida's," she muttered. "*The Woman in Black*—is that the ghost story about a small English town?"

"Yeah, that's the one." We started walking again, Aspen close by my legs. The air was getting chillier with the breeze blowing off the lake, and I wondered if we should have gone inside instead. All the same, we continued toward the dock. "The book keeps showing up on a chair or table in the library. I re-shelved it twice, but lo-and-behold, it will be out again."

"Why are you shelving it? Making work for the person who's reading it isn't very guest friendly."

"You think that's what it is? A guest leaving it out?"

"What else would it—" she stopped and stared at me. Through laughter, she said, "You thought it was the ghost?"

I waited until she got it together, hands on my hips. "Are you done?"

"Sure." Another chuckle escaped her lips, but she silenced it. "If a ghost wants you to know it's there, you'll know. Guessing will only drive you crazy. Crazy will drive you to drink." She took my hand. "Now tell me what's going on."

For the next half hour, we sat on the dock, legs crossed in front of us, Aspen between us. I relayed the conversation between Detective Griffin and myself before the conversation shifted to unrelated events, but a lively chat, as were all conversations with Sister Alice.

Finally, I said, "By avoiding the obvious topic here, are you telling me you think I have valid cause for concern?"

"I'm telling you that you cannot let this consume you, or it will bury you. There's nothing we can do about it tonight. Tomorrow, after you've met with him, we'll go from there. So get some sleep and be ready."

"Sister Alice, I'm already spending time tomorrow getting an attorney—if I decide to go that route. Having an attorney makes me look guilty when I'm not. I can't take any more time away from the inn. I need to help

Tony in the kitchen."

"We'll figure something out. I can talk to the ladies from the Spirited Women's Society at St. Michael's. They help with meals for funerals, weddings, and such. Maybe they can pitch in with kitchen duties."

I stuck out my tongue. "Church food tastes like hospital food. I remember the food they made for Grandpop and Honey's funerals. No, thank you." Then, just to get her goat, I added, "Maybe I'll check in with the Gals and Grace Society. We have pretty high standards here at the inn." Gals and Grace was the women's group at the rivaled Protestant church, Spirit Vineyard.

She studied me over the rims of her glasses. "Don't be a snob, Andie Rose. Some ladies in the Spirited Women's Society are better cooks than Ivan ever was. And they're definitely better than that *other* group."

I wrinkled my nose. "Okay. I'll think about it."

"You have no other options right now, Grasshopper."

My phone rang, and I looked at the display. "Great, it's Brad. I hope he's not calling for an answer." At the mention of Brad, Aspen crossed his paws and buried his snout between them.

"You've got an answer, so give it to him. What are you waiting for?"

"It's not that simple." Except I knew it was. Putting off the inevitable would only cause the wound to fester.

She waved at me. "Take the call. I'll head home and see you tomorrow."

I waved at her and clicked the button on my phone. "Hey, Brad."

"What the hell, Andie Rose?"

His tone left me dumbstruck. He rarely got emotional, much less upset, which, oddly, was one thing that made me question his feelings toward me.

"What did you do?"

I took a deep breath before replying. "First of all, how about a 'Hi, Andie Rose. How are you this evening?' "

"Sorry, but imagine my shock when I listened to voicemails and got one from some guy by the name of Detective Griffin, requesting my immediate response. Oh, yeah, and he just threw in a comment about a murder at the inn and that you're the one who found the body. What happened? Are you a suspect?"

"Your support is heart-warming, Brad," I said dryly.

"Tell me you didn't do it, and I'll believe you. You know I will."

"That you even have to ask leaves a big question mark in my head."

"About what?"

"About us." My retort was harsher than intended.

"Come on, Andie Rose," he said in a tone that attempted to placate me but only raised my ire. "You know I trust you. And we're perfectly fine. Nothing that we can't get back on track. But what happened?"

Doing my best to digest his ignorance about us, I filled him in on the latest news. "Long story short, the victim was killed with a corkscrew in the kitchen here at the inn. I remember fidgeting with one I'd picked up from the table next to us when we were talking."

"I don't remember you doing that. Why?"

"Why what?" His question confused me.

"Why did you fidget with the corkscrew? Were you

that upset at my proposal?"

Whether he was serious or it was an ill-timed joke, my nostrils flared. I took a deep breath and counted to five.

"I don't know, Brad," I said in exasperation. "I guess I was nervous. But the server cleared off the table before we left. I'm sure of it." Was I though? Now I couldn't remember.

"Did you take it home with you?"

I gasped at his nerve. "The corkscrew?"

"Yes."

Another deep breath, and another count to five. "Are you asking me if I used it on Ivan?"

"No. Only trying to figure out how it got to the inn."

"You and me both," I lashed out. "But I don't appreciate your implication."

"Andie Rose, be reasonable. I'm not implying anything. You know I trust you. I'm just trying to make sense of this."

"Worried about how it will look to your co-workers and employer if word gets out, Brad?"

"That's not fair, Andie. But, yeah, now that you mention it, it wouldn't look good, that's for sure."

Stupefied, I couldn't find anything to say that I wouldn't later regret, so I clamped my lips tight.

"Andie Rose? You know I didn't mean it like that. Come on."

"No, Brad."

"No what?"

"I don't want to get married."

I heard his heaved sigh across the line. "You're understandably upset, babe. Let's talk about this later."

I squeezed my eyes shut and bit my cheek. "I have

to go. There's a guest who needs attention," I lied.

"I'll call Detective Griffin back in the morning and let you know what happens."

"Okay," I said stiffly.

Without even realizing I'd done so, I found myself back inside the inn and by the front desk. Lily had already left, and a note lay in front of the computer. *Left at eight-fifteen. Didn't know where you were to say goodbye. See you tomorrow morning. Have a good night.*

"Too late for that," I muttered. I looked at my exercise watch—eight forty-five and only a measly 8,217 steps today. The way tomorrow morning was shaping up, I'd have to miss another day of running around the lake. As much as I hated to miss enjoying the brightly colored leaves, hearing them crunch beneath my feet, and the prominent smells of fall, I didn't know who would be more disappointed, Aspen or me. He gave a short whimper quietly at my side, as if sensing his morning doom.

Chapter 11

I slept fitfully that night yet woke feeling optimistic that things would work out all right. Motivational quotes bedecked the walls of my suite, and I zeroed in on my favorite: One day at a time. A colossal impact for so few words.

After a shower, I slipped into a pair of jeans and a long-sleeved T-shirt and pulled my hair back into a ponytail—again. I delayed leaving for a minute to inspect my appearance in a mirror. Other than my typically intense cobalt-blue eyes looking a little dull this morning, no one would be the wiser and know anything was wrong. Or so I hoped, anyway. Of course, Sister Alice would be the first to let me know if she thought otherwise.

Tony was in the kitchen putting together a sweet roll basket at the work island. I snatched one, grabbed a giant mug, and strode over to the coffeepot. "Morning," I said.

He glanced at me and then back to his project. "Look what the cat dragged in."

His hair was plastered in place with more than a dollop of gel. "I could say the same. How's the headache this morning? You look a little better, at least."

"I'm doing great. Benefits of being young."

I grinned. "Young is a subjective term."

"I'm choosing to ignore that observation."

"You're older than me by two years, and I feel

ancient this morning." I took a much-needed swallow from my huge cuppa joe.

"Anything happen after I left yesterday?" he asked.

"Nothing worth mentioning." My palms began to sweat as I thought about the phone call that ruined my night. I'd need to consume at least two mugs of coffee before delving into that this morning. "I'll be in the office for a while, and then I have to run an errand around nine. Do you have things covered here?"

"Ye of little faith. Of course I do. Where are you going? Or is it none of my business?"

"I told you, an errand. It shouldn't take me long. Jade and Lily are on their regular schedules today, so Lily will be in at eight."

"You know what they say about when the cat's away—"

"The mice—"

"Will play solitaire," he said.

"I'm installing cameras in the kitchen," I teased.

"Too bad you didn't have one in the kitchen the night Ivan died."

My eyes flew wide open, and I gasped. "Tony, you're a genius."

Tony studied me for a minute and cocked his head. "It's about time you realized that. But tell me why you think so."

"The cameras."

He narrowed his eyes at me. "*What* cameras?"

"The security camera doorbell and the one installed on the back that overlooks the lake."

He visibly relaxed and returned to grating the mozzarella cheese for a spinach and bacon quiche. "Oh, that. I never understood what possessed you to have that doorbell cam on an inn. You've gotta be getting a million alerts on your phone. From the back camera too, what with the lake, the bonfire pit, and everything else back there."

I assumed *everything else* he referred to was the fishers, ice skaters, and wanderers. "It's worth it."

"Your grandparents never had one, and they did fine."

"They never had a murder here, either."

He cast a look over his shoulder at me. "You had them installed long before the murder. Besides, I'm not sure what that says about you after being here for only six months."

I shook my finger at him. "You'll see what a benefit the cam will be. And if I can find someone coming in here around the time of the murder, that alone makes it worth it." When he said nothing, I said, "I know you think I'm crazy. I'm running things as close as possible to the way Grandpop and Honey did. I only added some extra precautions."

"Well, I'd say those precautions didn't work."

"Yet," I said. "And thanks for the overwhelming support. Maybe I'll change my mind about the lead chef position." I stole a glance at him to find my comment didn't faze him in the slightest bit. "For your information, I had them installed so I can see who's wandering around the property at night or at the door after hours. If it's not a guest with a key, they have no business here at night. Plus, I'm hoping to see the bear."

"And for *your* information, that didn't stop the murderer. Unless it was an employee you think is harmless but isn't. Like Jade."

"Tony Valentino," I scolded. "You take that back.

You know Jade didn't do it."

"No, I don't know that. And you don't either." He pointed a spatula at me. "We *hope* she didn't, but we don't *know*. She was the last one to see Ivan alive."

"No, she wasn't. The killer was."

"And who's to say it wasn't one and the same?" I cast him a long look. "I'm just sayin'."

As much as I wanted to argue my case, I waffled back and forth on whether I was a hundred percent sure. So I zipped my lips. Or so I thought.

"No. No. No."

"No, no, no, what?" Tony said.

Even though my mind had been miles away, I'd remained rooted in the kitchen. I shook my head. "Nothing. Just thinking. Apparently, out loud."

"Why haven't the police asked you for the camera footage?"

I squished my eyebrows together. "I don't know. Maybe they need a warrant first?"

"Or maybe they already have their minds made up without looking at all the evidence."

I shook my head. "I don't think so. But whatever the reason for the delay, it's to my advantage." I pulled up the security camera app on my phone, and leaned over the work island, resting on my forearms, the phone between my hands. Tony stood behind me, hovering over my shoulder.

I nudged him with an elbow. "Back up. I can feel your breath in my hair."

"Ouch. I've never had a woman complain about that before." He began covering the sweet rolls with sheets of plastic.

"First time for everything. Besides, you said I was

crazy for having this camera out there, so why are you so interested in seeing what's on it?" I scanned through the events until I reached the day and the suspected time of the murder. There were only a few captured events. The first was a bear, almost as elusive as the ghost, wandering around the campfire ring; the second was two guests coming in through the back entrance; the third was a fox trotting across the parking lot. I was losing hope when I opened the next one and caught my breath as I watched. "Tony. Com'ere and look at this."

He came up behind me. "Permission to look over your shoulder?" I elbowed him again, harder, and he grunted. "Ouch. Where's your dog?"

"I wouldn't ever let him hear you call him the D word."

"I've heard you do it," he defended himself, stuffing his hands in the pockets of his apron.

I turned to glance at him. "That's different. He knows I love him."

"So when you love someone, it's okay to call them names? No wonder you're single." He snickered.

I stared at him with narrowed eyes. "Again, thinking I'll hire a new lead chef instead of a sous-chef."

"You wouldn't," he said, narrowing his eyes. "You have to sleep sometime."

I gave him a tired grin.

"All that over calling a dog a dog," he said.

I pointed toward the kitchen doorway. "Aspen," I said, loud and clear, "is right over there within hearing range while he waits for me. Now watch," I ordered as I played the video again—a car's headlights pulled in slowly before going dark, lights off. The driver parked off to the left of the lot in a dark alcove beneath a giant oak tree. There weren't any security lights that way, and only the driver's side was in the camera's range. We waited, but no one got out. I zoomed in as close as possible but still couldn't get a bead on the person or the make of the car.

"Can you tell what kind of car that is?" I asked Tony.

He leaned in closer, and I moved over to the side a bit. "Breathing in your hair again?"

"No. Unlike you, I'm courteous and giving you space to see better."

"Um-hm." After a moment, he said, "I can't tell anything by looking at this. It's too far away and in the dark. And the clarity in this video sucks. Are they all like that?"

"I didn't say it was a state-of-the-art camera. It's a knockoff brand."

"I can tell."

"Whatever." I played the video again and waited for someone to get out of the car. The door began to open. "There," I said, pointing to the screen. I waited for the interior lights to come on, but none did. And then, as I held my breath, waiting to see the person, the door closed again. It didn't reopen during the rest of the video, and there wasn't any further activity to activate the camera again. I clicked on the following video eight minutes after the last, and the camera caught the car driving away, lights off.

"Darn it." I stood up and nearly knocked into Tony's chin. He jumped and wheeled around toward the oven. When he opened the door, the smell of cinnamon billowed out and wafted toward me. My mouth watered.

I sighed and logged out of the app. "I have to leave in a couple of hours, and I'll be gone most of the morning."

"So you've already said." He stopped what he was doing and looked at me as if I was a sandwich short of a picnic. "You okay? Considering, I mean."

"Yep. Disappointed, but other than that, peachy." I forced a smile. "I'll be back as soon as I can. For sure to take over by the time you leave."

"What's the plan for my replacement? I'm not the only one who can't continue two shifts every day. You can't work 'round the clock either."

I filled him in on Sister Alice's suggestion last evening. He abruptly halted and stared at me.

"What?" I asked.

"What we do isn't something just anyone can *fill in* for. It takes training."

I ignored the part where he sounded a little like Ivan. "No one said this person will be as good as you. But Sister Alice seems to have someone in mind who could have out-cooked Ivan."

"Well, as good as he was, *I* could have done that," Tony mumbled as he rolled his eyes. "It's just that—can we at least see what she can do before we agree to it?"

"Of course," I assured him. "You and I will agree together. This is your domain." When he relaxed a little, I said, "Now, I gotta get Aspen out for at least a short time before we run our errands." *Errands. Yeah, right.* "I'll see you in a while. Call if you need anything."

"Aye, aye, captain," he said with a salute, spatula still in hand.

I pivoted toward the doorway and scurried before he could launch more queries in my wake.

I snapped Aspen's leash on his harness, then decided to let him roam and unclipped it again. We headed toward a trampled path through the woods. Aspen perked up and pranced beside me, no doubt relieved we'd finally gotten going. There wasn't enough time to take him around Lakeshore Trail, but a short walk was better than none. By the time I got done talking with Detective Griffin this morning, I hoped this wouldn't be our *last* walk. My heart rate sped up faster than it should have for just getting started. But Aspen didn't seem to notice; his focus centered on two squirrels scampering around an enormous bright-yellow-leafed Eastern Cottonwood.

Maple trees with bright tangerine-colored leaves and birch trees with fluttering golden yellow leaves surrounded the path. And oak trees displayed deep red leaves that reminded me of the murder. I shook my head to cast the memory from my mind. Aspen trotted next to me, staying close as if sensing my worry. Which only made me worry more. What would he do if they threw me in the slammer? Jail was no place for a dog. I wondered if Sister Ida allowed dogs in the house so Aspen could stay with Sister Alice. I shook my head again. This was silly. I had done nothing wrong, so I wasn't going to jail. *Was I?*

After another twenty minutes of trying fruitlessly to focus on the beauty encircling me, we headed back toward the inn. Lily should be there by now. I could check in with her before going to my office to brainstorm ideas for someone to help in the kitchen until I found a permanent replacement. I could ask one of the several part-time employees who covered the coffee bar, along with other miscellaneous needs, but they were part-time for a reason; they either had other jobs, kids, were in school, or other variables. And at the risk of sounding like Ivan and Tony, not just anyone could be a chef. I sighed and switched gears as I thought about my search for an attorney. I camped there for a moment to process the decision that could make or break me. I still hadn't decided on that one yet. I was innocent. Innocent people don't need an attorney.

My phone rang. I snagged it from my coat pocket and looked at the display.

"Hey, Sister Alice. You must have been reading my mind."

"I talked to Sister Eunice. She said she'd love to help Tony until you find someone permanent."

"Really?" I exclaimed, causing Aspen to look up at me. "I mean, Tony and I need to talk with her first."

"Of course you do. But I wouldn't scare her away when she's the best option you've got right now. And I'm telling you, she could give Ivan a run for his money."

"Can she come by this afternoon between noon and two? I'll be back by then, and Tony will still be there."

"I'm sure that won't be a problem. She was helping Sister Ida at Lakes News and Reviews, but they cut her position. So she'll be happy to get out and about."

Lakes News and Reviews was the talk of the town last spring and summer when someone murdered a reporter for secretly working on a story about big pharma dumping drugs into the lakes, causing billions of dollars of damage. Worse, the owner of Lakes News and Reviews was in cahoots with the pharmaceutical company at fault. While the reporter's murder permanently silenced her, it busted the story wide open into a scandal. New ownership ensued at News and Reviews, and they brought Sister Ida and Sister Eunice on board immediately after. My guess? It was a purely political move to help improve the company's reputation.

"They don't feel they need her to improve their image anymore, or what?"

"That could be one argument, I suppose. The other could be that it wasn't her cup of tea to begin with. It was assigned to her without a say in the matter."

"Nice."

"Attitude problem this morning, dear?" she asked in a no-nonsense tone.

I stopped walking, kneeled beside Aspen, and wrapped my arm around his neck. "I have to talk to Detective Griffin this morning. What if—"

"Part of the coaching process is encouraging your clients not to entertain 'what if' scenarios, am I right?"

"Yeah, but—"

"Don't be a yeahbut."

"What?" I scrunched my face in confusion.

"Someone who denies themselves happiness or satisfaction regardless of the outcome. Don't be one of those. The outcome will be fine. You'll see."

"Easy for you to say. Will you take care of Aspen for me if it's *not* fine?"

"No."

"*No?*"

"Of course I will," she scoffed. "But if I tell you that, you'll concede easier. Don't do that. You've done nothing wrong. We'll find the person who did this."

"I wish I was as confident as you are."

"With age comes wisdom. You'll get there. Eventually."

I rolled my eyes. "I'll see you this afternoon," I said.

"That's my girl," she said. "And Andie Rose?"

"Yeah?"

"You're welcome."

I grinned. "No wonder you and Sister Ida butt heads."

"Well, all three of us know which of us has more fun. God knows I love her anyway. That's what matters."

"Keep telling yourself that."

Despite the heaviness hanging over me, our conversation somewhat lessened the funk I'd fallen into. At least now I was hanging onto a flimsy branch on the cliffside instead of falling to my death into the abyss. But, still, the usual sanguine person who often annoyed people had moved out. It needed to come back home and kick the residing wimp out. Better an empty house than a bad tenant.

I stood and took a long inhale, settled a fist on my hip, posture erect. I'd seen a lawyer on a television show do that to promote confidence before attending a court process, and I'd found it worked miracles. I even suggested it to my coaching clients who dealt with confidence issues. I stood, probably looking like an idiot, but I didn't give two hoots what anyone else thought about me. I was innocent.

I might be a life coach helping clients navigate tough spots and realize their potential, but Sister Alice helped me recognize the importance of *having* a coach. And how hard it was to follow the suggestions I so easily handed to others.

I saw Lily, Marcie, and Frank's cars parked in the lot when I reached the inn. I hopped up the stairs to the front entrance, my strength and energy revived a tad by Mother Nature, and almost bumped into Frank as he came out the door. Aspen was so close on my heels that he smacked into me at the abrupt stop and rubbed his paw over his snout. Frank's bib overalls already had dirt on the front.

"Watch it there, Petunia. Don't want to get hurt at the beginnin' of your day." He smiled through front teeth stained from years of chewing tobacco. He spit into the bushes beside the front stoop.

"Frank, that stuff will kill you. You know that, right?"

"It comes from a plant, Miss Andie. And my life is workin' with plants. Me and plants are one with each other."

"Marijuana is a plant, too, and you don't do that."

He looked down then back up at me. "Yeah? How d'ya know?"

I grinned. "Wild guess."

He sniggered and went about his way to the gardening shed with the attached greenhouse.

"Hey, Lily," I said as I strode up to the desk. "How're things?"

She held up her coffee mug and took a gulp. "Better now. Jade coming in today?"

"I haven't heard that she's not. Why?"

She tipped her head to the side, tilting her chin down. "That girl's as flighty as they come when there's *not* drama, much less if there is. How that child of hers is such a good kid is beyond me."

I smiled and rested my hand lightly on her shoulder. "Sometimes it's hard to understand other generations."

"You both are about the same age, and you're not like that."

"Everyone's different," I said, feeling a responsibility to defend Jade. "We need to give people room to be who they are, not who we expect them to be."

"Hm." She twisted her lips. "I guess not all of us can be that good."

"I didn't say I do that. It just seemed like the right thing to say."

Lily nodded. "Well, it's not a secret that she thinks I'm an old bat, so I guess we're even." She took another swallow. "Tony makes better coffee than Ivan did."

I looked at her mug, a picture of the Maxine comic strip character, that said "Going to check out a couple of antiques—yep, time for my mammogram."

I howled with laughter. That it was so out of her dapper and somewhat proper demeanor made it funnier. Finally containing myself, I glanced at my watch, shocked at how fast the last hour zipped by. "I'm going to fill a travel mug and run an, uh, errand. I should be back soon."

"Want me to keep Aspen here?"

"No," I said a bit too abruptly. I needed him with me. For one, I was going into a stressful situation. Second, Detective Griffin might be less inclined to throw me in the clink if a support animal was with me. "I'll take him. But thanks, anyway."

Chapter 12

The door to the police station weighed a thousand pounds. I scanned the surrounding area. Photos of police chiefs, past and present, bedecked the wall above a row of distressed black vinyl chairs. Most of the chairs' torn seats revealed a thin layer of white stuffing. No chance of anyone getting too comfortable here, no sir. My bra had more padding than these chairs. A wide staircase led to a row of closed doors. Probably offices, I'd assumed. I wondered if the facility had holding cells on-site or if they ushered the suspects directly to the big boy jail. Go to jail and don't pass go, as the Monopoly game goes. I shuddered. Hopefully, I'd never have to find out.

I plodded toward a counter surrounded by a glass enclosure, wishing I could evanesce. No such luck. A woman with readers perched on her nose, and a blouse that would make even Jade blush, stood behind the counter and looked up as I approached.

"How can I help you?" she asked, her voice silvery. "If you're here for court, it's upstairs." She pointed to the staircase behind me.

"I'm here for Detective Griffin. Andie Rose Kaczmarek. He's expecting me."

"One moment, please."

The woman picked up a phone receiver, punched in a set of numbers, and turned slightly left to talk. Her boobs, resting on the counter, almost knocked the grimy pen holder over. Apparently used to the drill, she nabbed it with expertise before it fell.

"Detective Griffin," she said, "there's an Andie Rose here…yes, sir…okay…yes…okay, sir." She hung up, turned back toward me, hand still on the penholder, and faced me again. "Officer Wilson will be here to get you."

"Get me?" I asked, my legs wobbling a bit. "I have my service dog here," I said, nodding toward Aspen.

She leaned forward, pressed her forehead to the glass, and looked at Aspen. "The little fella can go with you, of course."

"Go with me where?"

"To an interview room. I'll get a bowl of water for your guy."

"Thank you," I said as she turned to leave.

I looked around the room before Aspen and I trudged toward the row of chairs. I sat at the end nearest to the door. *Just in case.* I made a snorting noise, startling Aspen. *Like I'd stand a chance if I made a run for it.* It appeared more than a few others had the same thought because this specific chair was by far in the worst shape. As casually as possible, I switched the chair with the one next to it, but one leg let out an ear-piercing scrape on the floor, giving me away. A female officer happened by and said, "You're not the first one to switch around those chairs. They're in sorry shape."

I forced a smile. "I'm sure I'm not," I said, but she'd already breezed right on by and outside of hearing range. You could bet that if I'd said something I didn't want her to hear, she would have. Murphy's law; Sod's law; whatever.

"You're sure you're not what?" The woman

previously behind the counter laid a bowl of water on the floor in front of Aspen, her cleavage revealing impending disaster. I swiveled my head to avoid witnessing an awkward moment. But as with the penholder, she'd skillfully stood at the precise moment. I could imagine how many officers visited her at the front desk, accidentally on purpose dropping something. *Perverts*.

"Thank you," I said as I artfully multitasked— watching Aspen gratefully lap up the water and ditch my attitude.

"Anything for the innocent ones. We don't get a lot of those in here."

Feeling short of breath, I forced a deep inhale. Had they already made up their minds? Do they assume those of us who say *I didn't do it* were guilty until proven innocent? That's not how the justice system was supposed to work. But if I didn't do it, I would not say I did. I was in a lose-lose situation here. "Dogs," she added quickly. "We don't get many *dogs* in here." I glanced at her. "I saw the look of panic on your face."

Whew. "Overthinking things, I guess." I sighed through an exhale and sank on the edge of the chair. Despite it having the most stuffing, it was still unforgiving to my sit bones. I readjusted my position. Aspen lapped more of his water before sitting at attention beside me.

By the time Officer Wilson came out for me, we'd waited for what seemed like an eternity. So when I glanced at the clock on the wall across from me, just over his head, I was surprised to see it had only been seven minutes.

"Andie Rose?" he asked.

"That's me." I stood and nodded toward Aspen. "This is my service dog."

"I see that," he said, pointing toward Aspen's orange and yellow harness. "You can come with me."

Wait. I can *go with him? Did that mean I had a choice?* If so, it was a no-brainer. Deciding not to revert to the rebel of my youth and cause a stir at the onset, I acquiesced and followed him. "I hope this won't take long. I need to get back to the Spirit Lake Inn and relieve my sous-chef."

"I'm sure Detective Griffin will make it as quick and painless as possible," he said. He whistled as he led me down a harsh, fluorescent-lit hallway, both abrading my nerves.

"How long have you worked here?" I asked, an attempt to tranquilize said nerves.

"'Bout six years. How long've you lived here?"

"About six months," I said.

"Didn't take you long to visit us, did it?" I clamped my lips tight to avoid snarking at him. The nerve-grating whistling started again as we turned down yet another hallway. Happiness should be illegal at a time like this. I'd have to write to my congress person.

Striving to snap out of my mood, I decided small talk was better than stewing in my mental stink. "This place is bigger than I thought."

"It's not all for us," he said, turning into a room smelling of disinfectant.

At least the chairs were decent. And that it wasn't a jail cell was bonus.

"We share the building with the courts and the probation office."

"One-stop shopping."

"Depends which side of the law you're on. Hopefully, that won't be the case for you."

"You and me both," I muttered.

Once he left Aspen and me alone again—with a promise that Detective Griffin would be with me in just a moment—I sat on the chair I'd initially declined when we'd entered. Once again, Aspen planted himself by my feet. I stroked his neck and back. If this drama didn't trigger a panic attack, I was convinced nothing ever would again. *Now there's a silver lining.*

I'd just pushed myself back on the chair and crossed my legs, one arm wrapped around my middle, when Detective Griffin popped the door open. I shot up in my chair, both feet on the floor, and clutched Aspen's leash. The detective shoved the door closed with his foot and dropped a file on the table before he sat opposite me. He smiled at Aspen. Women softened toward men with babies or puppies. Too bad it wasn't reciprocal.

"Mornin'," he said, slapping open the file, wasting no time. "Let's get this show on the road. I'm sure you have places to be."

His words issued a tsunami of hope. "Yes, sir. I have to relieve my sous-chef and begin looking for a replacement for Ivan," I said, my words unintentionally clipped.

He looked up at me. I was surprised to see a somewhat warm look in his eyes. "Relax, Ms. Kaczmarek. I'm not the big bad wolf."

I nodded stiffly and kept my fingers buried in Aspen's silky fur.

"I just have a few questions for you. Shouldn't take long."

"Do I need a lawyer, Detective?"

"Like I said, it shouldn't take long," he said again, evading the question.

"Lawyer?" I said again.

He paused and closed his eyes momentarily, but long enough that I caught his vexation. "Are you asking for one?"

"I'm asking if I should get one."

"That's up to you. I'm sure I don't have to tell you it makes my job easier without a lawyer getting in the way. How about I ask you a couple of things and if you decide you need one, let me know and I'll stop the conversation."

I resented the way he said *need one*.

Our eyes met for an uncomfortable moment before I finally said, "I'm not guilty. So ask away."

The corners of his lips pulled upward ever so slightly. He sat back and crossed one leg over the other, hands clasped behind his head in a relaxed manner.

His gaze briefly rested on me. "Can you tell me how your prints got on the murder weapon?"

Boom! I had been right after all. I choked on the brutality of the verbal sucker punch. Aspen sat up, turning his face toward me. I cursed my stupidity in passing on retaining a lawyer. While it wasn't too late, I feared if I asked for one after piercing me with the zinger he had, he'd determine me guilty straightaway. His eyes were like lasers now as he focused on my every move. Heck, my every breath.

Four in; *hold for four*; *four out*; *hold for four*...Finally able to talk, I asked, "*My* prints? You know I don't even drink."

"Exactly. So you can see why this is problematic."

"This is all a misunderstanding. There's a very good

explanation."

He remained quiet, focused on me. I wondered if he was hoping I'd say something to trip me up. I shifted my weight, wrapped an arm around my stomach, and averted my gaze until I was unable to stand the silence anymore.

"You've already judged me as guilty, haven't you?"

"It's not my job to judge, Ms. Kaczmarek. That's for a jury to decide. My job is to collect the evidence and you can see what that's telling me. Evidence doesn't lie." He steadied his chair by placing all four legs on the floor and leaned his forearms on the table, tapping his pen lightly.

"I'm waiting to hear this explanation you don't seem to wanna disclose."

"I didn't kill Ivan."

"That's your explanation? That's a weak argument at best."

I squirmed in my chair. "Well, it's not like I can think clearly with you staring at me."

He nodded. "Okay, let's start with your prints. How did they get on the murder weapon?"

I relayed the events of the night Brad and I were at Brewski's, when I'd fiddled with the corkscrew during Brad's proposal. After half an hour of answering his subsequent questions (the same questions asked in several ways, only worded differently), he stopped jotting notes, turned off his recording device, and sat back. He tossed his pen and his readers on top of the file folder.

"So here's the deal." He leaned his chair back on two legs again and reached his arms behind him, clasping his hands behind his head. I only wished I could be so relaxed. "I gotta say I knew your grandparents, and I don't like you for the murder."

"Don't like me?" My heart thudded in my chest. I'd hoped Aspen had saved my bacon with that part.

"Cop speak; I don't think you did it," he clarified.

"Because you knew my grandparents?" I thought that odd, but still shot a silent thank you up to Grandpop and Honey.

"Everyone in this town loved your grandpa and Honey. But evidence is evidence, even if it is only circumstantial. The murder weapon has your fingerprints on it. That's a fact. But it also has two more prints. Presumably, one is the man who'd used it to open the bottle. And the server who cleared the table along with the corkscrew. She said she turned her back on the tray for about fifteen seconds while she attended to other business, but she swore no one was around the area at the time. Unlike the inn, no one claimed to have spotted any ghosts in Brewski's, and the corkscrew didn't strut itself down to the inn. See the hangup there?"

"But there's proof it was still there when I left the bar?"

"*A* corkscrew, yes. But we can't know if it was *the* corkscrew. Get my drift?"

"Well, I only touched one. So if my fingerprints were on it, that's the one it was. The one from the table."

"*You* claim you only touched one, but I don't know of a single suspect who claimed to have touched a murder weapon. That said, given the circumstances, I don't have enough to hold you on yet."

Yet? I swallowed hard. "So I'm free to go?" I had a murder to solve.

He sat his chair upright again, put his hands, palms down, on the table, and pushed himself to a standing position. "For now. But I don't need to tell you not to go anywhere."

I heaved a sigh of relief and said, "Innocent people don't run."

He nodded. "Not if they really are innocent." He gave me a sidelong look. "Don't prove me wrong, because one piece of solid evidence, and I'll be at your door."

"Yes, sir."

He led me back toward the front lobby. I pushed the door open, stepped outside, gulped fresh air, and hopped down the two stairs to the parking lot. "Come on, Aspen. We have work to do and a killer to catch."

When I returned to the inn, Sister Alice zoomed her moped beside my car. A woman hopped out of the sidecar and stood, smoothing her shirt. I couldn't determine if the disheveled look was her usual or from the ride here.

"Good gracious," the woman exclaimed. "I didn't think we'd make it here alive."

Aspen apparently sensed her emotional state and trotted over to give her some lovin' by licking her hand.

Sister Alice chortled and looked at me. "She was screaming like a little girl before we'd even left the house."

I laughed. "I assume this is Sister Eunice?"

"The one and only," Sister Alice said. "She will be your saving grace around here until you find a replacement."

"Sister Alice, I told you we need to—"

"Talk to Tony, I know. But he'll agree if he doesn't want to work himself to death. Finding a suitable replacement isn't as easy in a small town as he might think it will be. Tourists are on vacation, not looking for work."

Aspen turned his attention from Sister Eunice back to me, and we walked into the foyer. Lily was perched behind the desk on the phone; Jade leaned over the desk, studying the reservation book.

"Good golly, girl," Sister Alice said to Jade. "Tuck in the twins, honey. This isn't that kind of establishment. Not everyone wants to see your—assets."

Jade stood, gripped the neckline of her scoop-neck orange sweater and pulled it up. Lily laughed loudly. Jade scowled and grumbled, "Bat."

Avoiding further altercations, I took an arm of each Sister Alice and Sister Eunice. "Come on. Let's go to the kitchen and talk with Tony."

As we turned the corner into the kitchen, Tony peered inside an oven. A mouth-watering scent drifted toward us. When he closed the oven door, it whooshed the delightful aroma even more. I swallowed my hunger and said, "Tony, this is Sister Eunice. She's here to help until we find a permanent replacement."

"Do you have experience outside a convent kitchen?" he asked. His tone dripped with skepticism. I shot him a look to which he lifted his shoulders as if mentally relaying, *What*?

"Tony, since you're in the middle of finishing lunch and preparing for afternoon tea, maybe Sister Eunice could help. That way, you both can see if it's something that's workable short-term."

Without waiting for Tony's approval, Sister Eunice said, "Show me where the aprons are, kiddie, and I'll show you what I got. Watch out, Gordon Ramsay; I'm moving in."

I grinned. One of my coaching niches is confidence, but Sister Eunice could teach *me* a thing or two about it.

Tony jerked his head back in surprise, then grinned. He pointed with the butcher knife in his hand to a bank of drawers on his left. "Third one down."

Sister Alice and I turned to leave. "I think it's safe to assume they'll be just fine," she said. "And you're welcome."

"Have time for tea or coffee?" I asked as I led the way to the coffee bar. "I'll fill you in on my lovely visit with Detective Griffin."

Sister Alice stayed by my side as she followed me to where the green neon *Coffee Bar* sign hung above the alcove. "Wonder why they call it a coffee bar," she said. "I mean, they don't call it a beer bar or a whiskey bar. It's just a bar."

I shook my head. "Good grief. Only an alcoholic wonders about that kind of thing."

"Aren't you just a riot?" she scoffed.

"I'm told I used to be."

Chapter 13

Three part-time employees worked at the coffee bar. If all were gone simultaneously, I'd also trained Lily and Jade. Despite two magnificent coffee shops in town, locals and tourists often drove out to the inn for the coffee bar and ambiance. It was nothing exquisite or extraordinary, but it was unique, warm, and inviting. In contrast to the pine walls, the floors were reclaimed pine with ebony stains and a darker finish, adding a moody element. There were only a handful of tables with charging stations, and the rest of the seating was comfy barrel chairs with side tables. I'd even strewn about a few floor chairs—a mishmash of furniture that lent it an unusual, homey air. I supposed the suspected ghost presence didn't hurt business, either, since people had claimed to hear the espresso machine when no one was in there.

Matching the rest of the inn, colorful gourds and yellow, orange, and clear glass vases of sunflowers graced the room along with colorful fall leaf garland.

The barista, scrolling on her phone, stood on our arrival.

"I got it, Cindy." I waved her aside and went behind the bar. I looked at Sister Alice. "What'll it be?"

"What do you have?" She pushed her glasses up on her nose with her pointer finger.

"Name it."

"Well, how the devil should I know when I don't know what you even have? This coffee bar wasn't here when Honey was."

I chuckled and said under my breath, "How the devil, indeed." I pointed to the menu. "Your choices are up there."

"Can't see that far. The writing is too small."

"Clean the lenses on your glasses and you'd be able to see it better," I teased her. "We have plain coffee or any other drink—tea, latte, mocha, white mocha, iced, hot, flavored, chai tea—"

"Black coffee, room for cream and sugar. Lots of both."

I stopped and squinted at her. "You wanted me to list everything we have when you already knew you wanted plain coffee?"

"Remember, resentments are the death of an alcoholic," she said. Her shoulders trembled with repressed laughter.

I shook my head slowly, poured her coffee, and dramatically slid several packets of cream and sugar across the counter. "Enough?" I made a nonfat pumpkin spice latte for myself before choosing a table out of Cindy, the barista's, earshot.

"So?" she asked, doctoring her coffee. I shuddered as she dumped the fifth packet of sugar, followed by equally as many packets of creamer, and stirred. *Yuk.* Finally done, we turned toward a table, her free hand looped through my arm.

"Ivan's murder weapon has my fingerprints on it."

She stopped in her tracks and dropped her hand from my arm as if fingerprints were contagious. "Come again?"

"The murder weapon has—"

"Your fingerprints on it, I heard you. But how? You said you didn't touch it when you found Ivan. And what were you doing with a corkscrew?"

She was quiet while I filled her in.

"Sister Alice, there's no way that specific corkscrew could be the murder weapon unless someone is trying to frame me. Someone who saw me touch it." I stopped talking for a moment, trying to remember who could have seen it. *Wait. Brad*? It startled me when his name slipped its way into my head as a suspect. "No," I breathed.

Sister Alice gave me a sidelong look. "No what?"

"Brad was the only one who saw me touch it. The people at the table were already gone. But there's no way. The guy just asked me to marry him, for heaven's sake. He hadn't been happy when I made the situation incredibly awkward, but he's not vindictive," I said vehemently, shaking my head. I was rambling but I couldn't stop. "Brad and I had drifted islands apart, but he'd never been vengeful."

"Andie Rose," she said, covering my hand with hers. "Getting all twitterpated isn't helping anything right now. This turn of events only means we have work to do. And fast." Silence fell between us until she said, "Focusing on the positive a minute, you weren't arrested. I told you I wouldn't have to watch Aspen for you."

"Yet."

"Is there something you want to confess?"

I scowled. "Of course not. Why would you ask that?"

"If you're so sure you're going to get tossed in jail, what have you done that you haven't told me about?"

"Nothing."

"Then stop acting like you have, Andie Rose. Part of your coaching gig is to teach your clients that everything begins with their thoughts, right?"

"Yeah. But how do you know that? I've never coached you."

"Thank the good Lord for small favors on that one," she said, running her palm over her forehead in dramatic Sister Alice fashion.

"Just so you know, I'm siding with Sister Ida on any issues the two of you may have."

"I'm sure you will. But to assuage your flippancy, I've heard you talk about the whole thought/action connection on more than one occasion in the meetings."

"Oh."

"So if you keep telling yourself you're going to be pitched in the jug, you'll live in constant fear, right?" I nodded. "Well, that will wreak havoc on your mental state, correct?"

I nodded again. "Yes. Why does it feel like I'm getting a lecture from my mother?"

"Practice what you preach."

"Those who can, do. Those who can't, teach. I teach." I rolled my eyes as I realized I repeated my dad's worn-out phrase. Again.

Sister Alice guffawed. Aspen snapped his head up to check what disrupted his peacefulness; Cindy glanced away from her phone and at us before laying it facedown. She snatched a rag from the sink and began wiping the steam wand with a bleach solution, followed by the counters and the outside of the equipment.

I filled my cohort in on the security cam footage, then pulled it up and pressed play.

"Whoever it is just sits there. Doesn't even get out of the car. It can't be a coincidence that—"

"Yes, they did," she said.

"What?"

"I'd bet money that the person *did* get out of the car."

I frowned. "Nothing is missing in this video. You've seen it. It doesn't skip in the slightest."

"Nothing is missing in the video, Andie Rose, because the person got out on the passenger's side, which the video doesn't include. They must have covered the light with something when they opened the door."

I set my cup down with a thud, the latte sloshing over the side, and my eyes grew wide. "Why didn't I catch that? Of course they did."

Sister Alice removed her glasses, laid them on the table, and ran her hand over her hair and down her face before looking at me again. "You have much to learn, Grasshopper." She took a sip of her coffee—or milkshake with as much cream and sugar as she added—and said, "You're too close to the situation. That's why I'm inserting myself in this fiasco. You need a fresh set of eyes."

"I want your help. Trust me. Except what will Sister Ida say if she finds out? I can't imagine she'd be too keen on this."

"And how would she do that? Find out. Because I don't see any reason she will, do you?" She narrowed an eye.

I grinned. "None at all."

"I didn't think so." She nodded at our *understanding*. "Did you show Detective Griffin the footage?"

"I can't imagine he won't get a warrant and come to get it. Any detective worth his salt would know to do that. He just hasn't *yet*, so I'm using it to my advantage. If he somehow retrieved it the night of the murder, I don't know how because he didn't take my phone and the cameras are still in place. Of course, I'm not the most tech-savvy person."

"You're making an assumption and withholding evidence."

"No, I'm not. There's nothing usable in the video. We can't see anything or anyone. Not even a license plate."

"*We* can't see anything, but they probably have a tech geek who can make the visual clearer and get something from it."

I shook my head. "Just in case, I can't risk him taking my phone. I have a business to run. The inn's landline rolls over to my cell phone outside of business hours. What if we take it to Matt from the group? He's a techie."

"You catch on fast," she said as she slid her glasses back on.

"First, I have a burning question."

"What is it?"

"Did Father Vincent do a background check on you before taking you in? Maybe Sister Ida did, and that's why she has it in for you."

"Father Vincent wasn't at St. Michael's when I came. It was Father Tobias. And he was senile as they come." She tapped her palm to her forehead, knocking her glasses as she did. "I could have told him I was Mary Magdalene, and he wouldn't have disputed it."

I rolled my eyes. "Oy. Oy. Oy. No wonder Sister Ida

watches your every move."

"She's getting close to that senility point, too, so I've got nothing to worry about." She smiled at me, drained the last of her coffee, and stood. "Let's go check on Sister Eunice. She'll make some excuse why she has to stay here to get out of riding back to town in the sidecar."

"I don't think it's the sidecar that bothered her; it was your driving."

"Details."

We walked past the front desk, Aspen in tow. Lily waved and acknowledged Sister Alice, but Jade became hyper-focused on whatever she was doing, which involved *not* looking at Sister Alice.

"You might have burned a bridge there," I whispered.

"Sometimes taking one for the team isn't the popular thing to do. I could tell *you* weren't going to say anything about her risqué top."

"It's not me who it bothered."

We peeked into the kitchen to find Sister Eunice vigorously chopping vegetables on the large cutting board as Tony watched. We stayed in the doorway for a few moments before Sister Eunice noticed us.

"Ready to go?" Sister Alice asked her.

"Tony needs me to stay."

Tony jerked his head toward her. "Stay if you want, but I'm competent to run a kitchen by myself."

Fairly new to Spirit Lake and the convent house, Sister Eunice didn't have a vehicle yet. When she worked at Lakes News and Reviews upon her arrival, she rode to work with Sister Ida.

Sister Alice gave me an I-told-you-so look.

"It makes sense to stay. If Andie Rose and Tony are okay with it, I'll take the afternoon or evening shift until they find a suitable replacement."

"I'm more than okay with it," I said and looked over Sister Eunice's shoulder at Tony, who lurked there. "Tony? You good?"

"Yep."

Sister Eunice startled, and he took a step back.

"Three o'clock?" he asked her.

"I'll have her on the doorstep no later than two fifty-nine," Sister Alice said.

I said to Sister Eunice, "If Sister Alice gets called to the hospital and can't get you here, let me know. I'll come and pick you up."

"Even if she isn't working at the hospital, can you still pick me up? I'm not a fan of bugs in my teeth from that sidecar."

"I told you to wear face protection," Sister Alice said. "You opted out."

"Yeah, well, that was before I realized what a maniac you are on that thing."

"You could always ask Sister Ida for a ride. I know how much you enjoyed riding with her to work before."

Sister Eunice shot her a look, and I swallowed a giggle. They fought like biological sisters in the world of us outcasts and sinners.

"I'll start looking straightaway for a permanent solution, so transportation won't be an issue for any of you," I promised. "I already put out some feelers in the community and called the paper to see if they could get something in the next issue."

"That's the day after tomorrow," Tony said.

I squinted. "I know. What's your point?"

"I'm just surprised they got it in there so fast."

"The editor of the paper likes to come here for dinner."

"And he's afraid of Sister Eunice's cooking, or what?" Sister Alice asked.

I waved my hand at her. "You're just a laugh a minute, aren't you?"

"Maybe it's Tony's cooking that's got his undies in a bunch," she said, smirking.

Tony gave her a laser-eyed look.

"I also posted an online application." I glanced toward the doorway, expecting Aspen to be lying there, surprised to see he wasn't. Probably licking Jade's emotional wounds from Sister Alice. *Traitor*.

"Well, don't rush it," Tony said, to my surprise. "The devil you don't know is usually worse than the devil you do."

Sister Eunice's jaw dropped. "Did you just call me a devil?"

"No," Tony exclaimed. "I didn't mean to insinuate that you—forget it." He sighed and blotted his forehead with a white hand towel, then looked at Sister Alice. "See? You've got me all discombobulated." Back to Sister Eunice, he said, "All I meant was that I can work with you, and you're good. Not as good as me," he clarified with a grin, "but good. I don't want someone coming in here who's going to try to take over or who's not a team player. In other words," he looked at me, "not another Ivan."

"Except you're the one who took over Ivan's job, not the other way around."

"After he was dead," he said pointedly. "Big difference."

Sister Alice looked at Tony. "How badly did you want Ivan's job, Valentino?"

He shook his head. "I might not be sorry he's gone, but I didn't do it. And you know it."

She waved a dismissive hand, and her eyes twinkled. "I believe you. But it'd be negligent not to ask, at least."

"Yeah, well, Andie Rose already grilled me."

I rolled my eyes. "Oh, good Lord, Tony. Stop being so dramatic. I did *not* grill you. But whatever."

Sister Alice's phone rang; she looked at the screen and rolled her eyes. "It's Sister Ida." Tony and Sister Eunice returned to work, but I stayed and listened to Sister Alice's one-sided conversation. "Yes, she's here with me." A moment of silence. "She's going to fill in as the sous-chef at the inn until Andie Rose can find a replacement." Another moment of silence before her eyes grew wide. "When?" Silence as she held my gaze. "Any idea who?" A pause. "Of course not," she said, maintaining her patience. "I just thought maybe you had an idea. No, that's not what I said." The room became heavy with Sister Alice's irritation. "Well, we'll get to the bottom of this." Pause. "No, I'm not at the hospital today. I'm at the inn. I gave Sister Eunice a ride here." After more silence, more eye rolls from Sister Alice, and finally a sigh which she *attempted* to silence, she said, "Okay. I'll head there now."

"What was that all about?" I asked before she could even tuck her phone away.

"Father Vincent has noticed a few things go missing from the church. It wasn't anything big before, but this time the thief took collection money. A lot of it."

I narrowed an eye at her. "I think it's time we speak

with Deacon Luka Molotov. He's got a long-standing beef with a murder victim and works in a place missing money."

Sister Alice exhaled slowly. "Yes, I suppose it is."

Chapter 14

In a final attempt to escape the deadly sidecar, Sister Eunice once again offered—more like pleaded—to stay at the inn until Tony needed her to take over at three.

"The only purpose going back to town now would serve is to inconvenience you or Andie Rose."

I shot that suggestion down faster than terminal velocity. If Sister Eunice didn't ride back to town, Sister Alice would insist I ride with her instead of driving my own car.

"I won't hear of it. You'll tire of it here fast enough the way it is."

Sister Alice was no dimwit and caught on to my scheming.

"One who needs a ride takes what I offer or walks," she said, glancing at Sister Eunice. Then she stared at me over the rims of today's orange frames.

I swallowed a giggle, then said under my breath, "Walk." She either didn't hear or chose not to.

I glanced toward the doorway. Aspen lazed in the sun, nose propped on his crossed paws. Usually, we played with his favorite red ball daily, but as of late, it had gone by the wayside. He loved to take off at a dead run as I threw the ball, then gallop back, dropping the slobbery toy at my feet.

"Let's go," Sister Alice said, smacking her hands together. "I don't have all day."

Sister Eunice grumbled as she trudged outside and hopped into the sidecar. Before she could put on her helmet, I said, "Hey, Sister Eunice, if you can convince Aspen to jump into the back seat, you can ride with me into town."

With one glance at Aspen, sitting tall and proud in the front seat, she waved her hand in dismissal and slipped her helmet on. "Thanks anyway."

The drive into town was stunning, as usual. (I can't say Sister Eunice experienced the same as me.) Every season had its beauty: the lush green of summer, the light lime-green fresh growth in spring, the silent, pristine snow in winter, but the brilliant-colored foliage of fall was my favorite.

The businesses on both sides of Spirit Lane were decorated to the hilt in anticipation of the upcoming Harvest Festival; part of its festivities included a fall decorating contest. As a kid, I remembered participating in apple dunking, face painting, and the costumes most locals wore throughout the week-long festival.

When we arrived at St. Michael's, Sister Eunice jumped out of the sidecar before Sister Alice had even turned off the motor. She whipped her helmet off, scraped her teeth with a tissue, and stalked off.

Sister Alice placed the helmet in the sidecar and removed her own. "If she'd keep her mouth shut, the bugs wouldn't get in her teeth."

"It's hard to scream with your mouth closed," I said. "Have you tried it? My car windows were up, and I heard her. Aspen even howled."

She smirked. "The good Lord saw to it that she got here safely."

I scanned the empty parking lot. "Doesn't look like

anyone is here."

"Father Vincent parks in the alley behind the church. Luka isn't a full-time employee; he has another job. Add to that a lot of his diaconate duties are spent out and about, so…"

"All that to say he might not be here right now? Would have been nice to know that beforehand."

"Think of it this way; you got to get out of the inn for a while—someplace other than the police station. Does you good to clear your head."

"We should swing by Brewski's and see if Mike Swanson is there."

She shot me a sidelong look. "Liking the pub a little too much, aren't you?" Then she gave me the old eye roll. "Except, sadly, that's where we may find him. Talking with him after he's had a few could either be our friend or foe."

"Exactly. His alcohol-lubricated lips could offer up useful information, or he'll be defensive and argumentative." Aspen looked at me with his irresistible eyes and cocked his head to the side, as if suggesting a walk would make good use of our time. I rubbed his neck. "Later, buddy." He lowered his chin but kept his eyes on me, letting me know that wasn't the anticipated answer.

"Defensive and argumentative isn't all bad," Sister Alice surmised. "As long as he's uninhibited and talking at all, he'll give up something he hadn't intended."

I snorted. "That was my downfall as a teen when I lived at home. I couldn't keep my mouth shut. Got me in trouble more times than I could count."

"Why doesn't that surprise me?" Two tiny rhinestones on her eyewear sparkled in the sunlight.

She seized the large brass antique handle on the heavy oak door of the church entrance that led into the narthex and waited for me to pass through. I hesitated. Other than for AA meetings, I hadn't been inside a church for years. And for meetings, we used the small side entrance leading to the basement.

"I'd better stay out here with Aspen," I finally said.

"He's welcome inside. Mass isn't going on." I hesitated. "Come now," she said, her tone dancing with amused impatience. "You won't go up in flames. God invites and loves us all as we are."

I dipped my chin and glanced at her warily. "You, maybe." I stepped through the door, keeping Aspen close to me. I paused on the other side, waiting for the hand of God to strike me down.

"Look who just pulled up," she said.

I turned around as a white sedan pulled into the lot. "Is that Luka?"

"Sure is."

We waited for him to get out of his car—which seemed to take an eternity—until he finally reached the door. His sparse hair, long, narrow nose, and slightly down-turned lips reminded me of Ebenezer Scrooge. This guy wouldn't need a costume for the festival at all. He was set to go.

"Sister Alice," he said in greeting, sounding more like a question.

"Hello, Luka. Busy day?" The heavy door whined as it closed slowly behind him, and we stood in the narthex.

"Just came from the hospital. Marie Dayton is in there, you know. She asked for the anointing of the sick blessing."

"Is she doing any better?"

"Her daughter, Ella, says she isn't. But her daughter is also—how shall we say it—"

"Hoping for her inheritance sooner rather than later?"

Luka paused, frowned, then nodded. "Unfortunately."

"How are you doing with Ivan Laskin's death? I know the two of you used to be friends."

Luka stiffened. "Used to be, yes. That ended years ago."

"Still, it can't be easy," she said.

"When was the last time you saw him?" I asked.

Luka stopped and faced forward a beat before turning his attention back toward us.

"When we had a falling out years ago."

"Oh," I said, shrugging. "That must be awkward with Spirit Lake a small town and all."

"I've seen him in passing, but we haven't talked much."

"Not *much* or not at all?" Realizing how that might have sounded, I winced inwardly. The last thing I wanted was to shut him down.

"Surface talk. We didn't exactly socialize in the same circles anymore." His voice was as tight as Jade's jeans. The ones she would soon have to retire for something with a little give. His lips all but disappeared as he pressed them together.

"Did you see him the day he was killed?" I asked.

He turned his head, giving me the side eye.

"Young lady, I'm not sure I appreciate where you're going with this."

Sister Alice placed her arm across my chest to keep

me from moving forward. She should have put it across my mouth instead.

"I was just wondering—" I began before she interrupted me.

"If you saw him perhaps arguing with anyone that day."

Luka relaxed. "Of course. My apologies. It still seems a little crazy is all. Spirit Lake used to be a safe town." He leveled his gaze at me for a hot moment then said, "I saw him leaving Brewski's that evening."

"Oh?" The hair at the nape of my neck prickled.

"He got in his car and pulled a U-turn in the middle of Spirit Lane, heading toward your place, Ms. Kaczmarek. I was concerned he was driving in his apparent condition. You know, having been drinking and on his phone. Whoever he was talking to, it wasn't a pleasant conversation."

"How could you tell?"

"Flipped the bird at the phone. Kind of hard to miss."

"Hm." I considered this new information. "Do you know Mike Swanson, Luka?" I asked.

"Of course. He's been dating Ella Dayton for some time now. I've counseled her a time or two. Mike used to be a member of our congregation, but he has since fallen away. We've been praying for his return. And for yours." He nodded toward me, and I squirmed. "Why do you ask?"

"Someone saw him arguing with Ivan in the pub the other day."

Luka appeared to process the news. "I can't say as I'm surprised."

"Why not? Surprised, I mean."

"Both have tempers. Especially when they're drinking. Besides, I'm afraid they've been verbal sparring partners on more than a few occasions, even when alcohol *isn't* involved."

"Do you know what they've sparred about?" Sister Alice asked.

He shook his head. "Nope, can't say that I do. Like I said, I haven't talked with Ivan for years, and Michael has left the church."

"Ella didn't say anything about it to you in your sessions?" I asked.

"Sister Alice," he said, turning his attention toward her as if indicating I was too dense to understand the obvious. "I can't disclose what someone tells me in a counseling session."

"So she has spoken about it with you," Sister Alice said. He dipped his chin and looked at her under bushy eyebrows, a stern, what-did-I-just-tell-you look. Sister Alice said, "Father Vincent said a great deal of collection money has gone missing along with the miscellaneous items that have sprouted legs."

Luka sighed. "Yes, he mentioned that."

"Makes one wonder how much Ella needs money."

"Hm," he answered, pondering the suggestion. "It's possible, I suppose. About as possible as it is anybody else from the congregation. Or nobody from the congregation at all."

"Does everyone have access to the money? That seems a little risky," I said.

Turning his head toward me, impatient, he said, "Of course not. How does *anyone* acquire things that don't belong to them? Theft." He looked back at Sister Alice. "If you will excuse me, I need to go give Father Vincent an update on Marie's condition." He touched the brim of his hat, turned, and pushed through the doors to the nave, and walked up the aisle toward the altar.

After he disappeared around a corner, my eyes strayed to the nave's large stained-glass windows with beautiful images that, as a child, frightened me. I looked at the altar again, expecting something—well, I didn't know what to expect, but it filled me with serene peace. Peace was short-lived, however. Guilt shoved it right out the door, consuming me as I thought about how disappointed Grandpop and Honey would be at how far I'd strayed from the Catholic church. Or *any* church. I quickly glanced away and toward Sister Alice as I scratched the top of Aspen's head.

"What do you think?" I asked her. "He didn't seem too concerned about the missing collection money. And if Ella is dating Mike Swanson, and Mike and Ivan knew each other, that means Ella knew Ivan, too."

She looked at me and shook her head. "I disagree. Do you know all of Brad's friends?"

"No, but we don't live in the same small town. When we lived close to each other, it was in the city. Hardly the same thing."

Sister Alice shrugged, then said, "What does the missing collection money have to do with Ivan? Clearly, it wasn't him, or we have more than one ghost in this town. Not saying we don't. But Ivan's ghost wouldn't be as friendly as the one at your inn."

"I'm only saying we shouldn't rule out that the church thief isn't the same person who killed Ivan."

She pushed her glasses up with the back of her hand. "Unless we find evidence supporting that, I think it's a long shot. Thievery and murder are miles apart."

I sighed. "Well, what vibe did you get from talking with Luka? Think he could have murdered Ivan?"

She tilted her head side to side. "I believe Luka is hiding something, but I don't think that something is murder."

I took a deep breath. "Well, in order to get myself and my staff off the hook, I need something more solid than you don't *think* Luka did it."

"Have you talked to that man of yours? Does he have an alibi?"

"Brad?" A knot formed in my stomach. "Why does he need an alibi?"

"Because he saw Ivan threatening his hopeful fiancée. We don't know the exact time of death, so he might not have been with you at the time of the murder. I'm not the only one to realize that. Why do you think Detective Griffin wants to talk with him?"

I smacked my palm against my forehead. "That's it. If he was with me at the time of the murder, he's *my* alibi, too. We need to nail down a time frame."

She fingered and adjusted the crucifix hanging from her neck. "The police have talked to Brad already, yes?"

"He said Detective Griffin left him a voicemail, but I don't know if Brad has called him back yet." I took out my phone. "Hopefully they haven't. I need to talk to him before they do."

Sister Alice pressed her hand on mine, preventing me from punching in Brad's number. "So you can what, set up a fake alibi? As your sponsor, I'm telling you that's not a good idea."

"I just want to be sure we have our times straight."

"And you can't do that unless you conspire?"

My shoulders sank, and I exhaled through pursed

lips. "I'm trying, okay?"

"Trying to what, exactly—prove the innocence of you and your staff or prove you're not trustworthy?" I stared at her, knowing she was right and hating it. "We're to do the next right thing, Andie Rose. That's all. Not justifying what we *want* to do. Remember what we say in the program, justify is—"

"Just a lie," I finished, and groaned in frustration. "I know. I know." I rubbed my palm against my eye, then looked at her. "I need to get back to the inn and see if anyone has responded to my online call-out for a sous-chef. And I'm sure you have better things to do than solve a murder."

She smiled. "Yes, but none as fun."

"You have a sick sense of fun," I grumbled.

She touched my hand lightly. I absorbed the moment of comfort before Aspen and I walked to the car and headed back toward the inn.

I glanced at my phone in the carrier on the dash, tempted to call Brad. Eventually, the temptation grew to an inability to concentrate on anything *except* calling Brad. All self-control had gone out the window. I began requesting my smartphone to dial Brad's number, but stopped short when I saw Jade's husband, Tom, emerge from the alley alongside the Spirit Lake library and disappear behind the library doors. I had only seen him once, but given his unmistakable tough-boy strut, I was sure it was him. I zipped into an empty parking spot, grateful I'd recently mastered parallel parking after years of causing dings and dents. Aspen looked at me and cocked his head to the side as if to say, *Really? Can't we just go home? I deserve a biscuit.*

"Sorry, buddy," I said, rubbing the fur on his neck.

"This'll just take a minute." I was sure I heard him grumble his disapproval. As famished as I was from not eating, it could have been *my* stomach that grumbled.

Inside the door, I glanced around, finally spotting Tom, thanks to one of the half-dome safety mirrors more likely placed to catch people from committing the grievous crime of mis-shelving books than for safety or theft prevention. Whatever the reason, it worked in my favor now. Aspen obediently stayed by my side and was quiet. I popped him a dog chew. I tried to be strict about treats, but I hoped it would make up for the lack of attention he'd received from me the last couple of days.

I watched Tom, unnoticed, for a moment. When I saw the opened book in his hands, *HOW TO GET AWAY WITH MURDER: Evil Masterminds Who Evaded Capture*, I gasped, and he spun toward me.

"Can I help you?" he asked, glancing down at Aspen and then back at me.

I essayed to resume normal breathing. "You're Jade's husband, right?"

His jaw muscles clenched. "For now."

My heart pounded in my ears as my gaze flicked to the book, then back to him. "For now?"

He exhaled and rubbed the back of his neck. "Yes, I'm her husband." He planted his feet firmly apart. "Why?"

"Do you have a minute to talk?"

"You're her boss, Andie something-or-other," he said as if I'd forgotten who I was.

For now, I almost said. "Yes. Andie Rose." I looked at the book in his hands again and asked, "Planning something?" I hoped to convey a light tone so he wouldn't suspect anything and practice the tips given in the book to evade capture after killing me.

He looked at the book and then at me. "Nope. This kind of stuff fascinates me. Entertainment."

That's not disturbing at all. "Oh." We stood silent for a moment before I asked, "Tom, did you know Ivan Laskin?"

He scowled, his eyes hard as flint. He tossed the book on top of some shelved books. Instinctively, I glanced at the half-dome mirror to see if the shelving police had noticed. Seeing nothing, I looked back at him.

"If you're here to tell me about my wife, don't bother. She already came clean about her indiscretion. If that's what you want to call it. I call it cheating, debauchery, vile adulterer, disgusting, selfish... Need I go on?" Each word generated more and more loathing, spittle sprinkling the air.

"I understand—"

He jabbed his finger toward me, narrowing his eyes. "No, you don't."

"Okay."

"Unless you were married to a narcissist."

"Look, Tom, I'm sorry you're going through this, but it's not my place to get involved with your and Jade's marriage."

"Then what do you want to talk about? Because I have no desire to talk about that SOB Ivan."

My eyes grew wide, and I bit my lower lip. "You know he's dead, right? Murdered."

He gave a half-hearted shrug. "Yeah, I heard. Can't say as I'm upset about it."

I caught my lower lip between my teeth again as I watched him for a moment. Finally, I said, "Did you see him that night? The night of his murder."

He snorted. "Look, it's no secret I hated the guy, but I'm no killer."

"Do you have an alibi for that night?" I asked. *So much for keeping it light, Andie Rose.*

He leaned toward me, and I forced myself to stand taller and square my shoulders. He may have freaked me out a wee bit, but I wasn't about to let him know that.

"Why are you asking? You're an innkeeper, not the police. I don't have to tell you anything." The muscle in his jaw twitched again.

"I'm trying to clear Jade. Given the, uh," I cleared my throat and took a step back, "the circumstances, it won't look good for her." *Or for you, the betrayed husband.*

"I'm trying hard to care about that right now." I waited for him to say something more helpful. He exhaled, his posture sagged the tiniest bit, and he shook his head slowly. "No, I don't have an alibi. My daughter was staying at a friend's, and my wife was off seeing her lover, so she wasn't with me." His words dripped bitterness. He held his hand up. "And before you go assuming anything, Jade is a cheater, but she's not a killer."

"It'll sure be easier to prove that if we had concrete evidence. All we have is that Jade was with him around the time of the murder in the same room I found his body. And that they were arguing. That reeks of opportunity and motive." Anger flashed in his eyes, so I quickly continued. "Tom, I know as well as you do, she didn't do it. But we need to prove it to the police. They aren't about to take us at our word."

He took a deep breath, exhaling slowly as he leaned against the bookshelf. He tipped his head back, closed his eyes, and pinched the bridge of his nose. "I could just kill her for the spot she's gotten us into right now—marital as well as freedom from accusations." He sneered. "Now there's two words you don't normally hear in the same sentence—marriage and freedom."

I put my finger to my lips and glanced around us for anyone within hearing range. "Shh. You might not want to say that at a time like this. About killing your wife."

"Oh, good Lord," he guffawed. "It's just a manner of speech. But honestly, if I go down for one murder I didn't commit, what's one more? Given the circumstances, I don't think a jury would fault me for it."

Tom pushed himself away from the bookshelf and left without another word. I stood frozen in place, jaw hanging open in bewilderment. Seemed I'd been doing a lot of that for the last forty-eight hours.

When I finally gathered my wits about me, I checked into one more thing as long as I was here.

I waltzed up to the librarian behind the service desk and waited for her to acknowledge me three feet in front of her. Finally, she glanced up and peered at me over the rims of her stereotypical librarian cats-eye glasses attached by a chain around her neck. "Yes?"

"Sorry, I don't want to interrupt, but I was curious if you could help me find a book."

"Of course, dear," she said, slipping her glasses off with her thumb and forefinger and placing one of the temple tips of the earpiece between her teeth. "Which book would that be?"

"*The Woman in Black* by Susan Hill," I said.

She frowned, took the temple tip from her mouth, the corners of her lips curving downward. "Hmm. Now, why does that sound familiar?" She began keying in something on the computer to her right and said, "Oh, dear, that's why. Someone else was in here a day or two ago looking for it, but it had disappeared." She sighed, shook her head, and then nodded toward one of the half-dome safety mirrors. "That's why we have those, don'tcha know. But security measures can't catch them all."

Isn't that the truth.

Chapter 15

Sister Eunice was all too grateful to hitch a ride with me back to the inn to escape the risk of Sister Alice's sidecar. Aspen, however, appeared less than enthused— a passenger meant he had to sit in the back seat like the dog that he was instead of the human he *thought* he was.

Except for the cars belonging to the inn's employees, parked along the far edge, only two remaining vehicles were in the small lot. One of those, I believed, was from housekeeping.

After letting Jade and Lily know I was back, I left Aspen with them and went to my office to check my computer for any applications that may have trickled in. I swallowed my disappointment when the results yielded nothing. Sister Alice said she'd spread the word at St. Michael's, but I'd hoped the electronic call-out would have hooked someone's attention for efficiency more than anything. Seeing the application and resume beforehand could eliminate unnecessary interviews, a colossal waste of time for everyone involved. I heaved a sigh.

I snagged a red spiral notebook from the top drawer of my desk and opened it to a fresh page. To organize a legion of disconnected parts, I began writing suspect names to better see the whole. First was Luka: there was open hostility between him and Ivan. If I was to include mitigating factors, though, he was the church's deacon, a father, husband, and Godly man. *Or was he*? I camped here for a moment before deciding I'd pop into the coffee shop and chat with Roman. The quiet kid he was, he'd probably have few words to say unless Sister Alice was with me. People generally disclosed more information with laity or a clergy member. *Didn't they*? Next to Luka's name and probable motive, I wrote in parentheses *speak with Roman*.

Next, there was Tom. He had motive and opportunity—opportunity because he didn't have an alibi and motive because his wife had an affair with Ivan. Still worse, she was pregnant with his kid. Not to mention the temper I'd witnessed at the library. I softly tapped my pencil tip a few times on Tom's name. This didn't look good for him at all.

Then there was Jade. I scribbled her name next to Tom's. She, by her own admission, was with Ivan in the room I found his body shortly after. A lover scorned was as great a motive as any, especially pregnant and hormonal. I shuddered.

Tony—Ivan stole something of value from him; they worked together nearly every day, giving Tony's animosity toward Ivan plenty of time to pick up steam. And both had free access to the inn's kitchen at any hour.

I leaned back in my chair and chewed on the inside of my cheek. Considering Tony as the culprit was a struggle. Sure, he'd confessed disdain for Ivan, but so had several others. Even Marcie and Frank didn't like Ivan. And a stolen recipe seemed a weak motive. But then, I wasn't familiar with the life of a chef. I dwelled there a moment before sitting back up and moving on.

Mike Swanson. If he and Ivan had several

altercations, what's to say the last one wasn't the final straw? The coup de grâce. Maybe Mike had finally had it, went out on a bender, and snapped. I added him to my list of people to chat with.

And what about Ella? If she's dating Mike, perhaps Ivan said something to her about Mike, and she defended her man. *But murder*? I considered what Deacon Molotov said about Ella waiting for her inheritance. If she could be so cold about her own mother, choosing the inheritance over her mother's life, perhaps she was cold enough to kill. And she could also potentially be the one stealing the items from the church, connecting the dots between the two cases. But as I mulled it over, it was a weak connection at best. I added Ella to my *chat with* list.

Tossing my pencil on the notebook, I sighed and sat back in my chair. I reached my arms up and behind me, clasping my hands behind my head. While staring absently at the open notebook, a new email popped up in the lower right corner on my computer screen, followed by the quiet *ding*. I leaned forward and opened the email. It was an application with an attached resume. I skimmed through it as I chewed on my pencil, followed by a sharp inhale. I could hardly believe my luck. This had to be too good to be true.

I went back to the beginning and reviewed it more slowly. The applicant left a couple of minor areas on the application blank—her school attended, age, and sex—info easily gleaned from an interview. Given the name on the application, Izzy, the sex was a no-brainer. Maybe. And the age didn't matter—unless she was a hundred. I could even work with that. She demonstrated exceptional experience in her family's catering business despite her limited educational history. I'd take extensive experience over education any day. Not sure how Tony felt about it, however.

I reached for my phone and punched in the applicant's number, receiving a voice message. "This is Izzy. You know what to do." The voice sounded to be maybe mid-twenties, answering another blank on the application.

At the beep, I left my voicemail. "Hi, Izzy. I'm Andie Rose Kaczmarek from the Spirit Lake Inn. I'm calling regarding your application and resume for a sous-chef. I'd like to schedule an interview with you. Please call me back." After leaving my number and a final "thank you," I hung up with a hopeful smile. Until I remembered I was a suspect in a murder investigation, as well as my newly appointed chef, and may not be here to see how well Izzy does in the kitchen should I hire her. And who would run the inn for me? My folks? Sister Alice? I slunk back into my chair.

****

Sister Alice left Father Vincent's office, closing the door behind her as she chewed on his words. Sister Ida had sought out Father Vincent's counsel to improve the relationship between her and Sister Alice. He wanted to set up a date, the sooner the better. Sister Alice wasn't surprised, but she sure as heck wasn't happy about it. Sister Ida's last "I've had it with you" conversation with Sister Alice was about two missed prayer meetings in the past week. Also, that she hadn't been fulfilling her duties at the house. *Right*. It surprised her Sister Ida even wasted Father Vincent's time with something so insignificant as what happens at the house. It wasn't as if he gave two cents about what happens at the house.

Sister Alice fought the attitude rising in her throat. Somehow, she'd maintained control and agreed to the arrangement, albeit reluctantly. She'd gone to Father Vincent herself recently, confessing her contemptuous feelings for Sister Ida because of her impatient and critical nature. On one occasion, Sister Ida even apologized to her, yet nothing changed. Sister Alice suspected she'd have to spend an abundance of time on her knees to get past this one.

She perched on a bone-colored concrete bench in the tranquil church courtyard under the vibrant red leaves of a sugar maple tree. An antique finished statue of Mary, with pastel blue and pale-yellow clothing, roses at her feet, and a rosary draped between her fingers, stood before her. She could only hope to be filled with such grace and gentleness as the Holy Mother someday. Sister Alice bathed in the beauty of it until her mind persisted at replaying the conversation with Father Vincent.

"In my defense, Father," she'd said, "one meeting I had to miss because of an emergency at the hospital."

"You don't owe me an explanation, Sister. Sister Ida is the house Superior. She's the one you need to communicate with."

"I did, Father."

He held her gaze for a moment. "I see. Not that it's my business, but what caused the second absence?"

"I forgot about the meeting." Sister Alice shifted her weight. Father Vincent was the most congenial priest she'd worked with. Even so, she didn't like letting him down.

He frowned. "You—forgot?"

"Unfortunately. I was helping Andie Rose with a— shall we say, an *issue*."

Father Vincent sat back in his chair. "And that is what you told Sister Ida?"

"Not exactly, Father."

"I see." He leaned forward and looked at his calendar. "Let's get this scheduled, shall we?"

Sister Ida had given Father Vincent dates for her availability, and after deciding on a congruent date for all three, he marked it on his calendar.

"It's in pen, Sister. Let's get this taken care of." She nodded and stood when he said, "I imagine the *issue* you're referring to helping Ms. Kaczmarek with is the unfortunate death at her business."

"Yes, Father." She looked at the canvas painting of the Last Supper, made famous by Leonardo da Vinci, then back to Father Vincent.

He appeared to think a moment before replying, "Out of curiosity, what kind of help were you giving Ms. Kaczmarek? Grief counseling?"

Sister Alice shuffled her feet again. "Not exactly." Father Vincent remained silent, waiting for her to continue. "Andie Rose and her staff are considered suspects. I'm helping her find the actual killer."

Father Vincent let out a barely audible chuckle. "I see. And how do the police feel about that?"

"Probably not happy," she answered honestly.

"And how did you get involved?"

"I'm Andie Rose's sponsor. I figured it was the right thing to do." *How could he argue with that?*

"Does that fit within the scope of an AA sponsor?" he asked, clearly amused.

Sister Alice, grateful she was having this conversation with compassionate Father Vincent and not prickly Sister Ida, sat down in the chair across from him.

"Father, how well do you know Deacon Molotov?"

He raised his hand from his desk and rested it again. "Well enough, I imagine. Why do you ask?"

"He and Ivan—that's the murder victim—have been at odds for many years. Do you know anything about that?"

"Even if I did, you know I can't—and wouldn't—say anything."

"Do you think he's capable of murder?"

Father Vincent's mouth opened, but nothing came out. It closed again, and he leaned forward, clasping his hands on his desk. "Where are you going with this question?"

"Just wondering, Father."

"Wondering what, exactly, if he killed Ivan Laskin?" he asked incredulously. "Do you know how preposterous that sounds?"

Sister Alice nodded and said, "Yes, I do. But all humans are sinners."

"But Luka?" His thick, bushy eyebrows—in sharp contrast to his nearly bald head—drew together, and he sat back again, rocking his chair gently back and forth. "What motive does he have?"

"That's what I'm working to find out."

Father Vincent sighed and ran his hand over the remaining wisps of gray hair. "If I may intercede, Sister, see to it that you don't ruin lives by falsely accusing innocent people."

"Yes, Father." When he rose to a standing position, his hands resting on his desk, she followed his cue and rose to her feet. When she reached the door, she turned toward him. "Any news on the missing collection money?"

He sighed, sat again, and shook his head slowly. "I'm afraid not. I hoped it was an accounting error, but that doesn't appear to be the case."

Sister Alice hesitated, weighing her next question. "Deacon—"

Father Vincent's hand shot out, palm facing her. It was unquestionably the fastest she'd ever seen him move.

"Don't go any further with that thought." She nodded and turned toward the door. "Sister?" he said. She turned to face him again. "See that you don't forget our mediation session with Sister Ida. It would be easier on all of us if the two of you wouldn't aggravate each other so much." She could see the corner of his mouth twitch and curve upward.

"That's hard, because everything I do aggravates her," she murmured.

He cocked his head to the side, the curve in his lips growing ever so slightly. "What was that?"

"Nothing, Father." She smiled and pushed her glasses up with her pointer finger. "I hear Marie Dayton is doing better," she said, hoping to refocus his attention.

"Yes. That was wonderful news."

"I heard her daughter is—"

"Sister Alice," Father Vincent said with a sigh. "Gossip has no room in God's house. Or anywhere. It seems you have enough on your plate with Ms. Kaczmarek, Sister Ida, and the hospital without fretting about other people."

She nodded and silently closed the door behind her.

****

I busied myself with paperwork and mingled with guests that had returned, striving to keep that personal touch that Grandpop and Honey had always made a priority. "Andie Rose," Honey said on one of my long-ago visits, "you can have the best inn in the world, but if you don't give them service they'll remember, they'll forget to come back." I'd need to pay special attention to the inn while solving the murder. Connecting with the guests was a favorite part of owning the inn. Aspen seemed to enjoy it, too, lapping up the love and attention they gave him. To be honest, it was Aspen they were likely to remember more than the personal touch I provided.

After mingling with each one, Aspen and I trekked to my room for a brief respite and to call Sister Alice. Hopefully, she could go with me to Hallowed Grounds to talk with Roman.

As we passed the library, the copy of *The Woman in Black* lay on the side table alongside another book, *An Unlikely Suspect*. I looked at the author's name: Lisa Martelli. I'd never heard of the book or the author. I was familiar with the books in the inn's library, and *An Unlikely Suspect* wasn't one of them. A guest obviously brought it. Probably the same one reading *The Woman in Black*.

Floor-to-ceiling bookshelves covered two entire walls of the library, a set of wingback chairs with a reading lamp on a table between them against another wall, and another chair tucked in a corner beside a tall, narrow window, beside which set a floor lamp. Making it even more cozy was a gas fireplace that emitted a surprising amount of heat; a fireplace that some proclaimed turned on and off while the room was empty, giving credence to a ghostly presence. The library was one of the more popular rooms at the inn, and I often come here to read myself. After a pause, I left both books in place and continued to my room.

Chapter 16

Sister Alice waltzed through the door just as I'd come from checking on Tony and Sister Eunice. Tony had been getting ready to leave, and Sister Eunice was all but pushing him out the door so she could work without Tony lurching over her shoulder.

"How's the apprentice doing?" Sister Alice asked.

"Itching to get rid of her supervisor. I got an application today for a sous-chef. Sounds too good to be true."

"Then it probably is." She glanced around the room. "Where's Aspen?"

"Roaming. Pursuing the attention he hasn't gotten from me today. Or yesterday."

"Why'd you want me to come here instead of meeting at the coffee shop? You need a ride?"

I snorted. "That'd be a hard no." I crooked my finger so she'd follow me to the office. "I want your input on something. I could have brought it with me into town, I guess."

"Define 'it,'" she said.

I glanced back toward her as we reached my office door. "I pulled together all the information we have so far—suspects, motive, opportunity, you name it."

She parked herself in the chair, and I settled in the chair behind my desk. I pushed the notebook toward her. "I love those teal frames, by the way. Why'd you changed from the orange?"

She pushed them up with her pointer finger and smiled. "Because I could."

"You have more eyewear than I have underwear."

She looked at me over the teal rims. "You best get some more underwear." She studied the list before tossing it across the desk toward me. "Good work, Grasshopper. Organization is your strong suit." She sat back. "Keeping my mouth shut is mine. Not."

I chuckled and tilted my head. "Welcome to my world. What'd you do now?"

"Father Vincent called me into his office for a chat today."

"And?"

"He wasn't happy when I asked him about Deacon Molotov. And less so when I didn't stop asking."

"That's why he wanted to chat? How did he know about it?"

Sister Alice shook her head and waved her hand in dismissal. "Nah. The why has nothing to do with this case and everything to do with Sister Ida. She wants Father Vincent to mediate our differences."

"What did you do to Sister Ida?"

"Nothing. And that's the truth."

"Right," I said, striving to keep a straight face. "That's why she wants Father Vincent to mediate. Because you didn't do anything."

She looked at me, her lips pressed together. "It's the truth. I missed prayer group twice."

"And here you said you'd done nothing. Why'd you miss?"

"Once I got called into work at the hospital."

"And the other?"

"What are you, in cahoots with Sister Ida?" she asked, looking at me over the rim of her glasses again before standing. "I might have been caught up with helping you here at the inn. That presented the perfect opportunity to bring up Luka to Father Vincent. So I did."

"What did he say about him?" I caught my reflection in the window, my frizzed red curls wild. Slipping a hair elastic from my wrist, I whipped the mess into a ponytail.

"Nothing helpful. But he gave sage advice about not ruining lives by falsely accusing someone. It is a valid point, you know. I bet we could look at any of the people on this list," she nodded to the notebook on the desk, "and find something to make them appear guilty. We need to gather all the information carefully to assure the evidence fits the person instead of forcing the person to fit the evidence."

I sighed and stretched my arms above my head as I stood and led the way to the door. "I know." As I pulled it closed behind us, I said, "That same book was lying on a table in the library again earlier. Along with another one about an unlikely suspect. Maybe the ghost is telling us something about Luka."

"Ha," Sister Ida exclaimed. "Sounds to me like you've become a believer in ghosts."

I smiled. "Maybe. The verdict's not in yet."

"Don't look so hard to find something that you see what's *not* there, Grasshopper. The ghost isn't interested in trivial matters."

"How do you know that? Does it talk to you?"

"Everyone knows ghosts don't talk," she scoffed. "I'm simply realistic. Please tell me you didn't re-shelve the books again. You're only making more work for the poor person trying to read it."

"I didn't. I left both of them where they were."

When we passed the front desk, Lily and Jade were deep in conversation. Both stopped when we arrived.

"I like your sweater, Jade. It's festive," Sister Alice said. "And appropriate."

Jade scowled at Sister Alice, obviously not forgiving her for her last comment about her wardrobe.

"We have to run into town," I told them. "Either of you need anything?"

"Have you heard any more from that detective, Andie Rose?" Lily asked.

"Not yet."

"Does he still think it's one of us?" Jade asked.

I shook my head. "I don't know. But I'll let you know when I do."

"I'm riding with Andie Rose," Sister Alice called over her shoulder. "Don't let Sister Eunice take my moped."

"Like she's going to hot wire the thing or what? You keep the key in your bra."

"At least I wear one," she said, just loud enough for Jade to hear.

I elbowed her, and after closing the door behind us, I said, "You know that bit you said about not keeping your mouth shut was your strength? Yeah," I said without waiting for her to answer, "you need to find a different one."

She grinned. "Just because I'm a sister doesn't mean I'm perfect."

"Wonders never cease," I teased as we strode to my car. "Come on. We need to find the murderer before

Detective Griffin arrests someone from the inn."

"Any news from Brad yet?" she asked.

"No, but I—" My phone rang, and I slipped it from my pocket and looked at the display. "Creepy," I said. "It's Brad. It's like he heard you asking about him." I pushed the button on my phone. "Hi, Brad."

"What the hell, Andie Rose?"

Again? I jerked the phone away and took a moment and a breath before putting it back to my ear. "Let's try this again, Brad, starting with, at the very least, a hello."

"Hi," he grumbled. "Detective Griffin called me asking a bunch of questions."

My curiosity spiked; my breath hitched. "Like what?"

"Like about the altercation you had with the murder victim and how I felt about it."

"Did you tell him you didn't feel anything at all?" As soon as the question tumbled from my lips, I realized the tricky spot I'd put him in. I knew full well it hadn't bothered him, but if he admitted that to Detective Griffin, he'd look like the worst boyfriend ever. If he admitted he was torqued about it, he would look guilty.

"How can you even ask that?" he said, skirting around an impossible answer.

"I just meant that it hadn't bothered you, so—"

"It was a harmless spat, honey. It's not like it was dangerous."

His downplay of the incident raised my ire. "Wow," was all I could spit out.

"Can we talk about something a little more pleasant?"

The distinct sound of cracking knuckles traveled through the airwaves. It was a habit when he was either annoyed or uneasy about something. And it was one of the most emotional signs he displayed.

"What did you have in mind?" I asked, still a little miffed. Unlike Brad, I didn't have difficulty expressing my emotions. Not much ruffled my feathers, but when it did—well, let's just say people knew about it.

"Have you decided about my proposal? It'd sure be nice to put all of this behind us, get you out of that town to where it's safer. I want us to get married."

I sighed and looked at Sister Alice, who'd already gotten into the passenger side of the car. Aspen, albeit reluctantly, crawled into the back seat. "I believe you, Brad. That you want to be married. But not necessarily to me. And it seems like you want to get married for reasons that feel wrong to me."

"What's wrong with wanting to start a family? Andie Rose, we've been dating for over five years."

He didn't get it. In fact, during the past six months, perhaps longer, I wouldn't even call what we were doing *dating*. I looked at Sister Alice and Aspen again. Knowing it would turn into a debacle and an argument if I told him my answer—again—at this moment, I said, "We'll have to talk about this later. I was just leaving with Sister Alice."

There was a pause. "Sure. How about this evening?"

"Okay. Hey, Brad?" I said, hoping to catch him before he hung up.

"Yeah?"

"No accusations or judgement here, I promise. But I'm curious where you went after leaving the pub that night?" Silence, then more knuckle cracking. "Hello?"

"I'm here."

There was another, longer pause, and I thought he'd

hung up.

"I did not kill that guy, Andie Rose. Why would I do that? You say no accusations, but that's exactly what it was."

I admit shame fell on me, landing me as the worst girlfriend ever. *Ex*-girlfriend. I'd devised a new variation of breaking up. I cautioned my coaching clients not to use the overused, *It's not you, it's me*, because it skirted around the truth. Suspecting a partner of murder isn't what I'd suggest either, and it wasn't one of my prouder moments. I rolled my eyes, exhaled, and rubbed my temples with my thumb and middle finger. "Sorry. I'm just desperate to find out who killed Ivan, so my staff and I can get back to business without this hanging over us."

There it was again, the telltale knuckle cracking. "Well, I don't know what to tell you, except it wasn't me." And then the line went dead. His voice had been so sharp, it probably cut the phone line.

I glanced at Aspen before getting in the car, but he refused to look at me—punishment for backseat treatment. I sighed and slammed my door.

"Are Aspen and I safe with you behind the wheel right now?" Sister Alice asked, looking at me sideways. "Maybe we should take my moped."

"And what, Aspen can sit on my lap in the sidecar?" Although, when I glanced behind me to find him staring at me with the most pathetic and accusatory look, I thought he might prefer the sidecar. I sighed and rubbed the nape of my neck.

"What bit you in the butt?" Sister Alice asked.

I exhaled slowly before speaking. "That was Brad."

"Obviously. What happened?"

"He's mad because Detective Griffin asked him a

bunch of questions about the pub the night someone killed Ivan."

"And?"

"And then I asked him where he went that night after he left Brewski's."

Sister Alice looked out the windshield. "Ah. And he didn't like you questioning him."

I looked at her. "Would you?"

"He didn't seem to have a problem questioning you. Did you give him an answer to his proposal since he didn't want to hear it the first time?"

I turned the key in the ignition and began backing out of my parking space. "I didn't feel like getting into an argument. We're going to talk tonight."

"Seems like your plan didn't work. There was an argument anyway. Just shoot it and kill it already, for goodness' sakes."

Instead, I let my eyes do the talking and shot her a killer look.

The short drive into town was silent—I stewed, Aspen pouted, and Sister Alice remained cleverly cautious.

We got lucky with a parking space on the street in front of the door of Hallowed Grounds. Aspen hopped out right after me, and Sister Alice shut her door and came around the car. I opened the coffee shop door and held it for her, noticing for the first time that her eyeglass frames matched her teal and black jacket. Her white hair stood out, reminding me of meringue on a pie.

The smell of freshly roasted coffee beans met us at the door, a scent I never tired of and one of my favorites in the world.

I looked around at the packed tables in the coffee

shop, noticing a man and woman from the inn. I waved at them, called out a "hello," and then looked at the barista behind the autumn-decorated counter. Definitely not Roman. She had long black hair tied in a ponytail and coal-black eyelashes that looked an inch long. I instinctively scrunched my nose and touched one of my eyes. I'd tried lash extensions once and took them off the same day. I was used to wearing heavy mascara, but with the last extensions, every time I blinked, I thought my eyelids might fall off. They weren't for me. Unlike the dragonfly tat on my shoulder. Most of the time, I forgot it was even there; to be honest, I couldn't remember getting it in one of my drunken stupors. The price of sobriety—I actually felt things. Even if I didn't want to.

"Is Roman working?" Sister Alice asked the barista.

The girl grinned and stood straighter, as if her teacher had caught her cheating. "Hi, Sister. Roman's working today, but he left on a break with a buddy. He'll be back in about an hour."

"Wow, that's a long break," I said.

She smiled and looked at Sister Alice, her cheeks turning carnation pink. "Yeah. He just left. We kinda take longer breaks when the boss isn't here."

Sister Alice patted her hand. "No need to explain to me, dear. I'm not your boss. But remember, I have a direct connection to the Man upstairs."

"Sister Alice," I scolded, and she tittered.

"I'm teasing, Tara," she told the girl. "Say hi to your mom for me." She turned to me and said, "Let's take a stroll down Spirit Lane and enjoy the fall weather and the decorations. Maybe we'll run into Mike Swanson or Ella."

"Can I at least get you a coffee?" Tara asked. The

last word ended an octave higher, causing me to rock onto my tiptoes and back down.

After assuring her we'd be back in an hour and get one then, we turned and left.

"She's a sprightly young thing," I said. Sister Alice only smiled. "Why does it seem like there's a story between the two of you?"

Aspen stayed against my leg as if to remind me he should ride shotgun when we got back in the car. I reached down and scratched his head. When the door closed behind us, I asked Sister Alice, "Why did you say that to her?"

Her eyes widened behind the frames. "About the direct connection?" she asked. "I told her I was kidding."

"Right before you told her to say hi to her mom. Passive-aggressive much?"

Sister Alice shot me a devilish smile. "Tara and I have…let's just say we have an understanding." I stopped, tipped my chin down and looked at her, and she went on. "I caught her and Billy, a boy from her catechism class, together in the alley. Let's just say they weren't studying the faith."

My jaw dropped open. "And you're holding that above her head? That's cruel."

She turned toward me with wide eyes. "I'm not holding anything above her head. I agreed to keep quiet about it, but reminded her that God sees everything. Since then, she seems to get nervous around me and eager to please. I can't figure it out."

I rolled my eyes and scoffed. "I wonder why." I shook my head and reached for Aspen, ruffling his fur. "Good Lord."

"Hey," she said and winked. "I may have prevented a pregnancy."

Chapter 17

People, dressed in festive sweaters, coats, and scarves, filled the sidewalks. Most held cups of cider given out by Handy Hardware, sandwiched between Clips & Tips Beauty Shop and Lakeside Grocery. The Harvest Festival hadn't even officially begun yet, so I could only imagine the sheer number *during* the festival.

As Sister Alice and I reached Brewski's, I turned toward the door.

She grasped my arm.

I flinched. "Ouch."

"Sorry," she said, placing her hands on her hips. "But what are you doing?"

I rubbed my arm where it had pinched. "Aspen wants a whiskey."

She scowled. "Of course he does."

I raised my hands, palms up. "Checking to see if Mike Swanson is here." I continued in, Aspen by my side. Once my eyes adjusted to the dim lighting, I glanced around the pub, then strolled up to the bartender, busily wiping down the bar with a towel. "Have you seen Mike Swanson today?"

"Nope." He tossed the towel onto the counter behind him. "What can I get ya? Bloody Mary? Two for one all day today." He looked at Sister Alice. "We have Virgin Marys if ya like."

Sister Alice scowled and stared at him until he

squirmed—which gave her significant pleasure.

"Kidding," he finally mumbled, ripping his gaze away from Sister Alice and toward me. "Want me to let Mike know you're lookin' for him?"

"That'd be great," I said. I took a business card from my handbag and handed it to him. "Give him this. My phone number's on it."

"Can I keep your number? I like redheads."

"No."

Sister Alice resumed *the look*. He shut up, quickly averted his eyes again, and swiped the business card from the bar top. "I'll make sure he gets this."

Sister Alice paused, pointed two fingers at her eyes, then at him, and back and forth again in an *I'm watching you* motion. The warning lost all effect when her fingers jammed the lenses on her eyewear, landing them askew. The bartender smirked, I chuckled, and proceeded to the door. Blinded by the bright outside light, I crashed into something, feeling a solid thud. Rough hands grasped my upper arms as Sister Alice whammed into the back of me. I looked up at a man standing before me.

"In a hurry somewhere?" he said.

I stepped away from his grasp. "Sorry."

"Michael Swanson," Sister Alice said, straightening her glasses again.

"Sister," Mike said. "Last place I'da thought to run into you." He chuckled. "Literally. What are you doing here?"

"Looking for you," she said.

I studied the man who stood before me in the still-open door, my eyes now adjusted to the light.

"In or out, people," the bartender called toward us.

"I don't know about you all," Mike said, "but I'm

going in."

Sister Alice and I followed him back inside. Aspen let out a soft whine and followed. I sat on the stool beside Mike, and Sister Alice stood between and behind us next to Aspen. Mike held a finger up to the bartender. "The usual," he told him.

The bartender nodded, flipped a glass in his hand, pulled the handle to draw a beer, and set it on a cocktail napkin in front of Mike. "Do you ladies want something now?" the bartender asked.

"Nothing for me," Sister Alice said.

"A bowl with water for my furry kid here." I nodded toward Aspen. "Seltzer with lime for me."

"The hard stuff," Mike commented.

"Yep," I said. "The lime is the kicker."

He snorted a laugh and drew a large gulp of his beer, sounding his satisfaction. "Start a tab for me, Bill," he told the bartender. "And don't go too far. This one won't last long." He took another guzzle. As if remembering we were there, he swiveled his barstool to face us, the glass looking small in his giant hand. "Why were you looking for me?"

Bill slid a glass of seltzer in front of me, the lime wedge straddling the rim. I squeezed the juice from the lime into my water and dropped it into the glass, then wiped my fingers on my jeans. Aspen left his water, more interested in the lime. "I have a couple of questions for you about Ivan Laskin," I said.

Mike stopped his glass halfway to his mouth, set it back on the scratched and carved surface of the dark wood bar, and squinted at me. "What about him?"

"A witness said you two argued a couple of days before his murder."

"Yeah?" he said, eyes narrowing. "And who is this witness?"

"I don't know who it was," I lied.

"That so?" He drained his glass and motioned for a refill. "Someone just came up to you and said, 'Hey, I saw Mike Swanson argue with Ivan Laskin.' I ain't stupid, lady."

"Is it true about the argument?" I asked.

Mike leaned forward until his face was mere inches from mine and belched. I gagged on the beer breath that blew in my face, leaned back, and grimaced.

"I don't enjoy getting accused of something I didn't do," he said.

Sister Alice stepped in closer. "Take a breath, Mike," she said. "No one is accusing you of anything."

"So you *didn't* argue?" I asked him. Sister Alice shot me a *you're-going-to-get-us-both-killed* look before making a quick, ambiguous sign of the cross.

"I didn't say that," he said, wrapping his hand around the full glass Bill slid in front of him. "But if you didn't see it, you got no business talking about it like you're some hotshot cop." He gave me a pointed look. "Which you are not."

I took a drink of my seltzer water and set it back down. "Since you admitted to it, and I'm no longer assuming—" I winced as Sister Alice discreetly pinched my arm. I'd have to wear long sleeves for a month to cover the bruises. "Can I ask what the argument was about?" I quickly asked as I lurched away from Sister Alice.

"I refuse to answer on the grounds of possibly incriminating myself," he said.

"I'm not the police, Mike. There's no threat of

incriminating yourself with me."

"Forgive me if I don't believe that anything I say to you won't somehow find its way back to the cops." He looked at Sister Alice and dipped his chin toward his chest. "You too. No offense."

"None taken," Sister Alice said. She pushed the bent frames of her glasses up with her pointer finger.

"Can I ask where you were the evening of Ivan's murder?" I asked, earning an elbow jab. "*Ouch.*" I said under my breath and rubbed my arm. *Geez.* I was becoming a quick believer in the stories Grandpop and Honey used to tell me about the harsh discipline from the nuns back in the day when they were in Catholic school.

"With Ella. Ask her." His voice issued the warning his words didn't.

I sat there for a minute longer, prolonging the time, hoping he'd share anything else. Not that he'd shared anything up to this point except an alibi, most likely unreliable. I planned to check it out. When he faced forward, intent on pretending we weren't there, I slid my glass toward the inside edge of the bar, then pushed myself to a standing position.

"All right. Thanks, Mike."

"I'd say 'my pleasure,' but I ain't no liar."

Sister Alice patted his arm. "God is happy about that, Michael."

After the door closed behind us, I said, "What do you think? He has a temper, and he's not a sweetheart by any means, but I don't feel like he killed Ivan."

Sister Alice turned toward me and looked at me, chin tipped downward. "You don't *feel* like he did? Please don't tell me you're trying to make an informed decision based on emotion. I thought you were a life coach."

I scoffed. "This might surprise you, but that doesn't mean I don't fail to follow my own advice. By the way," I said as I attempted to straighten her glasses. "Now I know why you buy so many of these things."

"Sobriety can't fix everything."

We walked back to Hallowed Grounds. As luck had it, not only was Roman back from break, but Luka stood at the counter ordering a coffee. We quietly stepped up behind him. I nudged Sister Alice with my elbow and nodded my head toward the wad of cash in Luka's open wallet. I leaned in to look more closely at the bills. At the same time, Luka turned around, nearly bumping into me. I jumped back.

"Pardon me, Deacon Molotov."

He looked from me to Sister Alice. "Good day for a hot drink," he said, toasting us with his cup.

Another customer wedged her way in front of us, so I took advantage of the added wait time. "Do you have a minute to talk, Deacon?" I asked.

"If it's quick."

He and Sister Alice followed me as I stepped toward the side. Another customer stepped in line.

"Do you know if Ella and Ivan knew each other?"

"I suspect so. Mike and Ivan were friends, and Ella has been with Mike off and on for several years."

"Hm." Between hearing about their frequent rifts and the conversation with Mike moments ago, it didn't sound too friendly between him and Ivan. "Are you sure they were friends?" I made air quotes as I said "friends."

"I only know what everyone else in town knows. I've already told you that Ivan and I haven't spoken in years. Why do you ask?"

"I didn't get the impression that they were close. They don't seem to have any similarities."

He grunted and looked at me as though I'd just been released from the nut ward. "Men differ from women, Ms. Kaczmarek. They don't feel the need to—well, *bond*, shall we say, as women do. That makes similarities and differences a lot less important."

"Have you ever counseled Mike and Ella together?" I asked.

"That information is confidential," he said. "You know, like what's said and done within the walls of an AA meeting." He smiled, but it held no warmth. I gave him a sidelong glance. "Spirit Lake is a small, close-knit community," he said. "Of course, I know."

"I see confidentiality isn't popular with everyone here."

"Says the one trying to get personal information on someone else." His tone was one of impatience, as if explaining something logical to a teen.

I suspected my cheeks were now the same color as my hair. "Touché," I said, readjusting Aspen's leash wrapped around my hand.

He looked at Sister Alice, his chin jutting before giving a dismissive nod. "If you ladies will excuse me, I have an appointment."

As he passed, I stepped to the side, then looked at Sister Alice. "You know, I really hate that."

"Hate what? That you couldn't get the information you wanted?"

"Well, yeah, that too." I shook my head. "But the whole men differ from women spiel gets my goat. I wanted to wipe that smug look from his face."

Sister Alice looked amused. "Do I need to explain

the differences between men and women? I'd have thought you knew them by now."

"You know what I mean," I scoffed. "He thinks women are less than men. I help women with self-esteem and confidence issues so they don't lose themselves in a relationship. Men with Luka's mentality destroy that confidence. And to think I used to think he was nice."

"Think of it as job security," she said. I rolled my eyes. "I'm just saying that men and women *are* different in more ways than we like to admit sometimes." I opened my mouth to speak, and she held up a hand. "I didn't say we're inferior, but we are different. And thank the good Lord for that."

I begrudgingly nodded and took a breath. "Okay, I'll accept that."

"Good, because I, as your sponsor, have a responsibility to remind you what resentments do to an alcoholic."

"Yeah, yeah."

Five more customers now stood in line since we stepped out to chat with Luka. We moved in behind them. When it was finally our turn to order, I looked at Roman. "A medium two-pump pumpkin spice latte with oat milk, please. And a cup of whipped cream for my boy here." I nodded toward Aspen, who perked up at the mention of whipped cream. Three words he understood too well were "whipped cream" and "walk." Roman scribbled it on the cup, passed it off to the barista, then took Sister Alice's order, a black coffee, room for cream. "You'd better leave half the cup empty for cream," I said. "In fact, give her a two-pound bag of sugar and a gallon of cream." He chuckled and passed the cup to the barista. "Do you have a minute to talk?" I asked him. "Maybe a break?"

"I just got back. I don't get another one until my shift is over."

"What time is that?" I asked.

"Six. What's this about?"

"Ivan Laskin."

His eyes grew wider. "Oh. If you wanna sit at a table, I can stop by as soon as I can."

"We'll do that," Sister Alice said. "So long as it doesn't get you in trouble."

"The boss is gone today," he said with a shy grin.

"So we've heard," I said. "My staff probably feels the same way when I'm gone."

He chuckled. "Not probably. They *do*. Trust me."

I nodded soberly and pointed to the corner table facing the street. "We'll be right over there."

"I'll be with you as soon as I can."

Sister Alice and I each pulled out a chair, and Aspen lay by my feet. His body was mostly under the table save for his paws, which clutched the paper cup with whipped cream.

"Did you see the wad of cash in Luka's wallet?" I asked her.

"Is that what you were doing while practically leaning on his shoulder? Looking in his wallet?"

"It's not like I was looking for it. It was right in my line of sight."

"I saw it," she conceded.

The barista slid my order across the counter and called my name. After fetching it, I sat back down and said, "Well? Could I be right, and the church thief and the killer are the same person?"

She shook her head. "The crook stole more money

from the church than Luka had in his wallet."

"Well, yeah, but he wouldn't carry the entire amount around with him," I said. "He's arrogant, not stupid."

She shook her head again and stirred the cream in her coffee with a wooden stir stick. "I can't see it. What reason could he have to steal money? He's not destitute. He's got a nice house, a beautiful family, a good car. There's no rational answer."

"Not all criminals have a reason for what they do," I explained. "That would insinuate sanity. It's the thrill of the chase. Seeing if they can get away with it."

She leveled her gaze on mine. "He's a deacon, for crying out loud. Who's he trying to pull one over on, God?" She took a breath, gathering her wits. "Tell you what, I'm not ruling it out, but he's toward the bottom of the list of suspects I'd look at for it."

Not ten minutes later, Roman came over to the table and pulled out a chair. Aspen sniffed his leg, then licked his fingers.

"I think he likes you," I said.

"More like the syrup on my hands." He reached for Aspen again. "So, what did you want to talk about?"

"I was hoping you could give us some insight into the relationship between your dad and Ivan."

Roman visibly stiffened and looked down, wiping something off the table that wasn't there. "There was no relationship between them."

Chapter 18

"But they used to be good friends, right?" I said. "What happened between them?"

He lifted a hand loosely, palm up. "They had a falling out, but my dad won't tell me or my mom what happened."

Boy, could I relate to that. The falling out between Grandpop and my uncle demonstrated how secrets wedged themselves between family members. If Honey knew the basis of the argument, she kept mum as well.

"You've never heard anything around town?" Sister Alice asked.

He shook his head. "Nope. But it's not like anyone would talk to me about it since I'm his son." He looked at the counter, then back at us. "What's this about, anyway? I mean, I know Laskin is dead, but what's that got to do with my dad?"

I hesitated, pondering whether I should say anything and then figured, what the heck? It wasn't like we were getting any information as it was. "We're looking for Ivan's killer and nailing down suspects so—"

"Wait." He sat up straight in his chair. Aspen looked at Roman and cocked his head. "Is my dad a suspect?"

"I'm just looking at anyone who could have had motive and opportunity. The police are looking at me and my staff, and we didn't do it."

He shook his head vigorously. "Uh-uh. Not my dad.

He was home. I know because him and my mom argued in their room all evening."

"*All* evening? That must have been some argument."

"It was. My mom finally stormed out." He glanced out the window briefly, then scratched Aspen's head. "They didn't work it out until the next day."

"Do you know what it was about?"

"Uh-uh. I put on my headphones and tuned 'em out."

"But you knew your mom left."

"When I went to the can, I heard the door slam, and mom's car backed out of the driveway. Then I put my headphones back on."

I smiled when he reached down to touch the top of Aspen's head again. Pet therapy was the best. "So, theoretically, your dad could have left and then gone back home without you knowing about it."

"I don't see how. I came out of my room twice during argument intermissions, once for a can of Dr. Pepper and once for a bag of Cheetos and ice cream."

Sounds like a substance-induced binge. Even though it had been years ago, I remembered those binges all too well. Or it could have been an emotionally driven binge if his parents were arguing.

"Sorry, Roman, could you repeat that? My mind took a quick trip."

"The first time I left my room, my dad was in the bathroom, and the second time he was in his pajamas and reading something on his computer."

"Do you know what time that was, Roman?" Sister Alice asked.

He looked at her. "You can't possibly think my dad had anything to do with this. He's a deacon at the church."

I said, "We're not saying your dad had anything to do with Ivan's murder, Roman. We're trying to rule out whoever we can and leave the last man standing holding the weapon, so to speak."

"Well, you can rule out my dad," he said with brave confidence. "Between hearing him and seeing him both times, I know he was home the whole evening."

"And what time did you say you saw him?" I said. "So that we can rule him out a hundred percent."

"The first time was about eight and the second at nine or nine-thirty."

After Roman left the table, I whispered to Sister Alice, "What do you think?"

She took a drink of coffee and stood. "I think we should leave and talk about this outside instead of under Roman's nose." She nodded toward the door, and I followed.

I took my cup with me, unwilling to waste a drop of the pumpkin delight. When the door closed behind us, I said, "Well?"

"With the Molotovs' home approximately nine miles out of town and given what Roman heard—and saw—I don't see how Luka could have done it."

"So unless Luka has the speed and stealth of a ninja," I said, "he wouldn't have had time. Unless Roman is covering for him. He said he had on headphones so he wouldn't have to hear, but somehow, he knew there were argument intermissions. He said that's when he came out of his room. I think he knows more than he's letting on."

Sister Alice cocked her head to the side. "Hadn't thought of that."

"It sounds like he has some resentment toward his father. Or fear. Maybe Luka bullied Roman into giving him an alibi."

She narrowed her eyes at me, then said, "Careful when assuming things about people. Especially someone of Luka's stature."

"Why? Because he's more important than anyone else in this town?"

"Andie Rose Kaczmarek," she said with a sigh. "Don't twist my words. I'm just saying an accusation like that, even if it's not true, could damage his reputation and destroy his diaconate career."

I nodded, twisting my lips in acknowledgment. "You're right. Maybe we could speak with Luka's wife."

"Except if she left during their argument, she can't be his alibi for the entire evening, either. I think we're spending too much time on Luka instead of looking deeper into the other suspects. Remember what I said— you can mold any of them to look guilty by twisting the facts. Whatever you focus on is what you'll see. We need to find solid proof, not simple speculation."

"I know you're right, but that book in the library just got into my head. You know, the unlikely suspect one."

"It was a book—in a library. If there had been one sitting in sight about revealing bosoms, would you focus on Jade, for goodness' sake?"

I narrowed my eyes at her in defiance. "Maybe. But I swear I didn't have that book in the library. It got there by some other means."

"Like the ghost."

I slapped her shoulder lightly with the back of my hand. "Not funny. I thought you believe in ghosts."

"Oh, I wholeheartedly believe in spirits. But you're as wishy-washy about the subject as TV weathermen are about the weather report. I just think it's hysterical that you think a ghost is the one moving books in a library—where books are moved around all the time. By *people*," she stressed and chuckled. "Not ghosts."

"Whatever," I grumbled, endeavoring not to laugh at the absurdity I'd allowed myself to believe. Of course, Sister Alice was right. Someone had to have brought the book with them and liked to read it in the library, keeping it there rather than haul it back and forth.

My bet was now on either Tom or Mike as the murderer. I hadn't ruled out Ella yet, either. My gut was telling me something fishy was going on where she was concerned.

On our way back to the car, Mike Swanson stumbled out of the pub across the street. He squinted at the brightness of the afternoon. "Remember those days?" I asked Sister Alice.

"Not that, exactly. I wasn't a bar drinker."

"Not even with friends?" I tipped my sunglasses down and looked at her.

"I didn't have many friends back then. Not real ones, anyway. Until I met your grandpop and Honey."

I smiled at the memory of my grandparents. "My mom is planning a trip out here in the spring."

"Why wait until spring? She doesn't want to come back for a good ole' Minnesota winter? Farmer's Almanac says it's supposed to be a cold, wet one."

I looked up at the blue sky. Winters were beautiful, but they could be brutal, as the weather experts predicted the upcoming one to be. "Maybe she heard that report as well and that's why she's waiting until spring." In

Minnesota, we take what the Farmer's Almanac says about the weather to be gospel. I don't think I've ever known a state where the weather isn't at least partially the topic of nearly every conversation.

"Just a wild thought here," Sister Alice said. "What if Ivan's murder and the Lakeshore Pharmacy scandal are related?"

I frowned. "How so?" The owner of Lakeshore Pharmacy had retired, handing it over to his son to run. A friend and I had uncovered a scandal last spring where the son was in cahoots with big pharma, polluting the lakes, killing fish, and contaminating groundwater and drinking water. My friend, Melanie Hogan, was nearly killed over the discovery. The son running Lakeshore Pharmacy was incarcerated, and the owner had since taken it back over.

"Maybe he got caught up in the scandal somehow. Knew too much, and people at the top were cleaning up loose ends."

I pondered that for a moment. "Hmm. That's an interesting theory. Maybe we should investigate that a little more."

Sister Alice looked at me sideways. "Do you have a death wish? You'd be another loose end to clean up. I can't take care of Aspen permanently, you know." At the mention of his name, Aspen glanced up expectantly. "That whole pharmaceutical deal was—and might still be for all we know—way bigger than either of us can handle. You said yourself that your friend almost got killed over it."

I thought about it, then cupped a hand around the back of my neck and worked out a tight muscle. "I'm not looking forward to death, but if any of the people we're looking at for Ivan's murder did it, he or she is a killer as well. I can't see where one killer is more dangerous than another."

"Unless they have money like in the pharmaceutical business. Money talks." Sister Alice took a slow, long breath, letting it out just as slowly. "I say mention it to Detective Griffin and let him take it from there."

When I opened my car door, Aspen quickly jumped in and claimed his spot in the front seat before Sister Alice opened her door. She studied him for a moment, then slid into the back seat.

"You can't resist those eyes either, huh?"

"I am not inclined to argue with a canine in public. Humans always side with the animal."

I laughed and started the engine.

When we returned to the inn, Sister Alice strolled toward her moped, promising to call me if she heard anything. A car pulled up next to her as she put her helmet on. A teen of about sixteen or seventeen exited the vehicle and struck up a conversation with Sister Alice. She snagged my attention since we don't book minors at the inn without an adult present.

I stayed on the porch until their conversation ended, and the girl started toward me. She was the most striking girl I'd ever seen, with mesmerizing eyes that were brown around the rim and what looked like a green starburst in the center. Her long black hair was pulled back in a thick loose side braid hanging over the front of her shoulder.

"Are you here to check in?" I asked, trying not to stare into her eyes.

"I'm Izzy," she said through pouty, pink lips, earning her a petulant appearance.

"Come with me," I said, turning toward the door. "I'll show you the way to the front desk. Are your parents here?" I scanned the area behind her.

"I'm not here to check in," she said.

I turned toward her. "What can I help with, then?"

"I'm Izzy Carter. Here about the sous-chef job."

Taken aback, I studied her, remembering the name on the application. "I think there must be some mistake. This is a full-time job."

"I know. I read the ad before I applied."

"It wouldn't work with your high school schedule, Izzy. Even if you had free hours, it requires more than that."

"I'm not in school."

A dropout wanting a professional job? I'd heard of stranger things, I guess. "How old are you?"

"Sixteen." She held my gaze and didn't waver, her confident air impressive.

"Are you homeschooled? Where's your mom and dad?"

"They're divorced."

Answers too sparse to read between lines, I asked, "Where do you live?"

"With my mom here in Spirit Lake."

Okay, we were finally getting somewhere. "Izzy, this job requires a high school education and a minimum of some college or significant work history." My memory flashed back to the experience she'd listed on her resume about the family catering business.

"I know." When I said nothing, she continued. "I've worked in my mom's catering company since I was eleven and when I graduated high school at fifteen, I've been pretty much running it. I'm excellent in the kitchen and can prove I can cook better than your chef."

"You're a child genius?"

"I guess you could say that."

Since she'd begun working in her mom's business since eleven years old, I got hung up on the child labor law issue for a minute, and I almost missed her comment about showing up the chef. Her confidence impressed me, and I didn't have the heart to crush it by turning her away. I wanted to give her a chance to exhibit her skills, at the very least, even though I knew it wouldn't make Tony happy. Secretly, once he'd discovered Sister Eunice's skill, I think he was hoping to keep her. Not to mention there'd be no threat of her vying for his job as the lead chef.

"The chef—"

"Tony Valentino." she said, as if I didn't know his name.

"Yes. You'd need to come back when he's here, since you would work for him."

"Okay," she said, seemingly indifferent. "He's an okay chef."

I smiled. "An *okay* chef?"

"Yeah. I beat him in a contest."

"What does your mom think of you applying here?"

"She's the one who told me about it."

"Since you're only sixteen, I'll need to speak with her." Probably stupid, since her mother is the one who let her work for a business at eleven years of age.

"I've never heard of an employer having to speak with a sixteen-year-old's parents before hiring them."

I swallowed a chuckle. "First off, Izzy, this isn't just an ordinary part-time after-school job. And second, I haven't hired you yet. After we talk, and if I agree to it, you'd still need to come back and see Tony."

"Okay." She squared her jaw. "But once you see my work, I know you'll hire me."

I suppressed my laughter at the audacious certainty. "Tell you what. Come back tomorrow at nine. Tony and I can talk with you at the same time."

"Sure." She turned to leave. "See you then, Ms. Kaczmarek."

She got in her car and drove out of the driveway. As soon as I opened the door, Lily said, "Who was that sweet girl?"

Jade said, "That's Izzy Carter. And she's not *sweet*."

"Jealousy doesn't look good on you, Jade," Lily said. "She's just a kid."

Jade put her fist on her hip. "First of all, Lily, I'm not jealous. Second, she's a kid who thinks she's better than everyone else. It's annoying."

"There's nothing wrong with confidence," I said. But I understood Jade's opinion.

"What did she want?" Jade asked.

"The sous-chef job. I told her to come back tomorrow when Tony's here."

"You're considering it?" Lily asked incredulously. "Why not keep Sister Eunice until you find someone qualified?"

"Oh, she's qualified," Jade exclaimed, hand on her hip again. "That's the problem. You won't find a better cook. But she knows it." Doing a one-eighty, she grinned. "Maybe it's good for Tony. You know, keep his big head from getting bigger. It's already so big I don't know how Sister Eunice fits in the kitchen with him."

I chuckled and turned toward the stairs. "I'll be back down in a minute and mingle with the guests."

As I passed the library, I saw a woman curled up cozily in a wingback chair under the reading lamp, her feet tucked beneath her. The glow of the fireplace made it perfect.

I took a step back. "Reading something good?"

She held up the book cover. "*The Woman in Black.* It's a fabulous book and so much better than the movie."

I held back a giggle. Sister Alice had been right. "Were you reading the other book that was with that one?"

She frowned. "What other book?"

I waved a hand. "Someone probably borrowed it. Enjoy your quiet time." I smiled as she waved and went back to her reading.

When I reached the door, she said, "Andie Rose?"

I turned toward her. "Yeah?"

"Do you have the fireplace on a timer? It popped on all by itself about ten minutes ago."

A slow smile spread across my lips, and the warmth of the fireplace reached me. "Is that so."

She grinned and sank deeper into the chair. "The ghost," she whispered.

When I unlocked my door, I tossed my keys on the tiny table and went to my room to change shoes. I nabbed my tennies from my closet floor and froze when I turned. On my nightstand lay the book, *The Unlikely Suspect.*

Chapter 19

Holy wicked whiskey! I froze and took a gulp of air. How did the book get in here? The guest's experience with the fireplace was one thing, but my room stayed locked. No one else had access. Not even Brad. When I initially saw the book, had I subconsciously placed it here? There was no other answer. Unless... No. No way. I shook my head, trying to convince myself. Sister Alice was right. A ghost isn't interested in moving books around. Dear God, I was losing the last marble in my head. "You're losing your damned mind, Andie Rose," I muttered. But icy fingers ran up my spine and then up my neck, making the hair follicles on my nape tingle.

I stood utterly still and silent, cautiously looking around my room for anything unusual—like an open window. I rarely locked my windows, but even if one of them had been the access point, unless someone used a slingshot to catapult the book inside, the window was out of the question since it wasn't accessible from the outside without a ladder. I tiptoed toward the closed window and looked beneath as an extra precaution. Nope. No ladder. It was possible, I supposed, the slingshot not so much.

The book was too thick to fit under the door. Even if it did, how does that explain the book getting on my nightstand? I looked at Aspen, who remained calm, indicating no one had been in here. Otherwise, he would sniff the room like a hound.

I pulled out my phone and dialed Sister Alice.

"Miss me already?" she answered.

"Explain this—the book in question, *The Unlikely Suspect*, is on my nightstand."

"Why is that so strange?"

"Because I didn't put it there."

"Did you leave your door unlocked?"

"No. I always lock it. Habit."

"Maybe you're so preoccupied with all that's going on and forgot this one time."

"It's *because* of what's going on that I've taken extra precautions to be sure it's locked," I insisted.

She fell silent. "You're sure you didn't take the book when you saw it in the library earlier?"

"Sister Alice," I said, drawing an impatient breath, "I think I'd know if I took a book and set it on my nightstand." I wasn't about to admit I'd questioned that only a moment ago.

"Well, that is quite a puzzle then, isn't it?" She was silent again, then suggested, "Maybe it was the cleaning crew."

"They don't have access to my suite. I clean my own."

"They don't have a key to each of the rooms? How do they clean the others?"

"They get the keys from the front desk when they come in. I changed the locks to the master suite when I moved in."

"Hm." She pondered that before finally saying, "One key must be similar enough to yours that it works for both locks. That's the only answer."

I hadn't considered that. But if that was the case, I'd

be calling a locksmith again.

"The question remains," she continued, "if the crew doesn't clean your room, what were they doing in there?"

"Exactly," I said.

"Anyone new on the cleaning crew who missed the memo not to touch your suite?"

"I'll find out."

"Does it look like anything was moved or disturbed?"

I went into the kitchenette area. The glass and bowl were still in the sink where I'd left them this morning, and the pillows and blanket were askew on the sofa. Relieved I'd broken my neat-freak streak, I said, "Nope, nothing out of place. Only something *in* place that shouldn't be. When I find out who it was, they're gonna have to go."

"That's a little rash, don'tcha think?"

I sighed. "I suppose. This whole thing just has me off my center. I'll find out what I can and check my keys against the rest of them."

"Good idea. I'm sure you'll find there's a very plausible answer."

"What if—"

"Be reasonable, Andie Rose. The ghost didn't put the book there. You're giving me a headache."

"Let me finish my sentence." I combed my fingers through my hair as I realized my unintentionally sharp tone. "I was going to say, what if Tom got a key from Jade, and he was in here? Or since Mike and Ivan were friends, what if Mike somehow got it from Ivan?"

"How?"

"Maybe I left them lying around somewhere at some point, and he got a copy."

"And what, Tom knocked off Ivan for a copy of a key to your room so he could plant a book there? Andie Rose, you are one of the most organized people I know. You wouldn't just go leaving your key lying around."

"You just suggested a minute ago that's what I may have done."

"It was one of those nonsense things that comes out of my mouth."

I rubbed my hand across my forehead, then put light pressure on my eyelids with my thumb and forefinger, smudging my eyeliner and mascara. "You're right. I'm sure there's a perfectly logical answer, and I'm making something big out of nothing. I need to go for an evening run. It will do both Aspen and me some good." At the mention of the word run, Aspen sprung up, turned a circle, and cocked his head as he stared at me.

"That's a good idea, but do be careful. And hit up the meeting tomorrow."

"I will. That's where I get most of my entertainment."

"Indeed. Talk later."

"Hey, quick question before you go—how do you know Izzy Carter? I saw the two of you talking outside the inn earlier. Did you catch her in a compromising position with a boy, too? Like Tara?"

"Her mom belongs to the church. If you came, you'd know that."

"I'm not ready yet. When I am, I might go to the protestant church," I teased her. "Then what would you do?" The Protestant and Catholic churches in Spirit Lake each believed they were *the* answer. I'm the type that needs to do plenty of research before I find an answer to anything. But that meant I actually had to *do* the research, which I've not begun.

"I'd schedule an intervention."

"I'm sure you would. So, what can you tell me about Izzy?"

"She's a child genius. She pretty much runs her mama's catering company. She catered a few events for the church. Izzy has some serious talent. Unfortunately, she has a serious attitude to go with it. Because of her intellect, I think she needs a good challenge."

"She applied for the sous-chef position."

"Is that so?"

"She didn't tell you?"

"We were talking about her mom."

"She's only sixteen. I don't see how I could hire her for such a position. She should go to college. Did you know she was working for her mom's business when she was only eleven years old? That's criminal."

"Don't get your undies in a bunch. Izzy helped wash dishes. And she should go to college if *she* wants to go to college. Not because you think she should."

"I know that," I agreed. "But—"

"Maybe you could use your life coaching magic. You know, help her decide what she wants to do with her life. But I'd be willing to bet the money lost from the collection plate at St. Michael's that becoming a chef is her dream."

"Does that mean you have the money from the collection plate?" I asked, amused.

"Nope. That's why I offered to bet on it. That way, I can't lose."

I chuckled. "Good grief. Talk to you later."

****

When dinner was over, I helped Sister Eunice clean

up the kitchen, then drove her back home. When I returned to the inn, I changed into my running clothes, velcroed Aspen's harness around his chest, and snapped on his leash. "Come on, boy; let's go for a run." I could have sworn he smiled. I grinned and scratched his head before turning toward the door.

"We'll be back in about forty-five minutes, Jade," I called over my shoulder as we passed the front desk.

"You're going out *now*? It's dark."

"We're only going around Little Spirit Lake, not both Little and Big." Cutting out the trail around Big Spirit Lake shaved a lot of exercise from the run. But if shorter was safer, it was worth it. Better than an increased chance of getting axed by a maniacal killer on the loose. I held up my hand, showing her the pepper spray I clutched there.

"Why don't you stay on the road? There aren't a lot of cars, but at least there are some."

"That's precisely why we're *not* going on the road," I said. "It's too hard for drivers to see someone at this time of the night."

"It's not a busy road, Andie. It's only inn traffic, and dinner time is over. Whatever locals were here have already gone back into town."

One glance at her be-reasonable-about-this posture and I finally relented. "Fine. If it makes you feel better."

"A murderer is stalking around out there. Of course, it makes me feel better. Despite what the police are inclined to think, the killer isn't sitting here at the inn. Especially not behind this desk." She pointed toward herself.

"A killer is more likely to be on the road than hanging out by a lake enjoying the view after dark." At her attempted protest, I pushed my hand out, palm facing her. "I'll go on the road. Mom." I shook my head and exhaled through pursed lips. "See you in about thirty."

She smiled her win. "Thank you. And quit pouting. That's my job."

"And you do it well."

Aspen and I fell into an easy trot, the cold, fresh air reinvigorating my mind and body. No matter what it was, nature made everything better. Nevertheless, I wasn't stupid. I clipped Aspen's leash onto a strap around my waist, clutched the pepper spray in one palm, and my phone in the other. I played rock music from my phone, sans earbuds, so I could better hear my surroundings. Bear hadn't gone into hibernation yet. Just last week, a guest left grahams around a smoldering bonfire, and the bear feasted. There was also the one caught on the video cam. That said, humans frightened me more than animals. When animals killed, it usually served a purpose—food source or mamas protecting their young. Humans were capable of evil for evil's sake.

A pickup truck passed me, driving toward the inn. I waved with my hand that clutched the pepper spray, but the dark tinted windows prevented me from seeing if it was a guest.

As I ran, the murder, the investigation, the mysterious book in my room—all of it—released its stranglehold and nearly vanished from my mind, giving me energy to take deep cleansing breaths, the oxygen releasing all the bad vibes. Unfortunately, within the first five minutes, sirens wailed toward town, and it all boomeranged back.

Suddenly, Aspen stopped dead in his tracks, jerking me with him. "Ouch. What are you doing, Aspen?" I glanced toward the large cornfield nestled between groves of trees. He stared with earnest attention; my breathing picked up its pace faster than when I was running. "Aspen?" I whispered as I muted the music and listened for any noise. At the rustling of cornstalks, I strained my eyes through the darkness to see what it was. I held my pepper spray at the ready and screamed like a little girl, almost peeing my pants, when something lunged out of the field. A whitetail deer, more scared than I was, stood frozen mere feet in front of us before disappearing across the road.

I heaved a sigh of relief and bent over, my hands resting on my knees. "Holy wicked whiskey," I said, catching my breath. Aspen touched his nose to my cheek. I squatted, rubbed his neck and belly, then began trotting again. This time no music, only full awareness of my surroundings. It was a harmless deer, but it had heightened my senses all the same.

After ten more minutes, we were nearly to the town limits, so we turned around and headed back for the inn. By then, the sirens had ceased, but the blue, red, and white flashing lights pulsed against the inky, dark sky, a reminder of the emergency in town. I kept as calm as possible, trying to enjoy the run.

When we were within a quarter mile of the inn, I began a cooldown walk. Aspen followed my lead. Once again, he stopped and gazed into the cornfield sandwiched by groves of oak and birch trees.

Scanning the darkness in case there was something there, I came up empty. "The deer is long gone by now, Aspen. Come on." I tugged gently on his leash, but he didn't budge. The hair at my nape tingled, and I pulled harder. "Aspen. Come on," I urged, but he remained steadfast. I tapped the flashlight app on my cell phone and shined it in the woods, but it didn't carry far. Leaves crunched, followed by silence, then they crunched again, the sound getting closer. I held my breath and tried to look closer through the darkness when a truck came creeping around the bend. Seeing us, it sped faster, its tires sliding in the gravel toward us. The mirror narrowly missed my head and sideswiped a tree instead as I ducked and jumped back, yanking Aspen with me.

The taillights zipped out of view, my breath in ragged gasps. I crouched low and checked Aspen for any injuries. It appeared the only thing hurt on either of us was my leg from jumping back at an awkward angle. But it wasn't enough to keep me from taking off at a good pace toward the inn with continual glances behind me.

After what seemed like an hour, when it was hardly three minutes, we reached the parking lot of the inn. We slowed, and once again, I bent over, hands on my knees. I unclipped Aspen from the strap around my waist and unsnapped the leash from his harness. He eagerly sniffed the ground, his nose eventually leading him to the door. I glanced around the large yard. Despite the voices from the back and the smell of bonfire smoke, the front yard was empty.

When I opened the door, Jade quickly set her phone down. She leaned forward and stared through bloodshot eyes. "What happened to you?"

"Tom?" I asked.

"Tom?" She frowned, her brows nearly touching. "Where did you see him?"

"I didn't," I said, walking to the desk. "You were on your phone, and it looks like you've lost your best friend."

"Pretty much. But, no, it wasn't Tom."

I began taking my jacket off, and Aspen went around to Jade for the attention she doled out to him.

"Why do you look so stressed?" she asked. "Usually, running brings you peace."

"Yeah, when I'm not attacked by a deer and a truck doesn't almost hit me." I shook my head and shivered. "I told you, running on the road is dangerous."

"Attacked by a deer?" She scratched her head. "Tell me you're kidding."

"Well, he didn't exactly attack me," I stammered, "but he almost smacked into me."

She smirked. "I can see why the confusion. And what happened with the truck?"

"A truck hugged the side of the road as it came around a bend and almost hit us."

"Like the deer almost attacked you?" she asked, rolling her eyes. When she saw I wasn't kidding, she gasped and stood. "Oh, my God. Are you hurt?"

"I'll be fine. Scared the daylights out of me, though. Anything happen while I was gone?"

"Nope." She sat back down and loved on Aspen again.

"He plays you, ya know. I give him plenty of attention and affection."

"Says you," she said to me while staring into his big brown eyes. "Has mama been neglecting you, baby?"

"Stop baby-talking. He told me he doesn't like it."

She offered a bemused smile. "If you're hearing him talk to you, you have much bigger issues than my baby-talking to him." Her attention dove back to him as she crooned, "You're such a good boy, Aspen." She touched her nose to his, the only other person he allowed to do that except me.

I reached for the phone I'd moments ago laid on the counter alongside the pepper spray. The phone rang, startling me.

"Hello?"

"Andie Rose," Sister Alice said. Her voice sounded too serious.

"What happened? Is everything okay?"

"Someone shot Mike Swanson tonight. He's at the hospital. Father Vincent met the ambulance there."

I gasped, and my hand flew to my mouth. "Is he—did he—"

"He's alive, but it doesn't look good for him, Andie," she said gravely.

"I heard sirens a while ago. Must have been why." My head felt like the spin cycle on a washing machine.

Jade jumped to her feet and leaned over the countertop, practically in my face. "What happened?"

I shushed her, leaned back for space, and held up a finger, a nonverbal cue asking her to wait a minute. I turned away and strolled to the door, looking through the glass into the darkness.

I shivered and moved back toward the desk, turned away from Jade, and whispered, "This can't be a coincidence, Sister Alice. He was one of our suspects. Maybe Ella killed Ivan, and she was afraid Mike knew too much."

"Except the reason we suspected Ella in the first place was her protection of Mike. Shooting him hardly qualifies as protection," she said dryly.

I envisioned her running her fingers through her hair, causing it to stand on end.

"I hate to say this, but at least my staff and I won't

be suspects in this one."

"What makes you so sure?"

"None of us has a motive for wanting Mike dead." I inhaled sharply. "Unless Mike's shooting and Ivan's murder are related. And if it's not Ella, then who? Oh, boy," I muttered.

Chapter 20

When I turned around, Jade all but tumbled over the counter.

I caught her gaze and dipped my chin. "Boundaries, please."

"What happened?" she asked.

"How well do you know Mike Swanson?"

"What makes you think I do?"

"Because it seems all the long-time locals know each other. So?"

She took a breath and exhaled slowly. "I don't know. I mean, I know who Mike is, but that's about it. What happened?" she asked again, this time through an exasperated sigh. She clicked her long, black, polished fingernails on the counter.

"Someone tried to kill him this evening. I heard the sirens when I was running." I leaned against the desk, deep in thought, processing what this could mean in connection to Ivan's death. The two might not even be related to each other, but I suspected that wasn't the case. I snapped out of my bubble and looked at Jade when I realized she had said something. "I'm sorry, what?"

"What if the truck that almost hit you wasn't an accident at all. What if it was intentional?"

I frowned. "Hmm. It's possible, I suppose. But the shooter was in town, not driving on the road."

"*A* shooter was. But you don't know that it had

anything to do with Ivan's murder."

I narrowed my eyes at her. "Were you listening in on my conversation with Sister Alice just now?"

"Maybe," she admitted, pressing her shoulders back. "But it doesn't take a genius to put together a child's puzzle. Ivan was murdered; Mike was a friend of his and—"

"Wait." I held out my hand, palm facing her. "I thought you said you didn't know Mike. So how do you know he was friends with Ivan?"

"Well, I don't know if they were friends," she said, backtracking her statement. She picked up the stapler and juggled it from hand to hand. I wondered if I should duck. "Okay, so I know they knew each other. He stopped by one evening when I was at Ivan's."

"That's a pretty big clue you failed to mention." I covered my face with my hands in frustration, then looked back at her. "What was their interaction like?"

She set the stapler back down and made a sound I interpreted as *I don't know,* then began picking things together, taking extra care to set the guest log in the center of the desk just so.

"Jade, what other info are you withholding from me?"

"Nothing."

"You are," I countered. "What was their interaction like?"

"Not great." Her voice was quiet, and she shot a glance at me before straightening the guest log again.

"How so?"

She huffed and looked up at me. "Mike made an inappropriate comment about me and said he was gonna tell Tom about me and Ivan unless Ivan paid up."

I pursed my lips together. "If Ivan wasn't already dead, I'd name him as the one who shot Mike."

"My shift is up. Tom is going out tonight, so I need to get home for my daughter."

"Jade?"

She continued to avoid looking my way as she grabbed her purse from the bottom desk drawer. "Yeah?"

"Did you worry about Mike telling Tom?"

"Of course. But before you assume anything, you know I was here all evening. Even if I wasn't, Tom already knows everything, so I had no reason to shoot Mike."

"I'm wondering if Mike said something to Tom and—"

"No," she interrupted me. "Tom didn't shoot Mike. He doesn't even own a gun."

"Maybe he does. You know as well as anyone that marriage holds dark secrets."

"I know he didn't do it, Andie Rose. I know my husband."

I nodded. "I hope so, Jade. Go enjoy that beautiful daughter."

"That's the plan." She tossed a forced smile over her shoulder.

Aspen walked Jade to the door, and after she left, I unlocked the drawer that held the set of master keys. I withdrew my room key from my pocket. When the last key I inspected didn't match mine, I shivered again. Someone could have picked the lock, but who? Before killing brain cells over yet another mystery, I'd contact the cleaning crew supervisor first thing in the morning to see if they have anyone new on staff. One step at a time.

Before heading to my room, I circled through the inn

to be sure everything was as it should be. I locked the front door and swung through the dining room. As I did, I glanced out the wall of windows that faced the lake. I stopped and admired the moonlight shimmering off the water's surface, stealing my breath away. And then, off toward the edge of the property, I spotted someone hovering by the lakeshore. I stood in the darkness and watched for a moment, then turned from my voyeurism. It was probably just a guest. *Right?* But I couldn't shake the unsettled feeling that began consuming me again. I crossed my arms in front of me, the hair on my forearms erect from goose bumps. I turned to look one more time, but the person was gone. A brief tremor passed.

I shook my head and muttered, "Good Lord, Andie Rose. You're hoping to see ghosts that aren't there, but you're seeing *people* that aren't there." *Or were they the same? Can a ghost morph into human form?*

****

Surprisingly, I slept so soundly that night that I slept through the alarm and woke to Aspen's cool, wet nose against my own. I sat up in a sleepy fog, remembered Mike's shooting, and jolted upright, hurtling out of bed. I had work to do and people to talk with, starting with the cleaning crew supervisor. Given my key was cut differently from all the others, and the master key didn't fit mine, the chance of it being a newbie on the cleaning crew was next to zero. But for peace of mind, I still had to ask.

I glanced at the mystery book, *The Unlikely Suspect*, on my nightstand and shuddered. Luka Molotov's name returned and haunted my thoughts.

After throwing on some sweats and my Teva's, I brought Aspen down the back staircase and outside to do his morning thing and found the back door unlocked. All outside doors were locked at night, the guests having a key to come in after hours. Had I forgotten to lock it last night when I locked up the front? I was sure I'd locked it. But I couldn't have. Had Ivan's killer snagged his key? My mind played tug-of-war until all I could think about was getting back to the safety of my room.

Outside, and in fight-or-flight mode, I remained hypervigilant until Aspen finally lifted his leg. The second he finished, I yanked him back toward the door and inside, locked the door, and bolted up the stairs. I showered, dressed, and struggled with my long red locks, unusually frizzy today. Exasperated by the lack of cooperation, I groaned my frustration, split it into three sections, and threaded them into a braid. By the time I applied eyeliner, mascara, and lip balm, my frayed nerves had simmered down.

I scrambled downstairs to the kitchen to check in with Tony before guests arrived for breakfast. Maybe I'd even let him boss me around while I helped some. Maybe. After that, I planned to catch Luka at St. Michael's before hitting up the eleven o'clock meeting I promised Sister Alice I would attend. Unlock two doors with one key, so to speak.

****

Tony turned my way and smiled as I entered through the kitchen doorway.

"Hey, Tony. What's shakin'?"

"You're entering my castle. Don't touch anything."

"Okay, *Ivan*. You just lost the help I was going to offer you." He snickered, and I crossed the room, reached for an oversized coffee cup, and began pouring from the large pot.

I toasted him with my mug and took a drink of the instant pick-me-up. "Mmm," I said. "Good and strong. Perfect."

"Thanks."

Taking another sip, I said, "Not to hurt your feelings, but I was talking about the coffee."

His hand flew to his chest as he leaned back in a dramatic show of disappointment. "I'm crushed."

I chuckled. "Inappropriate much?"

"I guess it's a good thing I don't work for some big, stuffy corporation."

"I'd say. Everything going okay this morning?"

After a quick recovery, he said, "Couldn't be better."

"Hey, have you noticed anyone new on the cleaning crew? Or anyone new anywhere, actually."

He stared at me as if I'd fallen off my rocker. "This is an inn, Andie Rose. We always have new people." He shook his head and turned back to the oven.

I drew a breath and released it. "Don't play dumb. You know what I mean."

He tossed a glance over his shoulder. "I don't pay attention to the cleaning crew. Or anyone else. My nose stays in the kitchen."

"And in Jade's business," I said, pinching my lips together.

He scoffed and turned. "Why do you want to know if someone's new?"

"Someone was in my suite yesterday."

Tony stopped what he was doing and looked up at me. "What'd the person look like?"

"Hello," I sang. "I wasn't in there at the time or I'd know who it was."

"Then how do you know someone was in there?"

"There was a book on my nightstand that isn't mine."

He frowned. "That's weird. Why would someone put a book in there?"

"Good question. It's probably nothing." I shrugged it off and took another sip, refreshed my coffee, and started for the door. "I'll be in my office. Let me know if you need my help." When I reached the doorway, I pivoted back toward him. "Tony, did you unlock the back door early?"

He frowned. "Why would I do that?"

"It was unlocked when I took Aspen outside earlier, and I didn't do it."

"You seem to have a problem with locks here. I'd say get a locksmith to change them, but because of the cost and inconvenience you'd have with that, you might want to be sure *you're* not the one leaving them open."

"Noted."

When I opened my office door, I flipped on the light switch and glanced around the room, half expecting to catch someone. Between the murder, the book in my room, someone nearly hitting Aspen and me on the road, the attempt on Mike's life, and the person I might *not* have seen by the lake last evening, I was edgy and ill at ease. Strange occurrences didn't bother me too much, but when they kept piling up, it deserved pause for concern.

I looked at my watch. Before eight was too early to call the cleaning supervisor. I would have had plenty of time for a run this morning, but after last evening, it held little appeal.

I turned on my laptop and buried myself with business items: ordering things for the inn, checking stats and success rates from our advertising, and reviewing the P&L reports. Yet, hard as I tried, I could only focus on Ivan's murder and how I could clear myself and the staff. Finally, eight o'clock rolled around. I dug the cleaning supervisor's business card from my desk, picked up the phone, and punched in the number. She answered on the second ring. No, she didn't have anyone new on deck; yes, they knew not to clean my suite; and no, she confirmed, they do not have a key. After we hung up, I sat still for a moment, trying to come up with another logical answer. I couldn't. If I'd brought the book into my room, I was losing my ever-loving mind.

Next, I called Sister Alice, got her voicemail, and let her know I was going to the church a few minutes early and hoped to catch Luka. I also asked her to meet me if she was at the church early. I figured since she didn't answer, she might already be at the hospital.

I logged off the computer and ran upstairs to be sure I'd locked the door to my room. Aspen trotted up behind me and immediately made for his dog bed beneath the big window. He snuggled in with his stuffed hedgehog for an early morning nap.

"Slacker," I said, ruffling his fur. "I'll come back up in a couple of hours to get you."

He rolled on his side and closed his eyes in answer.

After triple-checking the door was secure and tucking the key deep into the pocket of my jeans, I scampered downstairs. I carried a coffeepot in one hand and a water pitcher in the other, refilling cups and glasses as I mingled—until I spotted Detective Griffin looming in the dining room doorway and nearly overflowed someone's coffee cup. Extending my apologies to the guest, I set the coffeepot and water pitcher down on the counter and reluctantly wove through tables over to the detective.

"I don't suppose this is a social call," I said when I reached him. I walked past him and led him into the hallway. The last thing I wanted was for guests to hear what he had to say. I directed him to the empty parlor, motioning toward the two wingback chairs beside a two-sided gas fireplace. The orange flames danced as if they were alive.

"I gotta say the food smells good, but you're correct. This is not a social call."

My stomach clenched in apprehension at what this was about. I forced myself to keep my mouth shut, so I didn't stick my foot in it. The ability to abstain was a credit to sobriety. I'd painfully learned what one thinks when sober, one says when drunk.

Detective Griffin took out a small wire notepad and a pen from his shirt pocket. "Where were you last evening between seven and eight?"

"Here."

"The whole time?"

"Well… I went for a brief run, but came right back."

"Where did you run? By the lake?"

"On the road. I turned back as soon as I reached the town limits."

"Anyone that can vouch for you?"

"When I was here, yeah, Jade can. But not when I was running. Unless you want to confirm that with Aspen."

"Your dog—right. Think I'll bypass that one." He cleared his throat and glanced around the room.

"He's upstairs napping."

"Anyone else?" he said.

"Yeah, a couple of vehicles, but I didn't see who they were, so I can't give you any names. A truck almost hit me, so apparently, he didn't see me either."

He stopped writing and looked at me, frowning. "Almost hit you?"

I nodded. "We were running along the side of the road—"

"We?"

I nodded. "Me and Aspen—my witness. Something rustled in the weeds, and while we were looking for what it was, a truck came around the corner. He cut it close and almost hit us."

"But you didn't see who it was?"

"Uh-uh." I shook my head.

"What kind of truck was it? Did you get a license plate?"

"I don't know, and no. I was too busy dodging the mirror on the truck that almost took me out. It was dark, and when I got back up, it was too far down the road."

"And you're sure he or she didn't see you."

I shook my head. "Obviously not. But I can't know for sure. If they did, I'd think they would have stopped."

"Do you always run at night?"

"Sometimes. When I do, it's usually on the lake trail because it's too hard for cars to see a person at dusk and after. Last night proved that."

"I want you to think real hard if you can remember anything more about the truck."

"The truck in question hit his mirror on the tree."

"His? So you saw it was a man?"

"No. Just assuming so."

"So a truck with a damaged mirror. Better than nothing, I guess." He exhaled and closed his eyes briefly.

"Anything else you might have seen that would help identify the driver?"

"Like what? I already told you I don't remember."

"Literally any little thing that can help us identify the person so they can confirm your whereabouts and the time."

I frowned and turned my head to the side. "I'm not sure I understand, Detective. Are you accusing me of something?"

"Just checking your alibi for the attempted murder of Mike Swanson. Someone saw you arguing with both the murder victim and, a couple of days later, the attempted murder victim."

"We weren't arguing, Detective. Who told you we did?"

"Doesn't matter."

"I disagree. It *does* matter if it's not a trustworthy source."

His gaze leveled at me. "Arguing with me to prove you weren't arguing with both victims. Do you see my problem here?"

I exhaled through pursed lips and looked down, scuffing the toe of my Teva on the floor. Finally, I looked back at him. "I was only asking Mike a few questions about his connection to Ivan. He got kind of huffy about it. Defensive even. Made him look guilty."

"Mike couldn't have shot himself, Ms. Kaczmarek." He rubbed his eyes with his thumb and forefinger and yawned. "Sorry."

"Did you look into his alibi for the time of Ivan's murder? Mike could have killed him. There was something fishy between those two."

He pressed his lips together, closing his eyes as he

did. "Please don't play detective and interfere in my investigation, Ms. Kaczmarek. I don't need your help. Stay. Out. Of. It."

Chapter 21

Sister Alice hopped on her moped and scooted to Lakeview hospital early to make her rounds, hoping to be back at St. Michael's on time for the eleven o'clock meeting. Except for Mike Swanson and Ella's mother, Marie Dayton, most had minor procedures or injuries, but she still made rounds to see all of them, offering prayer and communion. If time remained, she cast the net to other patients as well. Some welcomed her, some acted as if she was the devil himself. Today, she planned to save plenty of time for her visits with Marie and Mike.

After finishing the last of the patients on her list, she looked at her watch. Mike first. She hustled to the ICU.

"Can I help you, Sister?" a nurse said from behind the desk.

"Hi, Sally. I'm here to see Mike Swanson."

The nurse cocked her head to the side. "I wasn't aware he was one of yours anymore. I'm glad he found his way back to the fold."

Sister Alice shook her head. "He hasn't yet. Father Vincent is still praying he will. Nevertheless, I'm here to pray with him."

"No can do," Sally said with a sigh. "He hasn't regained consciousness yet. We're all hoping he does, but to be honest, it's not a positive outlook for him."

"What can you tell me about what happened to him?" Sister Alice asked.

"Hmm." Sally appeared to recollect details. "Not too much, Sister. Someone shot him in the alley beside City Hall. Missed his heart by a breath." She shook her head slowly. "He's lost a lot of blood."

Sister Alice had been around death so often it no longer bothered her. But if that was the expected outcome, getting information to help catch the killer was crucial. "It's imperative I see him, Sally." If Mike wasn't Ivan's killer, then perhaps finding Mike's shooter would also nab Ivan's killer.

"He's in a coma, Sister. But if he can hear you and something you say upsets him, that could turn the tides on whether or not he pulls through."

"Do you know if they have any suspects?" Sister Alice asked. Sally was a local who was up in everybody's business, so Sister Alice was confident she knew something useful to shed light on the situation.

"They don't tell me details of an investigation," she said. "But I overheard something about the gal who owns the inn. You know who I mean, the new gal that took over after Honey's husband died." She shook her head and pursed her lips in disapproval. "Sad when someone like that moves into our safe community," she said. "Terrible. Just terrible."

Overheard, indeed. "Innocent until proven guilty, Sally," Sister Alice said. "Not the other way around. I know that young lady, and I'd be hard-pressed to be convinced she did it."

"I only told you what I overheard."

"Did someone say she's the suspect?" Sister Alice said.

"Well, not those words exactly."

Sister Alice sighed with relief. "Then we ought not

to assume."

"Yes, Sister," Sally said quietly, her cheeks flushing.

Sister Alice bit her tongue to keep from saying more. She didn't want to stop Sally from revealing all she knew, but where Andie Rose was concerned, Sister Alice was a tad overprotective.

"Don't suppose you heard other suspect names. Positively heard, no assumptions," Sister Alice added.

"No, Sister. Ella's name came up, but I didn't hear the reason behind it."

Sister Alice pondered that for a moment. Ella's name could have arisen as a suspect or as Mike's significant other. She was grateful she'd stopped here before visiting Marie Dayton.

"I might just quietly peek in his room to give him a blessing," Sister Alice said, lightly touching Sally's arm. "A blessing won't upset him. As always, it was nice to see you today."

"You too, Sister," Sally said, brightening again.

Sister Alice turned toward Mike's room.

"Sister Alice?"

"Yes?" she said, turning back toward Sally.

"I just remembered something else."

"What's that?"

"Something about Ella knowing Ivan had been blackmailing someone."

Sister Alice's eyes grew wide. "You heard this from the police?" Sally nodded. "Any chance you heard who that someone was?"

"No. What I told you is all I heard."

After running possibilities through her mind, she finally said, "All right then. Could you let me know if you remember anything else?"

"Of course. Are you helping the police?"

Sister Alice hesitated a moment. "In a roundabout way, you could say I am, Sally."

She hurried to Mike's room, quietly slid open the glass door, then closed it behind her. He was hardly visible beneath all the tubes and machines hooked up to him. The rhythmic *whoosh, pause, whoosh, pause* of the ventilator, the consistent *beep, beep* of the vital sign monitor, and the hum of the blood pressure cuff as it kicked in were noisy in the otherwise quiet room. Any chance of Mike waking soon, able to recall what had happened, was slim to none. She watched him a moment longer and sighed.

After a whispered blessing, she slid open the glass door, startled at a shrill consistent *beep beep beep* from behind her, growing louder. A nurse pushed her aside. Another followed as a nasal voice blasted across the speakers: "*Code blue, ICU. Code blue, ICU.*"

Sister Alice remained fixed in the corner, praying, as blue scrubs and white lab coats rushed into the small machine-packed room, attempting to revive a heart that chose to stop.

"Does the patient have a DNR?" someone asked.

"Would we be trying to resuscitate him if he did?" another snapped.

Sister Alice knew DNR meant *Do Not Resuscitate* and the ramifications staff could face by disregarding the patients' wishes. She had seen it happen before and it wasn't a pretty sight.

Emotions and tensions were high until a male voice pronounced, "Time of death ten-oh-one." After which, mere sighs, followed by silence, as somber medical staff filed out of the room murmuring to each other:

"Another one gone too soon."

"He was so young."

"That was my second one in as many days."

"Sometimes I hate my job."

Sister Alice stayed visible should they need prayer or an ear. Sister Ida always chided her for her lack of soft compassion, but she could put aside her brusque, blunt honesty when the moment called for it. At least she tried. To prove Sister Ida wrong, if nothing else. Her job was to make sure everyone knew God's love, not to please Sister Ida.

After calling Father Vincent to notify him of Mike's passing, Sister Alice hung tight for half an hour before taking the elevator down to the chapel and then to Marie's room on the fourth floor.

****

Marie's door was closed, so Sister Alice turned toward the nurses' station to inquire about Marie's status.

"Hi, Sister," the woman said with a pleasant smile.

"Hello, Clara. As always, it's so nice to see you." She gestured toward Marie's room. "I noticed Marie's door is closed. Is a nurse with her?"

She shook her head. "No, no. Ella is here with her. They probably wanted privacy."

"Very well. I'll hang around until she leaves." Sister Alice leaned against the desk. "How have you been?"

"Been better. It's a little disconcerting when someone gets murdered in our town and another nearly murdered days later." She tsk'd. "What is this world coming to? Spirit Lake of all places. We'll soon be the hopping tourist town that turned into a ghost town.

Pardon the pun."

Sister Alice pressed her lips together, preventing herself from spilling the news that there now *were* two murders. Her mind traveled to Ella's disappointment about not getting her inheritance as quickly as she'd hoped.

"You know, Clara, I think I'll go to Marie's room, anyway. I'd like to check in with Ella as well. And I need to get back to St. Michael's."

"Okay. Have a good day, Sister." Clara waved and smiled again.

Sister Alice stood outside Marie's room, her ear pressed against the door. Hearing nothing, she knocked softly.

"Come in," Marie called, her weak voice weary.

Sister Alice slowly pushed the door open and peeked her head around it.

"It's Sister Alice," she announced before entering the room. She looked at the empty chair and then at the open bathroom door. "Are you alone?"

"Yes. Ella left a moment ago."

Unless Ella left before Sister Alice arrived or she took the back stairwell, it would have been impossible for Sister Alice to miss her departure. She peeked her head into the bathroom should Ella be hiding; finding it empty, she moved toward the bed.

"For someone who's getting better, you don't sound happy about it," Sister Alice said.

Marie sighed heavily. "Ella isn't happy with me. And she let me know it in no uncertain terms."

Sister Alice pulled up the chair and sat. "What happened?"

Tears escaped Marie's eyes. "Now that I'm not

dying, she won't be getting the inheritance she'd counted on. She asked if she could get it early, and I said no. She told me she incurred a significant debt, so she needs it now. That it's a matter of life and death. *Her* death." She sniffled. "She's always been such a dramatic girl. Worse, it feels pretty crappy when my own daughter is disappointed I'm gonna live and she can't get her money."

Sister Alice leaned forward and covered Marie's hand with her own. "Did she say what that significant debt was?"

Marie shook her head and stared toward the half-bare branches of the trees reaching toward the sky outside her window. "No. That's why I told her she couldn't get it." She smiled mournfully. "Ella has never liked the word 'no' from the day she was born. Her father treated her as royalty, and she's always resented that I didn't give her the same treatment."

"Could Ella be caught up in something that has spiraled out of her control? Something dangerous?"

She sighed again. "If she won't tell me, I don't have no way of knowing." She gasped and looked from the window to Sister Alice. "Oh—I just remembered something. The night I came to the hospital, before that I heard Ella and Mike talking in the front room. They thought I was sleeping, but I was on my way downstairs for a glass of warm milk. When I was halfway down the stairs, they talked about how Ivan was blackmailing someone for a substantial amount of money."

The ashy shadows beneath Marie's eyes were in stark contrast to her pasty, ghostly white complexion. Her hair, matted against her head, had at least two inches of gray regrowth at the roots of her lifeless brown strands. "Did they say who it was?"

"No. But what if he was blackmailing Ella? And why? What did he have on her? And what if Ivan was in on it with someone else, and that someone else is now blackmailing my Ella?" Her eyes widened, and her trembling fingers pressed against her lips. "Maybe that's what she needed the money for. Oh, dear God, what have I done? Maybe she wasn't being dramatic at all. I need to give her the money."

"You have done nothing wrong, Marie," Sister Alice assured her. "I can speak with her if you'd like."

"Oh, yes, please do," she begged. "And fast."

Sister Alice bit her lower lip and mulled over how to phrase her next question. Finally deciding the direct approach was best, she said, "Marie, do you think Ella could have killed Ivan?"

Marie's eyes misted again, and she whispered, "I don't know."

Chapter 22

When I drove to St. Michael's at ten thirty, hoping to catch Deacon Molotov, I left Aspen at the inn with Jade and Frank. Frank was third in line as his favorite human, after me and Jade. I assumed Sister Alice's silence was because of being caught up at the hospital or caught up with Sister Ida or Father Vincent.

I scanned the small parking lot for the car Deacon Molotov drove the other day, disappointed when I didn't spot it. Neither was Sister Alice's moped in sight. As I reached for my phone to call her, the door opened and out strolled Luka, pinching his overcoat together at the waist, dropping his keys as he did.

"Deacon Molotov?" I called as I trotted toward him. He scooped up his keys and stood. "Do you have a minute?"

"One," he said in a strained voice. "I need to get to the hospital."

"I didn't think you were here." I looked around the lot again. "I don't see your car."

"My car's in the shop, so I'm borrowing my wife's. But I'm sure you didn't come to talk to me about my car."

"No," I said.

He rolled his hand in a gesture to talk and get it over with. "Please hurry. I have emergency business to take care of at Lakeview Hospital."

"I'm curious about what happened between you and Ivan all those years ago."

He sighed. "Why's that." It was more a statement than a question, and he sounded almost–well, almost bored. Weird.

"I'm trying to get a better picture of the man who used to work for me. That being Ivan, of course. Seems I didn't know him at all." I tried to sound genuine.

"Ms. Kaczmarek, our falling out doesn't shed any light on that, I'm afraid."

"Did you trust Ivan?"

Luka let out a bitter laugh. "Now *that* is funny. Trusting is not a word I, or anyone who knew him, would use to describe Ivan. But he brought a lot of that on himself."

"How so?"

Luka looked at his watch and then jiggled his keys. "I don't have time to deal with this right now." He began walking away.

"Deacon?" I called after him. He turned, continuing to walk backward toward his car as he did. I said, "We lock the doors to the inn after hours." I remembered that just this morning it was unlocked, and my heart picked up a notch. "There was no sign of forced entry, so whoever killed Ivan was a guest with a key or someone Ivan trusted enough to unlock the door for."

"Well, that's my alibi, then. Because I guarantee you that wouldn't have been me."

He turned and stalked toward the car. I watched him, my head tilted. He had previously used his son as his alibi for Ivan's murder. And if Ivan didn't trust Luka, did Ivan have a good reason? Did Luka have a dark side? *The Unlikely Suspect* popped into my mind again.

*Un*likely was quickly turning into *likely*.

I descended the stairs for the meeting, drawn by laughter and the smell of burned coffee.

"Andie Rose," Matt said, followed by a few more hellos and more laughter. The thing I liked the best about this group was that laughter was usually present. And when we told stories of things we'd done that would horrify the average person, we shared the humor of it with each other. For a small town with only one bar, Brewski's, and a small liquor store, the room held more than its share of members.

I scanned the room for Sister Alice before opening the door to the small kitchenette. I checked my phone for a text. Nothing there, either. Despite telling her I'd be here, the rebellious part of me experienced a quick thrill that I could leave, and she'd never know. But my prefrontal cortex kicked in and overrode the rebellion. This was exactly where I *wanted*—and needed—to be. With my peeps, drinking awful coffee. I poured some of the thick black liquid into a Styrofoam cup and sat in the circle of chairs.

"Where's your sidekick?" a woman named Luna asked.

"Aspen's with Jade and Frank at the inn. And I don't know where Sister Alice is. She said she'd be here." I looked at my watch again. "Not a lost cause yet. She still has five more minutes."

"Whaddya know about the attempted murder of Mike Swanson?"

I dipped my chin and narrowed an eye. "You want me to break the AA traditions by talking about outside matters again?"

"Since the meeting hasn't started yet, neither have

the traditions, right?" a guy named Owen said.

I snorted. "I don't know anything more than you probably do. The police are keeping it pretty hush-hush."

"At least this one wasn't at your inn," Jim said. "Or was it?" He raised a skeptical eyebrow.

I shook my head vigorously. "Of course not. Everyone knows it was in the alley."

"Hey, Andie Rose," Shannon said. "I saw you running on the road toward town last night. You shouldn't be running out there after dark. It could be dangerous."

My antennae pricked up. "I only saw two vehicles while I was out."

"I have a small MINI cooper, but my husband has a big pickup truck I drive sometimes. I hate it though, because the truck feels like a semi after driving my little MINI. Makes me feel like I'm out of control."

"Which were you driving last night? I don't remember seeing a MINI cooper."

"My husband's beast."

"Which direction were you going, away from my place or toward it?" I regarded her carefully, watching for signs of something. *Any*thing.

"Why all the questions?" she asked, eyes narrowed. She crossed her arms in front of her and sat up straighter.

"No reason," I lied. "A dark truck almost hit me and my dog."

"You accusing me of something, Andie Rose?" Her shoulders pressed back, the corners of her lips curved down.

"Of course not."

Her posture relaxed a little. "You and your dog were

focused on something in the woods," she said. "I was going to honk the horn, but didn't want to freak you out."

I forced a smile. She had to be in one of the two trucks. Trucks were common in Minnesota, but I couldn't imagine I wouldn't have heard one going by when I was looking into the woods. I didn't even have earbuds in.

I studied her silently and as discreetly as I could. The last thing I needed was to get popped one by an angry Shannon. I had to get a look at her husband's truck. Maybe seeing the vehicle would jog my memory.

"Hey Shannon, how's your husband taking Mike's shooting?" Jim asked.

Shannon stiffened, and her eye twitched. "Mark and Mike may be twins, but they've never gotten along. Mike has thrown Mark under the bus too many times to count."

I bolted upright, nearly dropping my coffee. Mike had a twin? I'd seen Shannon's husband at a meeting when she picked up a chip, and he looked nothing like Mike.

"Still, it's his twin brother, man," Jim said, frowning. "That's tough stuff."

Shannon shrugged a shoulder. "Yeah. I suppose."

"Fraternal twins?" I asked, then shook my head. Not one of my brighter questions. "Disregard that."

She answered anyway. "They're as different in personality as they are in looks. Hard to believe they came from the same baby mama."

I took a minute to process the news. Had we accumulated a new suspect on the list? Maybe Mike's shooting had nothing to do with Ivan's murder at all, but was a family affair instead. The gang greeted Sister Alice, disrupting me from my thoughts. I glanced up at her as she removed her headpiece and ran her fingers through her hair. Despite the weighted look in her eyes, I bit my lip to keep from giggling at the visual of her riding her moped with the veil flying behind her.

"Thank you to whoever got the cookies out and coffee made." She shed her coat and tossed it over the back of an empty chair.

"That'd be me," Jim said, puffing out his chest.

Sister Alice took a sip of coffee. "Not as good as mine, but it'll do." She tittered at Jim's glare. "Where's Aspen?" she asked me as she sat down.

"With Jade and Frank."

She nodded, and the chitchat continued for another minute until Sister Alice called the meeting to order.

I kept glancing at her throughout the meeting. She wasn't her usual perky, outspoken self today. My phone vibrated in my pocket, and I snuck a peek at the text— Brad.

Detective Griffin has demanded I make a trip to Spirit Lake to ask me more questions about my whereabouts the night your friend died, it said. *This whole thing is a colossal waste of my time. But since I'll be there, maybe we can talk about my proposal. Will let you know when I finish with the detective.*

WTH? As long as he's here? Like it's a *convenience* thing? My lips pressed together. I couldn't decide if I was angry or hurt. But I *knew* I was glad I'd made the decision I had.

Okay, I texted back. *But at Hallowed Grounds this time. Not Brewski's.*

Maybe I'd run into Deacon Molotov again.

I looked up from my phone and spied Sister Alice looking my way expectantly. I sat up straight and looked around the circle. All eyes were on me. "What?" I asked. I dropped my phone, which clattered on the floor and under the chair next to me. I bent over to pick it up and knocked my head on the person's knee. "Ouch!" I sat up and rubbed my head.

"Problems?" Sister Alice asked with an amused smile. "Jim tagged you to speak next. We're waiting."

I took a breath and smoothed the hair at the crown of my head. "I'm passing today." I was afraid if I spoke, I'd inadvertently share what my mind was obsessing about—Ivan and Mike's cases.

For the rest of the meeting, I divided my attention between those in the room and those who weren't–Brad and Luka–and the case as a whole. *Both* cases. And learning that Mike had a twin brother—who had no apparent love for his twin—only jumbled things more.

As soon as the meeting finished, Sister Alice pulled me by my arm toward the coffee table.

"Help me clean up," she said. "As soon as everyone's gone, we need to talk."

"I'd say," I said.

She looked at me sharply. "Did something happen with Luka?"

"So you got my text?"

"On my way over here, yes. It was a little—shall we say, *eventful*—at the hospital."

"What happened?" I wrapped the remaining cookies—two halves, to be precise—in a napkin and tucked them in my purse.

"Hungry?" she asked.

"I don't like waste."

She rolled her eyes. "You have the most spoiled dog in the world."

I grinned. "He's not spoiled. He's loved. So what happened at the hospital?"

She nodded toward the two people lingering by the doorway. "Wait until they leave," she whispered.

We cleaned the refreshment table, put everything away, and wiped down the table before the two stragglers finally left.

"So what happened?" she asked.

"You first."

"Mike died right as I left his hospital room."

My mouth dropped open. "What did you do?"

"Prayed for him."

"Didn't do much good, did it?"

She narrowed her eyes at me. "Andie Rose, a man is dead."

The impact slugged me. I gasped and dropped against the counter. "Great," I exclaimed, blowing through my lips. "Now Detective Griffin will question me regarding a murder instead of an attempt."

Her eyebrows shot up above the smudged lenses of her frames of the day—cobalt blue, matching *my* eyes. "That's what you're worried about?" she asked.

"Shouldn't I be?" I looked at her as if there were anything that could be worse.

"I'd say we should be concerned about catching someone who's still running free. Killing."

"Yeah, but if I'm behind bars, I can't help catch said killer," I argued.

"Then let's catch him or her sooner rather than later, so that doesn't happen." She quirked one eyebrow, something I couldn't figure out how she did. I tried it as I looked at her.

"What's wrong with your eyes?"

"Nothing. I was trying to quirk an eyebrow like you do."

"I'd suggest you don't. It makes you look constipated."

I laughed. "You're ornery."

"What happened with Luka this morning?"

"The oddest thing, really. And it could be nothing at all." She waited for me to continue. "Before, he used Roman as his alibi. Now his alibi is that Ivan didn't trust him."

"That sounds rather cryptic. Care to elaborate?" She pushed her glasses up with her forefinger.

I snatched a Kleenex from a box on the table and handed it to her. "Clean your glasses."

She made a face. "I can see you as well as I want to." She plucked the tissue from my hand and began doing what she was told.

I relayed the conversation I'd had with Luka to Sister Alice. "So if Ivan thought Luka was so untrustworthy, could he have a dark side and be the one who killed Ivan? It seems the unlikely suspect is turning into the *likely* one." I thought for a moment, then said, "Maybe Mike and Ivan's murders weren't connected at all, as I thought they might be."

"It's anyone's guess at this point."

"What do you know about Shannon's husband, Mark? Other than he's Mike's twin. Which you didn't tell me about," I scolded.

"You never asked."

"Shannon is a bit of a hothead herself." I filled her in on the weird behavior from Shannon about Mark and Mike.

Sister Alice pondered the news. "I visited with

Marie this morning."

When she didn't say more, I said, "And?"

"It appears Ella was visiting her mother right before I got there. Had Marie in tears. That poor woman recently lost her husband, and Ella makes her grief even greater."

"What'd she say to Marie?"

"Marie mentioned Ella amassed a significant debt." She made air quotes when she said the word significant. "Ella wanted her inheritance early. Ella wouldn't tell Marie why she wanted it, so Marie told her no. Ella got mad and left." I opened my mouth to speak, but Sister Alice shot her hand up and continued. "Marie also overheard Ella and Mike talking in the living room a few days ago about Ivan blackmailing someone for a, quote, substantial, unquote, amount of money."

"Did she hear who it was?"

Sister Alice shook her head. "She got somewhat panicked that the someone getting blackmailed was Ella, and that it might be the reason Ella needed the money."

"That makes sense, except Ivan is dead, so Ella doesn't owe him money anymore. Which gives her the perfect motive for killing Ivan, but why does she still need the money?"

"Perhaps someone was in control of Ivan?"

"Meaning the mystery person could have killed Ivan and is now blackmailing Ella." I blew my breath through my lips and dropped into a folding chair.

Sister Alice leaned against the counter facing me.

"This whole thing keeps getting more and more confusing," I said. "If Ella killed Ivan, she could have killed Mike, too, for unknown reasons. Unconnected circumstances but same killer."

"I asked Marie if she thought Ella could have killed Ivan."

I snapped my head up and looked at her. "What'd she say?"

"Her exact words were, 'I don't know.' "

Chapter 23

"Well, that adds a layer of interest," I said. "A mother who doesn't know if her own child could be capable of murder."

Sister Alice finished giving me the last details of her visit with Marie before I filled her in on my near hit last night.

"Did you call the police?"

I shook my head. "Not then, no. I assumed it was an accident; there was only moonlight, and I was just around the bend. But now I'm wondering if Jade was right."

"About what?"

"She suggested maybe it wasn't an accident at all."

"Jade's judgment has proven not to be favorable, but I have to say I agree with her on this one. Especially with what you've told me about what went down with Shannon before I got here."

"If I knew where she lived, I could casually drive by to check it out."

"Let me do that," Sister Alice said.

"You have her address?"

"I've lived here a long time, Grasshopper."

"I can go to save you the time. Where is it?"

"If you want to hop in the sidecar of my transportation," she stopped and grinned, "you can come with me."

"Not on your life," I said.

She studied me for a minute, then shook her head. "I've already given you too much confidential information. If you repeat any of it, I'll deny it to the death."

"You'd lie?" I asked in mock horror. "Isn't that a sin?"

"I'm old. Legitimate dementia age."

I laughed and stood. "If you see a truck at Shannon and Mark's, check out the passenger side mirror."

"Why the mirror?"

I told her about the mirror sideswiping a tree, and she pressed her lips together. "Check out the area to see if the mirror came off or if you can find any damage to the tree that could shed some light as to the vehicle."

My eyes grew wide. "Great idea. I'll do it on my way home."

"I can't believe Detective Griffin didn't do it."

"I guess I don't know that he didn't, but he was more focused on telling me to stay out of his investigation."

"Like that's gonna happen." She snickered. "What was that with your phone during the meeting? Your attention never came back afterward."

My eyes grew wide. "Oh yeah, I forgot. It was Brad. Detective Griffin asked him to come in for another interview regarding his whereabouts on the evening of Ivan's murder. After he left Brewski's," I added. "Brad wants to meet up with me afterward. He let me know he wasn't happy about the interview because it was," I made air quotes, "a colossal waste of his time." I rolled my eyes. "Like any of us are happy about it and don't have better things to do. I told him I can see him, but we're meeting at Hallowed Grounds this time instead of

Brewski's."

"Good girl." She scrunched her face. "But I'm stuck on the part where you *forgot* about Brad's call. How does one forget about something like that?"

I extended my hands, palms facing up. "There's a lot going on right now, in case you hadn't noticed."

"Well then," she said, folding the chair I'd just gotten up from. "It's a good thing you've decided not to marry the man. You might forget you were married and pull a Jade."

"Sister Alice," I admonished.

"I'm not sure how one could have two more opposite people than Jade and Lily working in a small space."

When we left, I headed back to the inn. I'd planned to take Aspen out for a walk around Little Spirit Lake before Brad finished his interview and called me to meet him. But first things first.

I pulled off the road where the truck hit the tree and saw grooves in the soft dirt from tire tracks that weren't mine and too small for the truck. Looked like Detective Griffin had the same idea. I studied the tracks for a moment and searched anyway.

Swishing my foot back and forth through the weeds as I explored the area and, coming up empty, I leaned forward to look closer. Still nothing. I couldn't remember which tree it was since I was busy getting out of the way. I searched a few of them in the area about the height of the truck's mirror and caught my breath at one of them—scraped bark with dark blue paint transfer.

As I got back in my car, I shot a text to Sister Alice so she had more info when she checked out Mark's truck.

****

Before I left the inn with Aspen, I stopped in the kitchen to check in with Tony and Sister Eunice. Izzy was there shadowing today. I stood in the doorway listening, laughing to myself. Izzy was doing a little more than *shadowing*. She was pretty much taking over Sister Eunice's part of the process, telling Tony what she'd do differently if she worked here, to which Tony, as politely as he could—which wasn't very at this point—told her to mind her own business and do what she's told. *Please*, he emphasized.

I intervened before any injuries occurred. "How are things going?" I asked cheerily. Aspen sat, then stood, then paced, expressing his clear impatience at getting outside.

"Okay, for working with a murder suspect," Izzy chimed in, earning a stormy look from Tony. I winced, but Izzy tittered with obvious delight at getting his goat.

"Sister Eunice?" I asked, breaking up the tension between Tony and Izzy.

"Fine as frog's hair," she answered with a grin. "Izzy will be just fine here."

This time, it was Sister Eunice who earned a dark look from Tony. If she noticed, she showed no indication of it. Izzy, on the other hand, gave a victory smirk.

"After I check in with Jade and Lily, I'm gonna take Aspen for a short walk and play fetch with the tennis ball. I have a meeting this afternoon, so if anyone should need me, call my cell."

"I may call you with my resignation," Tony grumbled.

But I knew he wouldn't. For one thing, he loved his job too much. For another, I hadn't offered the job to Izzy yet. I had to have a good heart-to-heart with Tony first. I couldn't let unwelcome company into his *home*.

After a quick check-in with Lily and Jade, Aspen and I were out and in the great outdoors. Despite the cloud cover and the chill from the high humidity, it was still my favorite place to be. I wondered if Sister Alice had inspected Mark's truck yet and instinctively glanced at my phone. If she did, she hadn't called or texted me about it.

Aspen took full advantage of my distraction and stopped to sniff everything. I couldn't complain, though, with as negligent as I'd been. I worked with clients on how to live in the here and now, but this was just one more example of how I failed to follow my own instruction to others.

Halfway around the three-mile trail, on a bench by the lakeshore and almost hidden by an enormous willow tree, I glimpsed a man talking with someone completely obscured by the willow's branches. I backed up a few steps and leaned over a bit until I saw that the man's hat and overcoat were those of Luka. *What have we here*? I stayed as quiet as possible, trying to make out who the second person was. Aspen nabbed the opportunity to stare down a rabbit and yanked hard on his leash when the rabbit sped off. I gasped at the unexpected pull on my arm, and Luka turned around. I smiled to myself. Now I had to pop down there at least and say hello. *It'd be rude not to*, I told myself. *Thank you, Aspen*.

Luka wasn't the least bit happy to see me. And when I discovered Ella sitting beside him, I bit back my surprise.

"Ella? What brings you out here?"

"It's a personal matter," Luka answered. Ella nodded.

"I'm sorry to have bothered you," I lied. "Aspen loves to chase rabbits and tugs hard when he sees one." I smiled and stayed still. I looked at them, then at the lake. "I just love the autumn days, don't you?"

Luka sighed. "Let's stop the small talk, shall we? We're in the middle of a personal conversation, so if you'll excuse us."

"Oh, of course," I said, as if I'd just realized I might have been interrupting something. "Forgive my intrusion." I tugged Aspen's leash gently. "Come on, boy. We don't want to interrupt anything private."

Ella scrunched her face and said quickly, "*Ew*. It's not like that."

"Not like what?" I frowned, showing my best innocent look.

"Ms. Kaczmarek," Luka said, "you've been showing up at the most inopportune times. Are you stalking me?"

"Far from it, Deacon Molotov. I was at the church for an entirely different matter this morning, and you happened to be there." I waved my hand as if displaying the trail. "And Aspen and I walk this public trail all the time."

"All right, then." He forced a smile. "Have a good day as you go about your way. At this rate, I'm sure we'll be seeing each other again soon. Too soon," he grumbled.

"It's been a pleasure," I said over my shoulder in my sweetest voice. Which I pulled off quite well, if I had to say so myself.

Aspen and I were near the end of the walk when my phone rang. I looked at the display. Sister Alice.

"Guess who I just saw sitting on a hidden bench by

the lake?"

"Guess what I saw when I drove by Shannon's house?" she said in response. "But you go first."

"Uh-uh. You can't say something like that and leave me hanging."

"Fine. I saw a dark blue truck in the yard. Someone wedged it in the back between the house and the garage."

I caught my lower lip between my teeth. "Interesting," I finally said. "And the mirror?"

"I couldn't see that. Your turn. Who was on the lake trail bench?"

"None other than Luka and Ella. Don't you think that's a strange place to meet?"

"Not if they wanted to eliminate the risk of being seen," she said, sounding deep in thought. "I'll see what I can find out."

"Tell me as soon as you know anything." She didn't answer. "Fine. I'll do my own investigation."

"It's best you stay away from Deacon Molotov. He told Father Vincent he thinks you're stalking him."

"He hinted at that same thing when he saw me. It's ridiculous."

"Is it? We talked with Luka together, and you've gone out of your way a couple of other times to speak with him." I didn't say anything, and she continued. "Look, we both know what you're doing doesn't fit the definition of stalking, but all the same, let me handle Luka so we can both stay out of trouble. You focus on meeting with Brad."

"Won't it be worse if *you* ask him about it?"

"Trust me," she said in a honeyed tone.

"Sure." I rolled my eyes and sighed through a breath. "Fine."

After returning to the inn, Aspen wandered alongside me as I mingled with guests gathered around a picnic table in the backyard. Sister Alice may want me to focus on meeting up with Brad, but it was the last thing I wanted to do.

Peanuts, pretzels, the ingredients for s'mores, a twelve-pack of beer, and some cans of Pepsi tempted me from the center of the table. I looked around for a cooler but didn't see one. *Ugh.* Even in my drinking days, warm beer would have been last on my list to imbibe.

One of them held one toward me. I wrinkled my nose. "No, thank you. I'll take a Pepsi though."

"Don't drink?" he asked as he extended the soda.

I shook my head in answer and popped the top of the can, the fizz sprinkling my hand. A woman poured water from a bottle into a plastic bowl and lowered it for Aspen, who began lapping it before it had even touched the ground.

We made small talk about the weather, the scenery, the town, and the lakes.

"What drew you to Spirit Lake?" I asked.

"The infamous ghost," a woman said. "But we have had no luck yet." She sounded like a child who realized there's no such thing as Santa Claus. "We thought we saw something in a window upstairs there," she pointed to the window in my room that faced us, "but it disappeared too fast to be sure."

"That's my room," I said.

"You were seeing things," a man guffawed, taking a swig of beer.

"No, sir," she argued. "Mary and Pete saw it too, didn't you guys?"

"We definitely saw something. But like Carol said,

it disappeared before we could be sure what it was."

The mysterious book immediately popped into my head, and my antennae perked up. "When was that?"

"Yesterday sometime. I'd seen you leave shortly before, so it wasn't you. Probably a shadow of some sort."

"What exactly did you see?" I asked, trying not to sound weirdly desperate for information. "Could it have been a person?"

He shook his head. "Nah. Not a person. It seemed almost translucent." He lifted a hand. "But, hey, like I said, it was so quick; we couldn't discern what it was. It was probably nothing except the curtains up there." He pointed to the curtains, flowing gently from the soft breeze.

But it was something. That book didn't appear by itself. I thought again about seeing Luka and Ella by the lake when my phone rang.

"Hey, Sister Alice."

"I have some news about Ella."

"Were you reading my mind just now, or what?"

"She confessed to Luka about stealing the money from the church."

"I'm glad you're telling me, but can't you get in trouble for breaking confidentiality?"

"It's not a secret. She told her mom, who told a friend, who told a friend...you know how it goes. Charges are getting filed, so it'll be public record."

"Yowzers."

"Not only that, but I think she's scared, and who could blame her? She said Mike was, quote, up to his ass in alligators, unquote, and in deep trouble, that if he didn't pay, Mike would be the next one dead. Guess the guy meant business."

Chapter 24

My hand flew to my mouth, and my eyes grew wide. "We need to find out what Ella's debt is for and to whom. If she's involved in the same thing Mike was, Ella could be in danger." I processed the news when the realization struck me. "I think Ella knows she's in danger and believes being behind bars is the safest place for her right now."

"You no longer think she could be the killer?"

"If there's a connection between the two murders, then I don't think so. If they're not, I'd still say Ella's a contender for Ivan's murder, just not Mike's. Either way, I don't want her dead." Deeply rooted in thought, the line fell silent. Finally, I spoke. "A guest said a few of them saw something translucent in a window, but it was too quick to tell for sure."

"Which window?"

"The big one to my suite."

"Are you sure he didn't see you walking around? Or your shadow?"

"Nope." I shook my head, even though she couldn't see it. "He said I'd left the inn shortly before. It could have been pareidolia."

"Para what?"

"Pareidolia. It's when people see familiar objects or patterns in random, unrelated objects."

"Hallucinations? And you said it happened to more

than one? What, pray tell, were they drinking?"

I chuckled. "No, not hallucinations. Like when someone sees a rabbit in a rock formation. Or a dinosaur in the stars."

"The face of Jesus in the clouds," she exclaimed. "Except that's not para-whatever-the-word-you-used."

I sniggered. "Sure. But the weird part?"

"Like that isn't weird enough?"

"It was the same timeframe in which the mystery book somehow got in my room."

"That's curious indeed," Sister Alice said.

"What if the ghost is helping me solve this murder? Leading me to an unlikely suspect." Hearing how ridiculous it sounded, I instantly felt foolish. To save face, I told her the story about the fireplace turning on by itself in the library.

"I've heard of stranger things," she said, surprising the breath out of me. A call came through, and I lowered the phone from my ear and glanced at it. "Brad's calling. I'll talk to you later."

"Good luck," she said wryly. "Take care of this once and for all and cut the man loose. No more procrastinating."

"I have; he refused to hear it."

"This time make sure he does."

By the time I answered Brad's call, it was too late, so I dialed him back. He said he was on his way to Hallowed Grounds, and I told him I would leave straight away to meet him there. He hadn't sounded like he was in a bad mood, so I assumed his interview with Detective Griffin went okay. Not one to openly show anger, the couple of times he had since Ivan's murder were unfamiliar to me. And unfamiliar was uncomfortable.

****

Sister Alice called Sister Eunice to ask when to pick her up. Izzy was there, but she assumed Tony would want Eunice to stick around so Izzy wasn't in his kitchen while he wasn't there. Unless Tony planned to pull a double and stay himself. When Sister Eunice said as much to Sister Alice, she rolled her eyes. "Men," she muttered. "Makes me grateful I'm married to God."

Sister Eunice bounded out the front porch door and down the stairs as soon as Sister Alice pulled in front of the inn. She handed Sister Eunice a helmet.

"Why don't you borrow Father Vincent's car when you pick me up?" Sister Eunice complained.

"This or walk; your choice." She extended the helmet farther and grinned.

"But the bugs—"

"Won't bother you if you keep your mouth closed."

Sister Eunice reluctantly reached for the helmet in defeat and heaved a sigh. Before she put it on, she said, "I hope Tony doesn't kill Izzy one day while I'm not there to referee."

Sister Alice pressed her lips together. "Probably not a good thing to say when he's already a suspect in a murder that happened in that very kitchen."

"*Uffda*, you're right," she said. "I hadn't realized chefs are so territorial, though. But Izzy can be an irritating little devil. It's like she tries to find what bugs Tony and does it."

Sister Alice tipped her head from side to side and gave a bemused smile. "Sounds like Izzy. She's been that way since she was just a tot. Andie Rose may want to think hard before hiring her."

"I can stay on as long as needed if Sister Ida is okay

with it."

"Don't hold your breath," Sister Alice said. "Exactly how mad did Tony get?"

"He didn't talk much, but I could practically see the steam coming outta his ears from repressed emotions."

"Is that so." Sister Alice frowned. She'd always liked Tony and didn't want to believe he could get angry enough to kill. "Eunice, what's your impression of Tony after working with him the last few days?"

"Nice young man." Sister Eunice clasped her hands together in front of her. "And so handsome." Dreamy eyes and a goofy smile comedically transformed her expression.

"Eunice," she scolded. "I didn't ask how he looks. What is your impression of him as a person?"

Sister Eunice put her hands on her hips, dropping her helmet as she did. She reached over to pick it up. "I already told you he's a nice young man."

"Because he's handsome?" Sister Alice scoffed. "Do you think he'd be capable of murder?"

Sister Eunice's eyes grew wide. "Why, I'd hope not. I've been working in the same room as him. With big knives." She twisted her mouth, then shook her head.

Sister Eunice put on her helmet while Sister Alice started up the moped. This news on Tony's behavior was unsettling at best. She crawled forward before Sister Eunice was fully on the vehicle, earning a swat from Sister Eunice.

****

Brad's car was half a block from the door to Hallowed Grounds. I was stunned. He hadn't arrived first in eons. I pulled into the parking lot behind the building and sat momentarily, taking a couple of deep breaths to compose myself. We'd been together for several years, just not the *together* part very often. In fact, last time and now again today, he hadn't even come out to the inn. And there was that pesky little detail that I wasn't ever leaving Spirit Lake anytime in the foreseeable future, and he would never, in a dog's age, move here. He didn't want to accept who I'd become, and I didn't at all like who he had become. Respect had vanished as much as romance had. Reinforcement that it was time for both of us to move on.

I got out of the car, stood tall, straightened my jacket, and smoothed the front. I put my hands on my hips, took one more deep breath, let it out slowly, and started for the door. "Here goes nothing, Andie Rose," I whispered. Aspen looked up at me and then at the ground. I reached down and scratched his head. "I know I embarrass you when I talk to myself, but you embarrass me too, sometimes, buddy. Like when you lick yourself in public." He lay down and covered his face with a paw. I chuckled and gently tugged his leash. "Come on."

As I walked past the coffee shop's front windows to the door, I spotted Brad at a corner table, coffee in front of him, legs crossed at the knee, and focused on his phone. Probably looking up sports stats.

"Hey," he said as I approached the table. He leaned in to kiss me, but I turned my head, and his lips grazed my cheek. "What do you want to drink? I'll go get it."

I laid my hand on his arm. "Finish what you're doing on your phone. I can get my coffee."

"You sure?" He glanced at the screen on his phone and then back at me.

I felt a brush of irritation, and any apprehension I'd felt vanished. I was done being a convenience. A means for him to climb the corporate ladder.

"Positive." Besides, Luka was at the counter talking with his son. As Aspen and I approached the counter, I smiled at Luka and raised my hand. "Before you get any idea that I'm following you, I'd planned to meet my boyfriend here without knowing you were here. This is a public place unless you have a restraining order against me."

"Now there's an idea," he mumbled.

I nodded toward Brad, miles away on his phone, consumed by what he read there. "It's a small town, so we're bound to run into each other." I said, sounding falsely cheery.

Luka blew through pursed lips, then swallowed his annoyance. He looked at Roman, who observed our interaction. "Son, this is Andie Rose Kaczmarek."

"We've met," Roman said. "Hi, Andie Rose."

I held my breath, hoping Roman wouldn't elaborate on our last conversation. "Hey, Roman. Nice to see you again." I offered him a smile.

Luka said, "She's also the one who is intent on finding Ivan's murderer. She's been hounding me like a police dog on a scent." He pressed his lips tightly together, his nose appearing even more prominent.

I tipped my head a bit. "Hmm. That's an interesting choice of words."

"Andie Rose," Luka said, his pitch increasing, "let me be of some assistance to you. Give me space to talk with my son, and I'll bring your coffee to your table when it's ready."

"Why, thank you, Deacon. That's so kind of you." I offered him the most angelic smile I could muster, then looked at Roman. "I'll have a sugar-free caramel macchiato with almond milk. Please and thank you."

Luka grunted an unintelligible remark as I turned and left.

"Someone needs a hug," I said under my breath.

On the way back to the table, Aspen stayed beside me, none too pleased. His behavior had never demonstrated fondness toward Brad, but when we met at Brewski's, and again now, it was beyond his usual dismissive behavior. Brad continued to intently study something on his phone. I sat down, Aspen lay at my feet, and Brad placed his phone on the table.

"Where's your coffee?" he asked.

I gestured toward Luka, standing at the empty counter. "Deacon Luka Molotov was kind enough to offer to bring it to me when it's ready."

"Oh." He peeked at his phone again before laying it face down and focused on me. "About my marriage proposal."

Despite a glimpse of genuineness and sincerity in his eyes from days past, the way he said it sounded like it was some business transaction—a *business* proposal rather than a *marriage* proposal. Which, if one took everything into account, it's precisely what our relationship had become to him—a business deal.

"Brad—" I grasped the box that held the ring from my purse and laid it on the table. "I've already told you this, but you didn't want to hear it. I can't marry you." Aspen tipped his head and looked at me as if I'd just told him we would chase bunnies and squirrels for the rest of the day.

I'd gone through all the trite, pleasant-sounding rejections in my head (i.e., it's not you, it's me; you deserve someone better than me; you should have someone who can give you exactly what you want, etc.), but I finally decided honest and to the point was best. So he would know, without a doubt, that what I said is what I meant. I was *not* marrying him.

Surprised at the emotion collected there, I cleared my throat and took a breath. "A clean break is best so you can move on and find the woman who can give you the marriage and family you decided you want."

He heaved a sigh and sat heavily back against his chair. "Don't you think you're being a little hasty?"

His reaction baffled me. This was the second hard "no" I'd given him. And how could he have thought I'd accept this…arrangement?

He sat up, leaned forward, and met my eyes. "Andie Rose, we've been together for five years. Now you're telling me we wasted those five years?"

I flinched from the proverbial arrow. *Wasted? Ouch.* "Is that what you think our time together was—wasted?"

"It's time I could have spent with someone who wanted the same thing as me."

I had all I could do not to stand up and yell, "*What time? That's part of the problem—we didn't spend time together.*" Instead, I kept my composure as best I could and said, "First of all, I—we've—never discussed marriage and family. You'd never voiced or given any clue that's what you wanted."

"Be reasonable, Andie Rose." I bristled at the manner in which he said it. Like I was a child. "It's the natural order of things after a while."

"So after five years comes marriage and a baby in a baby carriage as the child's saying goes? Without so much as a discussion?"

"Now you're being juvenile." He inhaled slowly and

exhaled through his nose as he slowly shook his head. "This is ridiculous."

Forcing myself to stay put and not get up and walk out the door took all my strength. "I won't leave Spirit Lake, and you won't leave the city. That's a paramount detail with a marriage—" I struggled to find the right word. "Deal," I finally said. Silence followed for a beat. "Brad, I want you to be happy. But I'm not the one that can make that happen. I will not marry you." I slowly slid the ring toward him as he sat there, still as could be, staring at the box. When he looked up at me, his eyes were impossible to read.

"So I guess this is it then," he said quietly, cupping the box loosely. "For the record, Andie, I loved you."

Loved. Past tense. Words caught in my throat until I was finally able to whisper, "Yeah, me too." I reached to touch his hand, but he jerked his back, clutching the ring.

I leaned back in my chair and looked out the window at the gray skies. *How fitting.* Yet I felt freer than I had in a long time. Luka waltzed over to our table, setting my coffee in front of me. "You have your hands full with this one," he said to Brad.

Brad paid him no attention and didn't even grace him with a glance. Luka appeared not to have noticed as he strutted back toward Roman, said something to him, looked my way, then left. *Stupid to make an enemy of a murder suspect, Andie Rose.*

"How did your interview go with Detective Griffin?" I asked. Pathetic that murder was more pleasant to talk about than our relationship.

"I gave him a receipt and a suggestion to check the video cam footage at the Cenex station on the outskirts of St. Cloud to prove I was long out of the area during the time of the murder." Irritation tinted his otherwise flat voice.

"Oh. That's good, then. You're cleared, right?"

Brad pushed his chair away from the table, letting me know he wasn't up for further conversation. The chair's legs scraped loudly on the tile floor. "Let's not waste time on small talk, Andie Rose. Clean break, you said, right?"

"Talking about getting cleared in a murder investigation is small talk?" He remained quiet. "Okay, then, that's fine. Let's go. But first I need to use the ladies' room. Can you watch my things for me?" I gestured toward my purse and coffee, nearly gone after taking gulps between sentences to quell my nerves. I'd begun not feeling well and assumed the last several days were taking their toll. Aspen stood to follow me. I gave him the stay command, and he gave me a death stare. Even exchange, I guess.

"Sure," he said flatly. He tucked the ring box deep into his jacket pocket.

Five minutes later, feeling worse instead of better and wanting nothing more than to get home, I trudged back to the table. Brad stood and walked out ahead of me, letting the door shut in my face. I stopped to take a breath. Hurt feelings didn't look good on him. That I'd never noticed this before spoke volumes about our relationship from the beginning. *Dodged a bullet with that one.* And yet, it hurt how far we'd drifted from one another.

I shook my head, inhaled, and pushed the door open when a sudden bout of dizziness and nausea overcame me, followed by a stab of excruciating stomach pain.

"Oh," I gasped, bent over, my hands on my knees, and rested my weight there. Another wave came, and I crouched down. I sensed Brad hovering over me.

"Are you okay?" he asked calmly. *Too* calmly.

He extended a hand to help me stand up, but I couldn't grasp it. "Something's...wrong," I croaked, voice hoarse. I hadn't had a panic attack for a while, but one never forgets what they feel like, and this wasn't it.

Aspen sat close beside me and whined. His cool, moist nose touched my cheek, and he licked it. A legion of feet circled me on the sidewalk, but I couldn't look up to see who they were. I just prayed I didn't hurl on their shoes.

"I called an ambulance," a young man said. Roman's voice?

"I just hung up from them as well," a woman said. "I hope they don't send two."

I didn't care how many arrived so long as at least one did. Brad squatted beside me and held my hair back from my face. "Andie Rose, are you pregnant?"

If I wasn't in so much pain and discomfort, his question would have been laughable. We hadn't been together in several months. Then, in a pain-induced haze, it occurred to me that was his way of asking if I was seeing someone else. The absurdity brought with it another swell of nausea. Then the sickness waned a bit, enough for me to wonder if maybe it was Brad who had been seeing someone else, therefore the lack of intimacy. Maybe she dumped his ass, hence the marriage proposal.

Another spasm of pain barreled down on me, along with more nausea, and every thought vanished as I struggled not to pass out. And then, as sirens screamed, everything went dark.

Chapter 25

I awoke to the scent of disinfectant, a nasty headache, an IV in my arm, and oxygen flowing up my nostrils. I didn't have the strength or desire to open my eyes, but it didn't take an abundance of brain cells to figure out I was in the hospital. I struggled to remember how I'd gotten here. Whispers in the otherwise silent room reached me, and I forced open my eyes.

Running my tongue over my dried lips, I croaked, "What happened?"

Sister Alice appeared by my bedside. I was aware of someone bigger standing just behind and to her left, but I didn't have the energy to turn my head to see who it was.

"You don't remember anything?" Sister Alice asked.

"Sister, go get the nurse." Detective Griffin's voice.

I squinted as he came into view. "Why am I here?"

Sister Alice patted my hand. "I'll be right back."

"What's the last thing you remember?" Detective Griffin asked.

I closed my eyes again, a hazy recollection of Ivan's murder and some events that had occurred since then: being a suspect in a murder investigation—*Holy wicked whiskey*. Two murder investigations. Is Detective Griffin arresting me? A monitor beeped at my increased heart rate. A lady in blue scrubs rushed toward my bed and fiddled with the monitors, then laid her hand on my shoulder. "Ms. Kaczmarek, try to relax." She patted my shoulder before whisking out of the room.

"Easy for you to say," I mumbled under my breath. I recalled Sister Eunice working in the kitchen at the inn and Tony's resistance to Izzy. And then I remembered Brad, the coffee shop, and Luka.

Something was missing. "Aspen." I pushed myself to a sitting position. "Where's Aspen? Is he okay?"

Sister Alice laid a firm hand on my shoulder, nudging me to lie back down. "He's with me and he's fine."

I looked around and frowned. "Where?"

"Before I came here, I dropped him off at the inn with Jade and Frank. Thought he'd be more comfortable than at the house with Sister Ida."

I reclined back again. "I was at Hallowed Grounds," I said, willing my brain to recall more of the missing pieces. "Yes. I was at Hallowed Grounds with Brad." My gaze traveled the room. Why wasn't he here? "What happened after that?"

"You passed out. Two people called an ambulance, and here you are," said Detective Griffin.

"But what happened? I can't remember." Frustration crept across my chest and stuck in my throat.

"That's what we're trying to find out," he said. "All we know so far is the blood work showed signs of a toxin. We analyzed your cup and found it was in there. You'd ingested a significant amount."

I squinted at him again. "What kind of toxin? And why was it in my cup? Who put it there?"

"And that's the million-dollar question," said Sister Alice.

Detective Griffin asked, "Do you remember who you came into contact with while you were at Hallowed Grounds?"

"Where's Brad?"

"He left when the ambulance arrived. I've left messages for him, but he hasn't returned them yet."

"Do you have the right number? He's always on his phone for work." How sad that's the one thing I recalled with such certitude.

He nodded. "We haven't been able to locate him. I put out an APB. An all-points bulletin."

"Not Brad. He wouldn't—I remember he wasn't happy with me, but we have a lot of history."

"A witness saw him with your coffee cup while you were away from the table. Unfortunately, sometimes it's the ones closest to us. The ones we'd least likely suspect."

My mind became less foggy, and the book popped into my head. "*The Unlikely Suspect*," I said. Tears escaped my eyes and trickled down the sides of my face and onto my pillow. Before sobriety, I was a muddled hot mess. But since I'd been sober, except for the first year, I wasn't a crier. But these were unusual circumstances, to be sure.

"I'm so sorry, dear," Sister Alice said. "I'm just glad you finally turned down that man's proposal and that he finally accepted it."

I closed my eyes, took a deep breath, and exhaled. The lingering headache now felt like an ice pick in my brain.

"I'm not sure I'm so glad. That's what landed me here. Refusing his proposal. Can I please get a pain reliever for this headache?" I groaned, then winced.

"Ouch."

An irritatingly cheery—and too loud—woman breezed through the door, this one in green scrub pants with a Betty Boop top. "Shift change. I'm your nurse for today. How's our patient doing?"

"Better a minute ago."

"She wants some ibuprofen," Sister Alice said. "Headache."

She looked at the computer screen in front of her and blinked. "Huh. Looks like you have had nothing for pain yet. Is the headache new?"

"Since I woke up, yes."

"Well, darlin', let's take care of that pain."

"Got any whiskey?" I didn't have the strength to dodge the proverbial arrow from Sister Alice. "Kidding. And no narcotics. Only acetaminophen or ibuprofen."

"We have something stronger that works better."

"No narcotics," I said adamantly, visually pleading with Sister Alice to back me up.

"You heard what she said."

Nurse Betty Boop tsked. "All right," she sing-songed. "I'll put in the order, and it will be here shortly." She glanced at Sister Alice and Detective Griffin as she typed into the computer. "Perhaps the two of you should leave so she can get some rest."

Sister Alice leaned over, murmured a prayer, and thumbed a cross on my forehead.

"When will the burning start?"

"The what?" Detective Griffin asked.

"She's going to be just fine," Sister Alice said, slowly shaking her head. "She's back to her Catholic resistance."

As soon as the two of them left the room, Nurse

Betty checked my vitals and the IV bag attached to the stand and wrote on a chart. "On a scale of one to ten, where is your pain?" she asked.

"A twenty," I said.

She frowned. "Are you sure you don't want—"

"Yes, I'm sure I don't want anything stronger. Please stop pushing drugs on me. Twenty is an obvious exaggeration."

"Just trying to help, dear."

"I know. I'm sorry." I sighed. "Other than this headache, it's more fatigue than anything. My stomach upset has even all but disappeared."

She winked at me. "That's good to hear. Get some rest so you can get out of here, okay?"

She probably wanted me gone even more than I wanted to leave. I thought of Aspen and the inn. *Nah.*

An orderly appeared, holding a tiny cup with two white oblong pills and a cup of water. He tipped the pills into my hand and set the water on the tray next to me. I examined the pills.

"Acetaminophen," Betty Boop said.

I popped them in my mouth and swallowed them with metallic-tasting water.

"I'll come back to hook up a new saline bag."

"Thank you." I laid my head back and yawned, the weight of my eyelids pulling them closed. Nurse Betty patted my shoulder and said, "Get some sleep, honey. Hopefully, the pain reliever will help kill all your ailments."

"Kill," I mumbled through a yawn. "I don't like that word so well." Using the last of my energy, I ran my fingers through my tangled mop of hair and winced when the IV needle stung my elbow pit.

"I'm sure you don't, sweet thing," she said as she closed the door behind her.

For a fraction of a second, I entertained changing my mind and asking for the stronger medication she'd offered. If only there was something to make the emotional pain disappear from knowing Brad tried to kill me. Something other than booze.

As tired as I was, sleep wouldn't come. My thoughts were too active, memories firing rapidly. As unlikely as I thought it was, I could identify his motive for killing Ivan and trying to kill me. But Mike? I wasn't even aware they'd known each other. Had Mike been spying on me for Brad? Could Brad be the one blackmailing Ella and Mike? *An Unlikely Suspect*. As I tried to process and make sense of it all, the wheels ground in my head, making it ache like a vise.

Finally, I fell into a light sleep, dreaming of Brad. He was holding *The Unlikely Suspect* above his head with both hands, waving it in front of me like he was not only advertising the fact that he was the killer but also proud of it. His face held no expression. Suddenly, it turned into a look of horror. His mouth tried to form words that wouldn't come out. A clatter beside my bed woke me, and I stirred. A moment of panic that someone was putting a narcotic in my IV caused my eyes to flutter open. When I realized it was only a nurse changing my saline IV bag, I allowed gravity to take control, closing my eyes again.

"Thank you," I mumbled before trying to recover the dream. I had to find out what Brad was trying to tell me. The pain cooperated and completely disappeared. Who knew simple saline was a painkiller?

The door to my room squeaked open, and then the

latch clicked as it closed. I fell back into the dream. Brad was in Hallowed Grounds, but he'd turned into an apparition, then back to himself again. He pointed toward the counter. Smoke billowed from the kitchen. I couldn't smell it, but the smoke alarm went off, getting louder and louder, becoming deafening, the room hazy. Someone was trying to get me out of there, pulling, pushing, prodding, but I couldn't move. Suddenly it was still, and Honey stood beside me, holding my hand. She leaned over and kissed my forehead.

"Not yet, dear," she said. Comforted by her touch, I stared into her eyes, longing to go with her. A woman's voice rudely yanked me from Honey's gaze until I stared into eyes I couldn't recognize.

"She's back."

Desperate to find some kind of familiarity, my gaze shot around the room. "Back where?" I barely recognized my voice.

"Andie Rose?" Sister Alice. "Thank God." She touched her forehead, then below her chest, to the left side, the right, then bowed her head.

The vision of Honey faded into nothing, and I remembered the fire, sending me into a panic. "Brad—someone needs to get Brad out of the fire." I choked and coughed, wincing at the pain that sliced through my head.

"Brad is safe," Sister Alice said before a blue gloved hand pushed her aside to shine a light into my eyes, one then the other. I lifted a hand to push it away, and looked around the room, confused when I recognized the hospital room. I wasn't in Hallowed Grounds at all. "What happened? Where's Aspen?"

"You're one lucky non-Catholic," Sister Alice said.

"You had an unwelcomed visitor in your room."

"Aspen," I repeated.

"Aspen is fine. Misses you, but he's fine. He's bonding with Jade and Frank again."

The fog slowly lifted. "Was the visitor Brad?" I looked at Sister Alice through squinting eyes.

She shook her head slowly. "We don't know yet."

A nurse checked my vitals, switched out my IV, fluffed my pillows, and fixed a wire or cord of some sort. I tried to look around her as she hovered over me.

"Then who? What happened?"

"Don't get yourself worked up." She placed a hand on my shoulder, encouraging me to lie back. "The *who* we don't know yet. Detective Griffin will find out. For some reason, he has a soft spot for you. God only knows why."

"Nice try. I'm a pain in his backside."

"Well, he does, but I sure can't figure out why." She smiled.

The nurse, not Betty Boop, thank God, finished fussing with my equipment and pillow. "You have that way about you. I'll leave you two ladies alone to beat the police in solving your mystery. In the meantime," she gestured toward the door as someone poked his head around the corner and waved, "there's an officer posted outside your door."

After she left, I said, "I remember someone by my IV. Is that who it was? The killer?"

She shook her head. "That was probably a nurse. But someone subjected you to a dangerous amount of fentanyl. When you flatlined, the medical team saw patches on your arm and knew what they were. Thank the good Lord you were in the hospital where Narcan was readily available, or you'd be a goner, back in the lovely company of Ivan and Mike."

The severity of the incident drew close, and I shivered. "Someone wants me dead awfully bad." I thought for a moment. "Brad would never have done this."

"We know nothing for certain," she said reluctantly. "They still haven't been able to find him."

"I need to get back to the inn," I said. Although, I didn't have the energy or desire to go anywhere right now. I settled back against my newly fluffed pillows.

"What you need to do is relax. Everyone is pulling their weight, and then some. Things are running smoothly."

"Tony and Izzy?"

"I think Tony has grown to like the girl. Or at least accept her."

The news perked my mood. Izzy's age was a huge drawback for me, but with the references everyone seemed to have about her cooking and baking skills, I'd try to get past that if Tony could.

I closed my eyes and tried to process everything, struggling to focus on the dream I'd had. Nothing came to memory. But now I was surer than ever that the truck that nearly hit me was no accident. If only I could remember *some*thing about it other than it was dark blue.

I pushed myself to a sitting position. "I need to get out of here." A crucifix hung on the wall across from my bed. From spending time with Grandpop and Honey, I knew to a Catholic, they're a powerful visual reminder of God's love, and they served as a witness of hope to the world. But right now, it only served as a reminder of sickness and death. Of course, it could be an exquisite floral painting, and after the events of the past few days, my brain would twist it into looking like dead plants.

****

The next morning, Sister Alice stopped by my room on her rounds.

"Wow," I exclaimed. "To what do I owe the honor? I'm not even a Catholic and I still get a visit?" I held up a hand as if protecting my eyes from the glare from her eyewear—a combination of green, yellow, red, and purple.

She glared at me from behind the smudged lenses. "There's hope for everyone."

A nurse whizzed into the room. "Since your vitals all look perfect, it looks like you're getting discharged this afternoon. Considering it stays this way and barring any more unwelcome visitors."

I looked at Sister Alice. "You'll have to leave now."

Sister Alice snorted, and the nurse laughed. "You're just fine, I see." Then she leveled her gaze at me. "You don't fool me, Ms. Kaczmarek. You'll need to take it easy for a few days. No running marathons. Do you promise?"

Determined to be released to find out who wanted me dead—and why—I was willing to say anything I had to. So I did. "I promise I'll behave."

Sister Alice coughed, undoubtedly covering a retort. She strutted toward the door. "I'll be back in a while to pick you up."

"I'll call Tony."

"You'll take what you get, which is me."

At three o'clock, my discharge papers went through. Sister Alice was there, along with Aspen, to take me home. Seeing Aspen was the best medicine ever. He jogged over to me and jumped up on the bed beside me, licked my hand, then my face. I burrowed my nose in the soft indent just above his nose and between his eyes.

I grinned. "How'd you get him in here?"

"I know people who know people. Ready to go?"

I groaned. "They told me to take it easy. That means I'm not allowed to ride in the sidecar of your moped contraption." Aspen lay down, one paw on top of the other, and buried his nose beneath them, staring at me. "He's afraid, too. You didn't bring him here in that thing, did you? I'll have to get him into therapy."

She waved a hand in dismissal. "Relax. I have Father Vincent's car."

"Where's mine, by the way?"

"Your what?"

"My car."

She did that weird quirking thing with her eyebrows and looked at me over the top of her frames. "Why do you need to know that? Planning to go somewhere?"

"No," I lied. "I just want to know it's somewhere safe, and it didn't get towed."

"Tony picked me up and drove me to the coffee shop to get it, and I drove it back to the inn."

"How'd you get back home?"

"You worry about the smallest things."

I smiled. "It's curiosity. And it's what is going to solve this case."

"Or get us killed."

Nurse Frieda pushed a wheelchair into the room, her eyes zeroing in on Aspen. She planted a hand on her hip, not breaking her gaze from mine.

"If it makes a difference, he's a certified ESA," I

said sheepishly.

Sister Alice came to my rescue. "The higher up has approved it." She tilted her head up, then back, insinuating the Big Guy upstairs.

Nurse Frieda fought a smile. "I'm sure it was, Sister."

"This isn't any different from the therapy dogs brought in for patients." She looked at me. "I'll go get the car and bring it 'round up front to the door."

When she left, an orderly came through the door. I looked at the wheelchair and frowned.

"I'm not an invalid. I can walk."

"Hospital policy." His tone told me he wasn't a rule breaker.

I shook my head and scooted into the wheelchair, keeping Aspen by my side. The man pushed me toward the elevator. It stopped on the second floor; the doors creaked open, and in walked Tom. I was grateful I wasn't hooked up to the heart monitor any longer.

He nodded at me and said, "I see you're feeling well enough to go home."

"Yep." I placed a protective hand on Aspen. "What brings you here, Tom?"

"Business. I would have stopped in to see you, but I didn't have time."

"Thanks for the thought." When the doors opened, I said, "Tom, do you own a pickup truck?"

"Used to. Why?"

The orderly pushed my wheelchair outside the elevator doors and stopped while Tom and I talked.

"What color?"

"Dark blue."

"When did you get rid of it?"

He squinted. "Why all the questions?" When I didn't answer, he breathed a sigh of irritation. "I sold it to Deacon Molotov about two months ago." He began walking away and said over his shoulder, "Have you ever thought that your nosiness is what almost got you killed more than once?"

The orderly gasped.

"It's fine," I assured him, praying to God I was right.

Chapter 26

I relayed the latest events to Sister Alice when I climbed into the car.

"I don't know what you think about that," she said, "but to me, it sounds like a threat. Did Tom ever tell you *why* he was at the hospital?"

"No. Just that it was business."

She scowled. "I'm sure it was. I think you'd better let Detective Griffin know about that."

"I will. On another note, one thing in Brad's favor, I guess, is that he doesn't have a truck, so it couldn't have been him that tried to run me over." I sighed and looked out the window, keeping one arm stretched toward the back seat, touching Aspen. "I still can't believe he'd do anything to hurt me."

Sister Alice looked over her shoulder for oncoming traffic before she merged onto the street. "I'd swing by the cop shop so you can talk with Detective Griffin, but you need to get home. I can go there after I drop you off."

"Nah." I leaned my head against the headrest. "I'll call him. He can come to the inn if he needs to talk." Aspen leaned between the seats and nudged my hand with his cool nose, begging for continued attention. "Has Shannon said anything else since I've been gone?"

"Nope. But I've kept my eyes and ears open. Even drove by their house a time or two. Perhaps more." She cast me a sidelong glance.

I smiled. "Harassment is a crime."

"The blue truck hasn't been back there, so I assume it was a visitor."

"Yeah, like Deacon Molotov. Probably paying his respects and condolences to Mark. I've been wracking my brain trying to remember something else about the truck that could give us a lead, but I keep coming up with nothing. Nada. Zilch. Other than the mirror, and they coulda fixed that by now. *Grrr*." I slammed my hand against the dash, and the glove box fell open.

She glanced at me quickly, then back at the road. "Need a painkiller?"

"Yeah, a narcotic," I grumbled again and shut the glove box. "Sorry. I'm just so frustrated."

"I know."

Back at the inn, she turned off the engine and began getting out. I waved at her, dismissing her intent.

"I got it." I looped the long handle of my across-the-shoulder hobo bag around my neck and swung it to the side so it rested against my hip. I clutched the small white plastic hospital bag with my few belongings. "I'm going straight to my room to lie down as soon as I pop my head into the kitchen to be sure both Tony and Izzy are still alive."

"Good thing they took the corkscrew as evidence and didn't leave it behind," Sister Alice said.

I wrinkled my nose. "Really? That was bad."

"I'll try harder." She smiled and got back in the car. "Tell Sister Eunice if she's ready, get her tail out here, or I'll come back with my moped to pick her up."

I leaned over, resting my hand on the vehicle's roof, the other holding onto Aspen, to peer at her. "You enjoy tormenting people with that entirely too much. What do you do in the wintertime?"

"Father Vincent lets me use his car in inclement weather. Or like today."

"What about Sister Ida's car?"

She scoffed. "Right. She locks her keys in a safe during the day and sleeps with them under her pillow at night."

"How would you know that?"

"Even a fool who keeps silent is considered wise." I gave her a blank stare, so she said, "It's a proverb."

"Hmm. I'm going to lie down. I'll talk to you later."

Frank and Marcie were beside me before I could open the front door.

"Allow me, Miss Andie," Frank said, opening the door wide.

Marcie took the bag from my hand. "How are you feeling?"

"Exhausted. It'll feel nice to lie down in my own bed."

"I'll carry your things upstairs to your room," she said.

"You can leave them by the desk. My door's locked, and I'm making a few stops before going up."

"I'll bring them anyway, so you don't have to lug them with you." She continued holding onto the bag and my purse.

I paused to carefully choose the words to my question, so it didn't sound like an accusation. "Marcie, do you have a key to my room?"

"No one does that I'm aware of."

I eyed her carefully. She hadn't exactly answered the question but sidestepped it instead.

"Do you want me to use yours to put your things

inside? I can lock up behind me and bring it back down to you."

I shook my head and reached for my things. "No. Thank you, anyway. I can drop them in my office until I go up." Without knowing who was trying to kill me, I didn't want *any*one having excess access to me. I couldn't be sure if I was relieved or concerned that she, in a roundabout way, denied having a key. Because that provided no further answers or explanation for the mystery book left in there. The ghost looked more and more likely, and, at this point, I welcomed that scenario.

After getting gentle hugs from Jade and Lily, I went to the kitchen and poked my head around the corner. Tony and Izzy appeared cordial with one another, and I smiled.

Sister Eunice noticed me first and clapped her hands together in delight. "Andie Rose, how nice it is to have you back."

Tony looked up from the cutting board and beamed. "Hey there, slacker. Some people will go to any lengths to get out of work. Good to have you back."

Izzy spun around from the sink. "Welcome back," she said, giving me a small smile.

"Sister Eunice, if you're ready to go, Sister Alice is outside in Father Vincent's car. If not, she'll come back to pick you up on her—"

"Mother of God, no." She untied her apron and dropped it in a pile on the counter. "I'll take the car ride."

Tony and I laughed. Other than a trace of what I discerned to be amusement, Izzy remained stoic. She obviously had never had the pleasure of riding in the sidecar.

"I'll be lying down in my room," I told Tony. "Buzz

me if you need anything." I was through the doorway when Tony called after me.

"Hey, boss?"

I silenced a groan from escaping my lips. *Please don't gripe about Izzy. Not now.* I stopped, turned, and he nearly ran into me. "Can it wait for a couple of hours, Tony?"

He nodded and wiped his hands on a towel hanging on his apron belt. "I only wanted to tell you not to worry about the sous-chef. Izzy'll be fine."

For as tired as I was, my eyes flew open and my jaw dropped. "Are you serious?" He nodded. "What happened? I thought you were going to give me a giant no on that. I'm not even sure how *I* feel about it yet."

"It was an insult that you thought a sixteen-year-old could do the job, and she's an obnoxious and irritating kid, but she's better than Ivan ever could have hoped to be."

I took a moment to digest the change. "I've heard that from a couple of people." I thought about it for all of a second more. "Okay, then. Break the news to Izzy and let her know I'll have the paperwork ready for her tomorrow when she gets here. Assuming she can start tomorrow."

"I'll take care of it. Go get some sleep. You look like hell."

"Gee, thanks," I said dryly, but couldn't suppress a half smile. I knew I was fortunate to be standing here right now, considering in the past two and a half days, I'd been nearly hit by a truck and poisoned not once, but twice. I still didn't know what someone poisoned me with at the coffee shop, and I hoped Detective Griffin could enlighten me on that when I called him from my room.

Dragging my feet up to my suite sucked up any remaining energy I had. The moment I unlocked the door, I spotted the foot of my bed from around the corner, and its siren call was too strong to resist. I dropped my things on the floor, locked the door behind me, and dragged myself to the bed, where I flopped down face first. I kicked off my shoes, curled up on my side, and pulled the comforter around me and up to my chin.

The next thing I knew, I woke to a darkened room except for the moon which shined in my bedroom window. I moved to sit up and winced at the stab of pain from a crick in my neck, earned from sleeping on my side without a pillow. I looked at the bedside clock—one thirty-three a.m. I groped around the bed for my phone to check for missed calls or text messages, finally finding it in the far corner. I held it up—no missed calls, two text messages: one from Sister Alice checking to see how I was and one from Detective Griffin that said simply, *Call me*.

I groaned. *Shoot*. I'd have to call him in the morning. I stripped out of my clothes and pulled an oversized T-shirt from my drawer. Seeing it was one of Brad's Minnesota Timberwolves shirts, I tossed it in the garbage, feeling a pang of something uncomfortable and indescribable. I reached for a new one and slipped it over my head. I lay back down, and it was lights out again in a matter of seconds.

When I finally woke, it took a moment to figure out where I was. I hadn't even had any dreams to confuse me. Finally realizing I was in my own bed with Aspen curled up beside me, I stretched and yawned. After a shower to feel human again, I planned to take Aspen for a brief walk before making quick rounds of the inn, then head into town. I wanted to stop at Hallowed Grounds and see if I recognized anyone who had been there the day I was poisoned. See if anyone remembered something that could lead to answers. I also wanted to talk to Luka one more time about the truck he'd purchased from Tom. Hopefully, he wouldn't call the police to have me arrested for stalking. Sister Alice hadn't told me where he lived, so I planned to start at Hallowed Grounds. It seemed he spent a good deal of time there.

After artfully applying thick black eyeliner, black mascara, and drying my hair, I stepped into a pair of yoga pants and slipped a hoodie over a clean T-shirt. Despite expecting to be completely exhausted by now, the level of energy I possessed was a pleasant surprise.

As I walked past my kitchen table, I spotted *The Unlikely Suspect*. I couldn't remember putting it there, but in my frame of mind over the past few days, I could have put it in the oven and not remembered. I picked it up, looked at it, front and back, and dropped it back on the table.

Before I pulled out of the inn's parking lot, I called Detective Griffin and left him a message that I needed to talk to him. I said I'd be in town for a few this morning and could stop by the station unless he wanted to meet at the inn later.

As tempting as it was to stop at Sweet Temptations for one of their famous breakfast tarts, I drove past, eager to find Luka.

People had already filled the parking spots on the street in front of the coffee shop, leaving only one space too small in which to parallel park even Sister Alice's moped. Parking at Spirit Brew Coffee House and the Spirit Lake Café had also been full. Between the three businesses, it appeared they consumed half of Spirit Lake's population this morning.

Countless people wandered the streets, admiring the decorations for the first day of the week-long Harvest Festival. They weaved in and out of open stores and waited for the still-shuttered stores to open.

I turned into the alley toward the back lot, surprised to see it, too, packed, with only one remaining spot.

I squeezed between two vehicles, then slid out of my car, stepping aside for Aspen. I shut the door after him and hit the lock button on the key fob. Most people in town didn't even lock their house doors, much less their vehicles. But recent events had warranted it.

I began toward the front of the building when I stopped dead in my tracks. Aspen bumped into the back of my legs at the abrupt halt. Alongside the building, partially hidden by an even larger vehicle, was a dark blue pickup truck, one mirror at an awkward angle. Luka was here, and this was the evidence I needed to prove he was the one who tried to run me down.

My feet had a mind of their own, and I strode over to the truck and peeked inside the tinted driver's side window. I reached for the door handle, touched it, and squeezed my eyes shut as I hesitated a beat, expecting an alarm that didn't come.

"Be my lookout, Aspen," I whispered as I scratched his head. He sat down and looked behind him as if he'd understood.

Slowly, I slipped my fingers beneath the ledge of the handle and pulled. Still no alarm. I took a deep breath and opened it farther, then glanced around the parking lot before I got down to business, snooping for any clues. A few people came around the corner, laughing amongst themselves, got into their cars, and left. Two more followed suit.

I scanned the floor of the driver's side and then the passenger's side before opening the center console. Nothing but a lot of food wrappers and loose change. Lying low on my stomach, across the seat, my legs sticking out the door, I opened the glove compartment but found nothing of value there, either.

I began feeling discouraged. Voices came my way again, and Aspen whined. "Good boy," I whispered and reached over to rub his neck while I pretended to be on my cell phone. They waved to me as they got into the vehicle directly behind the truck. I waved back while engaging in my one-sided phone conversation. After they pulled out, I tucked my phone in my back pocket, leaned over, and fumbled around under the truck's passenger seat. Nothing. I jammed my hand under the driver's seat. "*Ouch.*" I said under my breath. I pulled my hand out to spot a few beads of blood on my pointer finger. "Shoot," I said in a harsh whisper as I evaluated the damage. *When was my last tetanus shot?* I couldn't remember, which meant either my brain function hadn't fully returned, or it had been too long ago. I made a mental note to get one ASAP.

I stepped down from the truck's running board, put my head down low to the floor, and shined the flashlight from my phone underneath the seat. In view was a dirty green microfiber rag stashed there. I used yellow ones to keep the inside of my car dust-free, so I thought nothing of it. But when I saw what looked to be something tucked inside of it, I pinched a corner between two fingers and pulled until it was in full view. I slowly unwrapped it to find a case for a pistol and a small glass vial, mostly empty save for a drop or two. And under another fold of the cloth was a bag filled with a significant amount of white powder.

A small click sounded behind me. I froze.

"Stand up and put your hands behind your head." I recognized the voice, but it wasn't Luka's. My gaze darted down to meet Aspen's. I hoped he could read the desperation in my eyes and crawl under a car and out of sight.

Chapter 27

Lacing my fingers behind my head, I took one deliberate, slow step at a time until I faced him. My breathing became shallow, and I tried to remain calm.

"Roman."

"What are you doing in my truck?"

The young man I knew as kind and quiet looked like a kid playing cops and robbers with a toy gun. Except the gun, pointed at my chest, failed to reveal the orange tip, proving it was a toy. I squeezed my eyes shut and then looked again. Nope, no orange.

"I thought it was your dad's truck."

"That makes trespassing okay?" His tone was low and even, almost bored. Or perhaps defeated. He took a slow step forward.

Over Roman's left shoulder, I caught sight of a man on his cellphone turning the corner. Engrossed in his conversation, he didn't spot us. Roman glanced back to see what held my attention, then lowered the gun while keeping it pointed at me.

"Don't do it," he said.

"Do what?" I asked, stealing another glance at the man, my potential savior.

"Scream or say anything. It'll be the last thing you do."

In the brief moments of waiting for the man to leave, any hope I had evaporated, and any optimism I had crashed. My life the past few days flashed before my eyes at lightning speed, a film on a movie projector spinning out of control—the meeting between Ivan and Roman at Brewski's Pub on the night of Ivan's murder; Ivan stalking out; the server clearing the table next to Brad and me. She'd left the tray unattended on the bar as Roman was leaving, and the murder weapon was on that tray. It had nothing to do with me at all. It was because of Roman.

"It was you," I whispered.

Roman tilted his head and heaved a sigh. "Why, Andie Rose?"

"Why what?" I said. I tried to remain calm, but it was proving harder under the circumstances.

He said nothing, only appeared bored and as though he had nothing to lose, which could prove to be the biggest loss of all. For *me*.

Finally, he said, "Why couldn't you have just kept your nose in your own business?"

The blackmail allegations that'd become the topic of conversation lately popped into my head. My eyes grew wide as I suddenly grasped what was missing.

"Ivan was blackmailing *you*, wasn't he?"

"Ivan was a POS," he scoffed. "He caught me in the middle of a deal—"

"A drug deal?"

"What else?" He shook his head at my blatant stupidity. "He got a video of it on his phone. All he had to do was hand over his phone, and it wouldn't have been a problem. Or even delete the stupid video in front of me. It's not like I didn't give him options. But no. He was too greedy for money so he could leave the inn."

I frowned at the unexpected revelation. That meant

the confrontation between us at the pub didn't even have to happen. "He was planning on leaving?" He took another step closer. I had to keep him talking long enough for someone to notice the predicament I was in. "What about Mike? Did you kill him too?"

He gave a short, bitter laugh. "He was just like Ivan. Ivan told him about the deal he'd caught on his phone, and Mike picked up where Ivan left off. They were bullies." His voice was quiet, but seemed to pick up steam. His eyes had gone cold and empty, but I knew that sweet young man I'd gotten to know was still in there somewhere. He had to be. I could only hope he came back before he used the gun.

"But why try so hard to kill me? I did nothing to you."

"You wouldn't let it go. You were relentless in sticking your nose where it didn't belong." His voice raised, his hand holding the gun punctuating each word. "What are you, some kind of Sherlock wannabe?" He put his other hand under the one holding the gun, ready to shoot. "When you started looking at my dad, I knew it wasn't long before you put it together." He drew a deep breath and shook his head slowly as he exhaled. "I'm so sick and tired of being picked on. My dad, my friends, now you." His voice quivered, and I thought he might cry.

"I've heard your dad is hard on you," I said, hoping sympathy would be my ticket to escape unharmed.

He snorted. "You have no idea. And people expected me to be this saint because of my dad. My dad is the biggest bully of all." He blinked rapidly and wiped his eyes with the back of his hand.

"No one likes to be bullied, Roman. I get it. But—"

"How could you get it? People like you have it all."

He stabbed the gun in the air toward me with each word. I closed my eyes and held my breath. When I thought it was safe, I opened my eyes and said, "People like *me*? Roman, kids made fun of me all the time in school because of my red hair. And I was always taller and scrawnier than all the kids in my class. Do you know how many derogatory words there are to call someone with red hair? Too many." I looked down at Aspen, ready to nudge him to run, but he was no longer there. I prayed he crawled under a car.

Roman seemed to consider what I said, the pistol's muzzle dipping slightly. He snapped back to angry mode. The muzzle lifted back toward my chest, and I held my breath.

"Whatever," he said. "It's too late now, anyway."

"I won't say anything, Roman. I swear. People will hear the gun. You don't want that, do you? Listen," I rambled desperately, "we can get in the truck and drive somewhere else. Or we can take my car. No one needs to know."

He appeared to think about it for a moment, then said, "I liked you, Andie Rose. You treated me nice. But my dad can't find out about this. He'd kill me. I'm in too deep now."

"Killing me won't help, Roman," I said as gently as possible. "Your dad will find out. You know that."

"What, is *God* going to tell him? You're the last loose end to putting this behind me."

I attempted one last desperate plea. "That's not true, Roman. I've been working with people. They know everything. If something happens to me, they'll know it was you."

He flipped back to resigned, expressionless. Who knew sociopaths could look so innocent?

"You're bluffing."

"Do you really want to take that chance?"

He cocked his head. "Who else knows?"

"I'd be stupid to tell you that, because then you'll kill them, too."

"Tell me, or I shoot."

"I'd say you're in quite a predicament, Roman," I said, feeling a sliver of bravado. "Shoot me, and the others go to the police."

"I don't believe you."

A trace of fear shimmered in his dark eyes, and a fragment of the fear I felt turned to hope. It was a good sign that he cared.

"Try me." I took a slow step toward him. Over his shoulder, I spotted a group of people turning the corner to the lot. Hoping to catch him off guard, I yelled, "Gun!"

Roman startled at the unexpected loud command, his lack of focus giving me the upper hand. I lunged toward him, pushing his arm down. The gun fired, sending the bullet through Roman's foot. He cursed and jerked his knee upward, then regained his balance and aimed the gun at me again and fired. The bullet grazed my arm.

I gasped and clutched my arm. "Son of a—"

"Roman?"

I looked up to see Luka behind Roman, slowly reaching toward his shoulder. Roman flinched as if his dad's touch was a hot poker.

"Son, give me the gun," he said in the calm tone I knew before he revealed his not-so-charming self.

Roman put his weight on the uninjured foot and kept

the gun, and his gaze, trained on me.

"Go away, Dad."

"I can't let you do this, Roman." Luka's tone was low and steady.

"How is that different from anything else?" Roman asked. "Everything was about how you looked to the people in this town. It was all about your standing in the community and all about you. Everything was about *you*. All you ever do is yell at me and Mom. I don't know why she stays with you."

Tears from apparent years of pent-up anger shone in his eyes. One escaped from each and trickled down each cheek. I held my breath. An angry person with a gun was never a good thing.

"Son, please," Luka said. He touched Roman's shoulder.

Roman jerked away from him and I squeezed my eyes shut. *Keep your hands off the kid, Luka.* An unsteady hand holding a gun wouldn't end well for any of us. Then the gun cracked. I cringed and kept my eyes pinched shut as I waited for the bullet to hit me. When nothing came, I slowly opened my eyes, one at a time. Roman stood completely still, gun pointed at his father, who lay flat on the ground, eyes wide, holding his stomach.

"You shot me," Luka gasped, his eyes round with disbelief. He pulled his hand away and looked at the blood there.

Roman, transforming back to the caring boy beneath the angry surface, dropped the gun by his side and fell to his knees. His hands covered his face, and his shoulders shook as he openly sobbed.

Detective Griffin materialized from nowhere and

slapped cuffs on Roman. I wondered if I'd fallen into another dream; or worse, if I'd been shot and was dead, getting a panoramic view of the scene. I hadn't even heard the sirens. I pinched the arm that the bullet grazed, and I winced. Aspen sidled beside me and rubbed his head against my leg. I breathed a sigh of relief and wrapped my arms around his neck. Yup, I was alive.

****

An ambulance pulled into the narrow alley. This time I didn't have a problem hearing the ear-splitting wail of the siren. After a paramedic inspected and bandaged my arm, he wanted me to go to the hospital for further evaluation. I gave him a death stare.

"Not a chance. That place is deadly."

I trotted over to the stretcher that held Luka. Ironic how he ruined the life of someone he loved and saved the life of someone he didn't even like.

"Thank you," I said.

He tipped his head toward Aspen. "Thank your dog friend."

Between spasms of pain, he told me how Aspen slipped through the door behind a customer into the coffee shop. He'd gone up to Luka and persisted in nudging him with his nose until Luka got irritated and looked around for me. When he didn't see me in the coffee shop, he looked down at Aspen, who then led him out the door and to the back parking lot. Aspen hadn't hidden under a car as I'd hoped he had. He knew better. Thank God Luka listened to him. When we returned to the inn, I would let Aspen take *me* for a walk. And I would play fetch with his tennis ball every day for the rest of my life. Which, if I wasn't more careful, wouldn't be a long life.

****

Once in my room, I looked at the clock—ten thirty. I sighed a long breath and fought the urge to climb into bed and start the day over. I flopped onto the sofa, reclined against the back, and rested the forearm of my bandaged arm over my eyes. I thought about Brad. Relief that he had had nothing to do with it competed with a twinge of shame that I'd thought he even could have. I reached for my phone to call him, then set it back down. He and I were through. Detective Griffin could tell him about it.

I stood and walked past the table toward my bedroom. I abruptly stopped and took a step back. The mystery book was no longer there. I ran my fingers lightly over the cool Formica of the tabletop as if that would make it reappear. I was positive the book had been there when I left this morning. I glanced around me, then continued. "I don't care what Sister Alice says," I whispered. "If there is a ghost, it brought that book in here to help me solve this mystery." Roman was a more unlikely suspect than even his father had been.

I glanced in a mirror on my way toward the door. With a little smoothing of my hair and the long-sleeved T-shirt I'd changed into, I was ready to roll and answer the million questions I knew were coming. As I locked the door behind me, Lily texted me: *Det G here to see u.*

For the first time, I was happy he was here. We could wrap this up, and I could put it all behind me. Spirit Lake had given me a welcome I'd never forget.

The lobby was unusually quiet, but given the number of people in town for the Harvest Festival, it didn't come as a surprise. Aspen flanked my side as I greeted the detective, then marched to the kitchen to fetch Tony and Izzy. I texted Sister Alice on my way.

In the parking lot and on my way in, she'd texted back.

Next, I asked Jade or Lily to please message Frank and Marcie. After surviving the past week, this was cause for celebration for the entire team. I flipped on the gas fireplace in the parlor, and Aspen sprawled on his side in front of it.

When all of us were finally gathered, Detective Griffin began filling in the missing pieces, as well as what had happened this morning, saving me some time and energy. When he finished, all eyes stared at me, mouths agape, before they peppered me with condolences and scolded me for not telling them.

"Is Luka okay?" I asked Detective Griffin.

"He came through surgery okay, but he'll be in the hospital for a few days."

"He resigned as Deacon," Sister Alice added.

"Shocker," Jade retorted. "They shoulda fired him without the opportunity to resign."

"What will happen to Roman?" I asked, saddened by so much loss. Not only had Ivan and Mike lost their lives, but Roman's was as good as gone now as well.

"He's an adult, so he'll most likely get a life sentence."

"Just one?" Jade asked incredulously. Her nostrils flared. "He killed two, shot his own father, and worked at killing Andie Rose three times. Four if it was him behind the wheel of the truck that almost took her out."

"Ultimately, what happens to Roman is up to the court—if it goes to trial, it will be the jury's call. If he pleads outright, it will be up to the judge." Silence descended momentarily as we each drifted in our own thoughts. "If it's of any comfort, Andie Rose," Detective Griffin said, "Roman said the incident on the road was only to scare you."

"So it *was* him," said Jade, her fists clenched.

Sister Alice pressed her lips together and frowned. "Tell him it didn't work. It takes her a while to catch on." She looked at me over the rims of her pickle-green eyewear. "That means you've used four of your nine lives in the span of a few days."

Detective Griffin snorted and said, "I've officially put in for retirement, so Spirit Lake will soon have a new detective." He looked at me. "Don't be mistaken; I'll be warning him or her about you and the unsolicited assistance and meddling to expect from you." He looked at Sister Alice and pointed at her. "And you, too."

"Do you know Mike's motive for blackmailing Roman?" I asked, ignoring Griffin's jab. "Other than greed."

"Since Ella's mom wasn't dying, Ella wouldn't get the inheritance they'd been counting on to pay their debt."

"Debt from what?" Sister Alice asked.

"He'd left a gang. One doesn't just *leave* a gang without repercussions. Usually, that doesn't bode well. Mike's death proved that."

Failing to put together the last piece of where the money came into play, I stared at him blankly.

"They offered him a buyout. But it didn't come cheap."

"So Roman killed Mike, but ultimately it was because of leaving the gang." I nodded slowly as the reality sunk in. "The gang was behind the whole fiasco."

"Thank God you get it, because I don't," Marcie said

and sighed. "I think I'm still confused."

I thought about Roman again as silence settled in the room. Scooting to the edge of my chair, I stood and grimaced from a shooting pain in my bandaged arm.

"Was Ella involved too?" I asked. "Since they didn't get the money from Mike, will they come after her now?"

"We're putting her in the witness protection program," Detective Griffin explained.

"Getting her away will be good for both her and Marie," Sister Alice said. "Ella hasn't been good to Marie for a long time."

"Were you able to reach Brad?" I asked him, my tone sober.

Detective Griffin nodded. "Yep. He'd made a last-minute decision to go to Minneapolis for a few days to clear his head."

"What about his phone? He never turns that off," I said, once again confused.

He coughed, reached in his pocket, and pulled out a throat lozenge. He took his time unwrapping it and popped it in his mouth, tucking it in his cheek with his tongue. "Never say never."

"I have some good news to add," Jade said. "Just so you all stop looking at me like a villain." She rolled her eyes and zeroed in on Tony. "The baby is Tom's, not Ivan's."

I reached my good arm around Sister Alice's shoulder and clamped my hand over her mouth.

"That's wonderful, Jade," I said. "That's great news for both you and Tom."

"Oh, we're not staying together." She jerked the neckline of her sweater a little higher.

I clamped my hand tighter over Sister Alice's mouth. Jade snickered and said, "Let her get it over with, Andie Rose."

I removed my hand and held my breath as I waited.

"I'll treat you to a spin on my moped anytime you wish," Sister Alice said and grinned.

Jade said to Detective Griffin, "You heard her. Isn't that attempted murder?"

****

After Detective Griffin left and everyone returned to normalcy, Sister Alice followed Aspen and me to the porch overlooking the lake. We each leaned against a pillar, admiring the tranquility of nature. Despite the billowy clouds overhead, beautiful in their own right, the vibrant colors of the leaves were breathtaking, even the big, old, gnarly cottonwood tree next to the lake. The willow tree looked graceful once again, and the water was without a single ripple, the leaves' reflection stunning on the smooth surface.

"So what do you think?" Sister Alice asked.

"About what?"

"The ghost."

My gaze traveled to the boat shed, and I offered her a bemused smile. "I'll see it one of these days."

"So you're now a believer?"

I cocked my head to the side, then looked at her and wiggled my eyebrows. "I'm still riding the fence on that one."

Out of nowhere, a gust of wind swirled across the yard, picking up leaves in a cyclone-like manner. As quickly as it came, it quieted, and the leaves settled into a pile. Sister Alice and I glanced at each other, the pile of leaves, and back at each other, neither saying a word.

Finally, she said, "And when you fall to one side or the other?"

I grinned at her. "I'll never tell."

A word about the author…

Rhonda is a retired paralegal and victim witness specialist, an exercise enthusiast, avid reader, lover of words, and coffee and dark chocolate connoisseur. She is the author of The Inheritance, a contemporary women's fiction novel; seven books in the Melanie Hogan cozy mystery series; and Finding Abby and Abby's Redemption, a romantic suspense duology. She is also an indie author consultant and was awarded the 2022 Master of Literary Arts Award from the Brighton Chamber in Colorado. She can be found at her online home at www.rhondablackhurst.com.

Thank you for purchasing
this publication of The Wild Rose Press, Inc.

For questions or more information
contact us at
info@thewildrosepress.com.

The Wild Rose Press, Inc.
www.thewildrosepress.com